DISCLAIMER

The opinions expressed in this book
are those of the author only and not of the
Federal Bureau of Investigation
or any other federal agency.

Appreciation is expressed to LTC John Krysa, US Army Infantry (Retired) and Past Chairman of the Board, Institute of Certified Records Managers for his help with archival records storage descriptions and more. Appreciation, as always, to Denise Kearns for her contributions as Beta reader.

My lovely wife, Georgia, always asks "When are you going to write another Jack Landers book?" Well, this one's for you, Georgia!

HEARTLAND DEPUTY

CHAPTER ONE

SHERIFF JACK LANDERS looked proudly at his staff, gathered for their Tuesday morning meeting. He hated meetings, like most action oriented people in law enforcement. Since he knew they were necessary, he kept his weekly ones quick and organized.

Tac, his wheelchair-bound communications officer, still wearing his ear pods and mic, changed expression. Jack knew he had just gotten a radio call from someone outside the agency.

"Thanks, we'll get a deputy rolling. Probably fifteen minute ETA. He'll be leaving from the office," Tac said into his mic.

"What do we have, Tac?" the sheriff asked.

"Highway Patrol got a call about a pickup in a ditch on County Road 52, ten miles out of town. They don't know from the caller whether it is a rollover or what. The caller thinks there is a fatality. Their closest unit is twenty minutes away."

"Rich, roll on it now!" the sheriff said to thirty year old Sergeant Rich Ammon. Rich nodded and stood. He

1

adjusted his holster and walked fast towards the door. "Call if you need any backup, okay?" he added. Rich waved as he cleared the door and went to his vehicle.

His new Ford Police Responder pickup was parked out front. He fired up the four hundred horsepower twin turbo V6 and energized the red and blue LED emergency lights as he headed out of town. Rich kept his speed reasonable until he hit the edge of town, then he put his siren on and his foot down.

Though the top speed was only one twenty, the acceleration was actually faster than his former hemi-powered Charger patrol car.

As Rich approached slower moving vehicles—which meant all vehicles—he blipped the air horn and the alert tone on the siren and swung around them smoothly.

Jack Landers had taught him to use his gun and his vehicle smoothly and fast. Clearly, Rich had learned well as he nudged the pursuit-rated truck up to just over one hundred miles an hour.

As most people who had run all out in an emergency knew, running code at high speed with lights and siren is not exciting. It is nerve wracking. Drivers are guaranteed to do exactly the wrong thing. Instead of pulling to the right and getting the hell out of the way, they often slam on brakes in front of the responding emergency vehicle or cross in front of it, or do something else stupid to endanger the officer, firefighter or ambulance driver, as well as themselves.

The OHP had dispatched an ambulance before calling Warrior 911. Rich knew this because it was running Code-3 in front of him and he passed and quickly left it in his rear view.

Rich dropped his speed as he approached the area where the accident was supposed to have occurred.

He saw a light green Ram pickup in a ditch up ahead and pulled in blocking it with the front of his truck's edge on the stripe in the county road and the rear end in the red clay on the edge of the road. The truck had travelled down a steep hill and come to rest with all four tires on the ground.

Rich looked behind before he hopped out and walked around his vehicle. One passenger was inside. He was dead. It did not take a doctor to pronounce him so. The bullet had entered his temple and exited the other side was proof enough he was dead. He put on nitrile gloves and carefully opened the door for sign of a gun. The placement of the shot did not suggest suicide, but he had to check anyway. No gun was obvious between the seat and the door, by the pedals, or under the seat.

He found a Smith & Wesson Shield semiautomatic on the passenger side floor. There was no way somebody could shoot himself in the left side of the head and the gun could end up on the right side of the body. Therefore, he concluded, it was not a suicide weapon. And, when he smelled the muzzle, it did not appear to have been fired recently.

The deputy sergeant was on his hand-held radio changing the call from accident to murder as the ambulance pulled in. He waved them back. This was clearly a crime scene.

Tac had switched the radio so it could be heard in the office. It was the only call in process in the large county with the whole sheriff's department, minus Rich, sitting in the front office.

"Our case. Let's let OHP handle traffic control," Jack said as he headed for the door. A former Oklahoma State Bureau of Investigation, or OSBI, agent, the sheriff had a full investigative kit in the back of his Expedition. He took off towards the scene.

An OHP trooper was arriving as the sheriff pulled up.

"Hey, Fred. Looks like a murder here. We will need a forensic team. Want to find out how soon y'all can get one here?"

The trooper called in. Minutes later, he said. "Not for about two hours."

"Radio, Warrior-1," Jack said into his mic as he drove to the scene.

"Go ahead, Sheriff," Tac responded.

"Call OSBI and see if they can get a criminalist team to our location in less than two hours."

"Will do. Stand by."

"Just call back on my cell, I am going to be tied up here for a while."

Jack walked over to the truck.

"Rich, your call on it?" he asked.

"Jack, somebody shot him in the side of the head. The caliber was significant enough to come out the other side, doing massive damage to the right side of his head. I used gloves when I opened the door and when I removed his wallet. He's out of state. But not by much. He lived in Wichita Falls, Texas.

"What's odd to me is the driver's side window is down, but there are limited powder burns on the left side of his face. So, nobody walked up to talk with him and blasted him from beside the door.

"I found a 9mm automatic on the floor and lifted it out with my pen stuck in the barrel. I suspect only his prints will be on it and am guessing he dropped it there or dropped it on the seat and it fell onto the floor when the truck came to a stop. I do not believe it has been fired. It looks like to me he felt threatened by another motorist, put his window down, and drew his own gun from his person or a glove box or console.

"It's pretty clear he was hit before he could use it," Rich said.

Jack listened thoughtfully. He had a lot of faith in this young deputy he had mentored from the start. He had promoted him to sergeant early in Rich's law enforcement career. His version of what happened made sense. The forensic team, called criminalists at the OSBI, and subsequent autopsy would clear things up a lot.

"Okay, Rich. I agree with your line of reasoning. Once we get forensic and autopsy reports, we will focus on the who and why questions. OSBI may want to take lead. I will give it some thought. They are certainly better equipped. We are stretched pretty tight from a manpower standpoint right now, but dammit, it's our county.

"Let's you and me walk through this," he said as he walked around the side of the RAM and looked at the missing portion of the victim.

"Like you said, not enough powder burns on the entry for a suicide or close-up. The shooter was either standing some feet away or sitting in a tall vehicle. It appears the exit was lower than the entry. Perhaps the other vehicle was taller. Let me get my laser pointer while you get your yellow 'police line, do not cross' tape. We might be able to help the criminalist folks get a head start on their work."

Two minutes later, the nitrile-gloved sheriff was in the back seat of the truck. Rich was outside the passenger window.

Jack held the strong laser pointer with its end adjacent to where the bullet exited and the green laser beam going through the bullet hole in the window and into the scrub beyond.

"Rich, walk over to where the laser seems to end. Watch for rattlers!" The deputy did as requested and stopped for a moment by a sapling.

"Jack, the bullet nicked this sapling."

"Good! Now keep going to where the laser beam ends."

Rich Ammon moved aside some brush in front of a tree.

"I got a bullet hole in the tree, Jack!"

"Perfect! I'll be there in a second," Jack said.

He got out of the rear door and looked around on the ground. He spotted a stick and whittled it to size with his pocket knife. He then tied the end of the yellow plastic tape around it and pushed it through the bullet hole in the window from the outside. Slightly opening the door, he moved the stick perpendicular to the bottom edge of the window and pulled it tight against the damaged pane. Keeping slight pressure on the stick, he walked towards Rich, unwinding the yellow tape.

When he got to Rich and the tree, he wrapped a couple of winds of tape around the tree a couple inches above the bullet hole and tied it off.

"Now, we have the path of the bullet," he said almost to himself.

Rich was opening his pocket knife.

"I'll dig it out," he volunteered.

"No, wait for the forensics folks, Rich. There are two reasons they may want to study the trajectory and remove the piece of the tree with the bullet in it carefully."

The young deputy sergeant looked at his boss quizzically.

"One, they may wish to remove a section of wood at a time to avoid prying the bullet out and possibly damaging it and the identifying rifling marks. The second reason is to identify the ammunition and weapon type. Think about it a moment.

"Let's say this was a handgun round and not a high powered rifle bullet. They and we would want to know whether it was fired in a rifle or handgun and the type of ammunition.

"There are a number of handgun rounds that have a less powerful alternative and a more powerful one. You can shoot the lesser one in a gun made for the more powerful one, but not vice versa. For example, you can shoot a weaker .38 special in a more powerful .357 magnum, but not the reverse. The same is true for a .44 special and a .44 magnum and a .45 Colt and a .454 Casull. All of those are available in both handguns and rifles. As you know, the rifles will have a lot more velocity because of longer barrel length. See how much they can learn from studying the bullet and the depth it penetrated? Plus, we need to check the back of this tree to see if it is still inside or whether it penetrated it and kept on going."

Jack leaned around the tree, brushed a spider web and its inhabitant aside and examined the bark.

"We are at the end of the trail, Rich. The bullet is still in the tree. They will have to saw the tree down and take the section back to the lab after they do the distance measurement. However, I think we will learn a lot about the murder weapon when they are through," Jack said.

They left the tape up and added a bow around the sapling the bullet had clipped on the way to the tree.

Back at the truck, Jack shot the laser beam from the

entry wound towards wherever the shooter was. He had to approximate from the angle going back to the tree.

Though no more than an approximation, it appeared the shot had come from a tall person standing or anyone sitting in a tall vehicle, like an 18 wheeler tractor or a raised 4x4 pickup. Both lawmen realized these were educated guesses and could be exactly wrong.

"Now we think we know where the shooter was, let's look at the area closely for empty casings. It's been walked all over, but if there was brass there, it was either picked up or is still there," Jack said.

"Unless the shooter used a revolver or a rifle and did not eject the empty. It appears from the one hole in the passenger window just a single shot was fired," Rich said.

"Exactly!"

They scoured the area and did not find any brass. The empty casings would have confirmed the shooter's approximate location and the caliber of the murder weapon. They simply were not lucky and would have to wait for the criminalists to study the bullet in the tree for the latter information.

Rich wrote everything they did and their conclusions in his notebook.

Tac called the sheriff and advised an OSBI agent was about ten minutes out. He was coming from the opposite direction of MacKenzie, where the county seat was. A forensic team was thirty minutes behind him, coming from Oklahoma City.

"Rich, you have this. Use your phone's camera to take photos of the body from each angle, the vehicle, the line of bullet travel tape, where the bullet landed, the victim's gun, and anything else relevant. When you get back to the office, you and I will begin a murder board in the meeting room. We can blow up the driver's license photo for the victim's picture until we get a better one. We will develop an investigative plan tomorrow. Brief Ray Colton, the OSBI agent. If he wants, include his forensics team. I have done all the damage I can do here, so I am going to pack up my little green laser and head back to the office," the sheriff said.

"I learned some things, sheriff. I'll keep in touch in case there's a new development."

They walked over to the trooper, who was directing intermittent traffic rubbernecking past the RAM in the ditch.

"Fred, I'm going to put a cover over the window so the dead man is not visible to passersby. Then, I'm going back to the office. Not much going on. I know you and Rich can handle it. OSBI and a criminalist team are on the way.

"If you would, let Rich know about any speeding or odd traffic stops between maybe ten this morning and now. Somebody shot this man and they left. Maybe we'll get lucky.

"Rich, make sure to use your phone to photograph everything in the guy's wallet. I am sure OSBI will want the originals.

"Be safe and I'll see you soon."

"Okay Jack. Looks like y'all may have solved half of it anyway," the trooper said.

"Naw. We just tracked the line of the bullet. Feel free to listen in while Rich briefs the OSBI agent. You add in anything you think is important, Fred."

He lightly punched his deputy in the shoulder and got back in the Expedition. Once the way was clear, he locked the wheel and spun it around in a U-turn and powered hard back to the county seat.

Colton was the OSBI special agent who covered the

same multi-county area Jack used to cover. Fairly recently assigned, he was about thirty-five and a former Oklahoma City patrol officer prior to joining the state agency. Jack knew he was a good cop, but only had a year's worth of investigative experience at this point. Jack had a feeling this was going to be a difficult murder to solve.

The office had a small bullpen where deputies could come in and do reports and computer research. A small cubicle was set aside for the OSBI agent who covered the area. Jack had stopped using it, due to his and his predecessor's several years of bad history. The prior sheriff had taken a strong dislike to Landers upon his election. Then-deputy Jack was in line to become chief deputy under the previous sheriff and was pushed aside. He was offered a job with the OSBI and resigned from the sheriff's office. The new sheriff's conversations grew more acrimonious over time and Jack avoided the cubicle and worked around the sheriff. He solved a serial bank robbery case in which the sheriff was shot to death and Jack was appointed county sheriff himself. The new permanent agent had not used the cubicle. Jack was not even sure he was aware of it.

The layout of the office was good, Jack thought. One entered a reception area with chairs and a bulletin board with information deemed helpful for the public.

There was a waist high counter separating the public from a small work area where the office manager and radio control were located. Beyond were the offices for the sheriff and the chief deputy, Rose Custalow. Down a hall was an interview room with a two-way window and an audio and video recording system. The bullpen and a conference room were past it. There was a break room with a microwave, refrigerator, tables and chairs. There were four cells located at the end of the hall.

The cells were equipped with a cot and a stainless-steel toilet and sink. They were for overnight holds until their residents were either released or transported to the regional jail.

Sheriff Jack Landers walked in and surveyed the lobby. Several citizens were waiting in chairs. He saw Helen, the office manager, was handling their needs. Tac was on the radio and computer.

He nodded and smiled at everyone and walked to his office. He was still getting used to the fact he was now a politician in addition to being a lawman. In two and a half years, he would have to campaign to keep his office as sheriff.

Jack sat back and considered the layout of the office. Did it meet their current needs? The building was fairly old and did not invite easy change. He thought about equipment changes and whether more were needed.

Upon appointment, he had loosened the dress requirements from uniform shirt, striped matching trousers, and a smokie the bear campaign hat. He approved uniform shirt, creased blue jeans and either cowboy boots, combat boots or running shoes. He did away with the campaign hats and substituted white Stetsons or Resistols. He specified the models designated for the Texas Rangers. He ordered a supply of Warrior County Sheriff ball caps for general use in the field.

He had approved tactical vests in tan to match the uniform shirts. They not only carried the Kevlar bullet resistant plates, they spread the weight of radios, handcuffs, knives, extra ammunition and other items a rural deputy had to carry. The amount of belt equipment and its weight had increased geometrically over the past few years. Studies were showing deputies and officers even at young middle age were suffering severe back issues as a result. The vests helped. Plus, they were simpler than having to wear a vest under a uniform shirt.

Pepper spray was an option. He had several TASER guns in the office and one in his Expedition, but nobody wore them daily.

Jack stuck with the white cowboy hats and cowboy boots for himself most of the time. He carried fatigues and combat boots in the Expedition along with a first aid kit, fire extinguisher and investigative kit, and a bugout backpack. It had food, water, and camping gear. Each patrol unit was equipped with a shotgun and a patrol rifle. The later was an Adams Arms M4 carbine with a red dot sight. Except for the sheriff, who carried his great uncle's former Winchester lever action .30-30 he used in the Texas Rangers.

Tac had proven very proficient at getting government grants from the state, the US Department of Justice and the Department of Homeland Security.

Grants had bought the patrol rifles, vehicle radios and the tactical vests. The sheriff's department had even been offered a former Marine Corps MRAP.

These Mine Resistant Ambush Protected armored vehicles were often used by SWAT teams. He reckoned he did not need one. He did not have a SWAT team anyway and would not for the foreseeable future.

He hung his straw Resistol on the coat rack in the corner of his office and walked to the conference room. An aficionado of British cop shows, he had a large white-board installed to use as a murder board. While he was sure murder boards were used all over America and the rest of the world, he still associated them with the Brits.

Jack would help Rich set up the board and he and SA

Colton would add to the thinking points and evidence copies placed on it. They would start as soon as the two returned. Which reminded him of something.

He walked to the front.

"Hey, Tac. Call Rich on the radio. If he is still with Ray Colton, have him ask Ray to return here with him. If not, call Ray on the radio and invite him for a quick meeting."

"Roger, boss," the affable communications officer responded.

Jack had tested Tac with increasingly demanding duties from day one. The young man always knocked them out of the ballpark and asked for tougher ones.

Jack had given him the nickname the day he showed up in a blacked out tactical looking wheel chair festooned with black web gear on it.

An ex-con had tried to assassinate Jack Landers a year ago at his wedding. Tac and a young college student, Polly Antrim, had seen the man fire the first shot and moved in. They shot and killed the man. Jack walked away with a minor .22 bullet quickly removed at the regional hospital, which then sent him home.

He knew he owed a lot to the two. Subsequent shots might have killed his new wife, his parents, uncle or others.

Jack had rescued the female college student from a kidnapper a year before. The experience had spurred her to pursue a life in law enforcement. She was currently partially through her degree in Criminal Justice with a goal of working for the Warrior County Sheriff's Office. Unfortunately, she was madly in love with the sheriff.

He stayed busy with paperwork until Rich and the OSBI special agent came in an hour and a half later. Rich told him they needed fifteen minutes or so computer time to give him a better picture of the victim.

The two walked in twenty minutes later with folders full of photos and documents.

"We are ready when you are Jack," Ray said.

"Let's go to the conference room and load up a murder board," he said, rising and heading down the hall.

"Who was the deceased and what do we know about him?" Jack asked.

Rich started off first.

"His name was William Lee Strauss. Ray and I checked him every way but loose for wants and warrants. He was clean as clean could be. Not even a parking ticket. The RAM truck was his, financed through a bank in Texas."

"Was he from Texas?" Jack perked up.

"Yeah, Jack. He was from Wichita Falls," the OSBI agent said.

"I know the area. One of my serial killer victims floated over to Wichita Falls when I had your job. My buddy Zack Bodeway worked the case with us. And, he's exactly who I am going to call right now."

"The famous Texas Ranger?" Ray asked.

"The very same," Jack said as he hit a button on his speed dial to call the ranger.

"Well, damn, boy. I was worried the little old .22 bullet had killed you of lead poisoning on the day you got married," said the deep familiar voice from Texas. His audience all knew "boy" was a way of speaking with friends which had nothing to do with age.

"Uncle Bud had his pocket knife out to dig it out, but Lily wouldn't let him."

"Should have let him. I could have held you in a

restraint hold. But, since you grew up wrestling mountain lions in Texas, it probably wasn't even necessary."

"Now, Zack, before you tell any more of my secrets, I have OSBI Special Agent Ray Colton and Sergeant Rich Ammon on the line here. You met Rich at the wedding, I believe." Rich nodded.

"I did. The boy has class. He's going to grow up and look like us. Hi, gents."

"Zack, we have a dead body up here in Oklahoma. Looks suspiciously like an assassination. One very powerful round to the side of the head. We found the round in a tree. It's being studied now," Jack said.

"What's the decedent's name, Jack?" the ranger asked.

"William Lee Strauss of Wichita Falls, Texas. We cannot find any wants, warrants, parking tickets or anything else on him," Rich said.

"When did this happen?"

"Somewhere around nine this morning. More or less," Ray said.

"What kind of vehicle was he in?"

"One year old Ram four door truck. It's a personally-owned vehicle in his name. He had the window down. Blew out the other window," Jack said.

"Jack, let me poke around a bit. I'll get back to y'all when I find something. The name is well known to me. I'll call back soon and will do the next of kin notification personally."

"Thanks, Zack. We'll be speaking later," Jack said and rung off.

"It's interesting the Texas Ranger is going to do the next of kin notification instead of passing the information to the local police or sheriff," Jack mused aloud.

"Okay, Rich. Put the DL photo you enlarged and printed on glossy photo paper in the top center of the board. Write Strauss' name and everything we know about him." Jack said.

"I have a meeting of some sort with Lily tonight. Don't stay too late guys. I have a feeling tomorrow will be a long day," he said as he left the room and headed to his office. "Ray, do you know you have a cubicle here with a phone and computer for you to use? I stopped using it because the former sheriff and I were at odds constantly. But it's yours whenever you need it," Jack said as he left.

As Jack walked out to his truck, he saw the criminalists for the OSBI directing a tow truck driver depositing the victim's RAM in the sheriff's impound lot behind the office. He was slanting the flatbed and getting ready to lower the truck to level with the wrecker's winch.

He knew the OSBI criminalists would give it a thorough going over in the morning. The privacy of his secure lot would beat the side of the road with rubberneckers driving by. By then, he, Rich and Ray would be working out an investigative plan and beginning to fill up the murder board.

Now, he needed get home to the Doolin's Cave Ranch and see what social or civic event Lily had roped him into. It was just part of being an elected official married to a successful doctor and community leader. He wondered if great uncle Bud was coming too. His beloved great uncle was spending about every other month with them in a renovated bunkhouse. He was far too vital to be languishing away in a retirement home in Ranger, Texas. Though the name of the town was appropriate to the man.

Jack found Lily and Uncle Bud were dressed a little more formally than usual. He took a shower and put on tan slacks, a white shirt and a blue blazer with an obvious sheriff's lapel pin. Less obvious was his every day carry .45 Colt Commander with the stag grips. His great uncle had carried it during most of his Texas Ranger service. Cocked and locked in an inside the waistband holster, it literally disappeared beneath the blue jacket.

They took the county Expedition instead of Lily's BMW. With such a large geographic area and so few on staff, the sheriff had to be able to respond every hour of the day. So, he was expected to use his official vehicle for virtually everything.

"So, Doctor Wife. Where are we going tonight?" he asked the gynecologist with long dark red hair.

"We are going to the library. They have asked me to chair the Library Patron's Council. We need to grow the number of books significantly. This is a fund raiser."

Jack looked over at his great uncle riding shotgun and the two rolled their eyes at each other.

"I saw what the two of you just did!" Lily said. She handed each an envelope.

"What's this? A detention notice?" Jack asked.

"No. It is a contribution from each of you. Don't worry, I am paying. As a community leader, Jack, you are giving five hundred dollars. So am I as a prominent physician. Uncle Bud, you are giving two hundred fifty as the region's most famous retired Texas Ranger."

"I believe I paid two fifty for my first car. And, it was close to new!" he responded.

"Well, times they are a changing' dearest" Lily noted and smiled sweetly.

Neither the current nor the past lawman had figured out how to counteract Lily's smile. They had spoken about it several times and decided to just accept whatever she wanted as a done deal. Luckily for them, she was hardly ever unreasonable.

Jack pulled into the library parking lot. There were no spaces. He let Lily and Bud out and pulled around front and parked illegally.

Though he had one of the two vehicles in the fleet without a big star on the door, it was pretty obvious the big Expedition was a law enforcement vehicle. A push bar on the front, LED blue lights behind every window. Wide high speed tires and the ugliest black wheels anyone ever saw on a luxury SUV. Like the .45 under Jack's blazer, the computer chip in the engine was not so obvious.

As he parked, he thought about the other unmarked vehicle. It was the last Crown Vic in the fleet. He decided to keep it as a backup vehicle. It was in great shape, mileage notwithstanding. It has just been repainted in navy blue. Like his Expedition, it was clearly law enforcement. If his idea came to fruition, he would let Rich use it in his investigative trips, especially out of state. It looked like he was going to go to Texas at least a few times in the Strauss murder case.

He walked into the library. There was quite a crowd and he spent his initial ten minutes shaking hands and speaking with voters. Both his wife and his great uncle had their own crowds of people mesmerized by just being around the charismatic and beautiful doctor or listening to the stories of the legendary ranger. For very different reasons, they were more in demand than Jack. He liked it just fine.

The librarian rang a small bell and called everyone to order. People shuffled around and found seats at library research tables.

She welcomed everyone and called on Lily to speak.

Jack knew she was a wonderful speaker and what the pitch was going to be. So, he let his mind wander back to their first lunch. It had been interrupted by a nearby call he had to take on a fight at a bar. He had taken and left her in the questionable parking lot with his backup revolver for protection and she had ended up saving him.

If he had not loved her before, he certainly did watching her daring a whole barroom to take her on.

As he thought, he heard his wife call his name and snapped out of his reverie.

He looked up at her as she motioned him up to the front of the room.

"Who better to lend emphasis to our book needs than Warrior County's very own sheriff?" she asked the crowd rhetorically.

"Hi folks. I knew what my wife was going to say, except for the part about calling on me to speak. She's like the teacher we all had crushes on in school. You loved her but could bet the herd she would call on you the moment you were daydreaming.

"She is brilliant, sweet, kind and beautiful. However, there is a side to Lily you may not know. Indulge me in the story I was daydreaming about when she just called on me.

"It was several years ago. We were on our first lunch date when I got a call to respond to a knife fight at a certain local bar about five miles outside of town. I won't mention the name of the place, but I suspect everybody here knows which one I'm talking about.

"Now, a knife fight at a bar is something a law officer does not want to respond to alone. There was no back up available for this call. Not for a long time.

"I could not leave the woman I hoped to become the

19

love of my life sitting in a police vehicle in a parking lot of dubious safety. However, I did. With a .38 snub nose revolver I handed to her. She assured me she had grown up shooting and could handle it.

"After putting several combatants on the floor, I found myself about to be overtaken by a small crowd. The one in front had a knife. The scene was frozen with the very loud crack of a two-inch snub nose revolver with a +P round fired into the ceiling. At the very least, the person I had had ordered to stay in the car had saved me a serious beating.

"From the floor, I watched the doctor swing the revolver in an arc around the bar room. The look in her eyes was unforgettable. The drunks—and there must have been twenty of them—were not up to taking on an angry redhead with a gun. By the time the backup and ambulance had arrived, the attackers were subdued, and the wounded ones were awaiting care," Jack said.

"Sheriff?" the owner of the local hardware called out.

"Yes, Hank?"

"You said a stabbing had happened. Then you said the 'wounded ones'. Were there multiple stabbings?"

"No, Hank. Just one stabbing. The others were injured while assaulting me."

The audience laughed and several clapped. This was the still the West. Folks expected their sheriffs to be tough and enjoyed hearing about the law winning against the lawless.

"To the point of why Lily called me up here, how many of you are like me? You wonder what's going to happen to our kids. They keep their noses stuck in a phone sending texts and selfies or playing computer games. Often violent computer games.

"Perhaps they'd benefit from actually reading a book,

huh? We've had children's books for years. Now, there is a whole class of books called Young Adult or YA. Many of them even have a religious theme. If our kids could be reading those instead of electronic communications, wouldn't they be better off?

"Let's expand the library and get a bunch of books appealing to our youth. And whatever other books our librarian needs. Also, some books for our senior citizens who can't get out but want something other than TV to keep their spirits up. Many of these folks fought for this country of ours and they raised their kids and paid their taxes. It's their time to sit back. They earned it.

This is an inexpensive and easy way to accomplish a lot of good goals.

Thank y'all and be safe."

Jack received applause. More importantly he left some thoughtful expressions on folks' faces.

The meeting continued for another thirty minutes. Lily kept her audience captivated.

The three got into the Expedition.

"I think it went well. Several people promised contributions in the hundreds of dollars. Some were personal, some were corporate," Lily said.

"Y'all did a good job," Uncle Bud commented.

"Jack, how do you know about YA books," Lily asked.

"I saw a story about their growth on the Internet news channel I almost believe. I don't even bother with cable news anymore. Seemed like a good trend and I recalled it off the top of my head just now."

"That was some story you told about Lily and the short barrel revolver. I bet she scared the dickens out of those old boys when she popped off her gun!" Bud said.

"Well, it was my backup gun, but she wanted it. You

21

already know how hard it is to turn her down when she lays those eyes on you," Jack said.

"She sure has you wrapped around her little finger, Jack."

"And not you at all, Uncle Bud? Ha!"

"You two realize I am sitting right here listening to you, right?"

"We do. No secrets in this family," Jack said.

Except for the story behind Jack's girlfriend who was stabbed to death in a café and I could not save, Lily thought to herself.

They stopped off at Mix's Barbecue for dinner. Uncle Bud thought their brisket was almost as good as brisket in Texas.

They returned to the ranch afterwards. Lily fed Jasmine, their tiny black and white cat while the men checked on the feed and water for the horses. Uncle Bud bid them adieu and retired to the bunkhouse which was his new home away from home.

Lily curled up in the big sheriff's arms and was asleep almost immediately.

Jack continued to wonder about the murder of the man Strauss in the RAM pickup. They knew who he was. Apparently, from what he said, Zack was very familiar with him. Which should lead to why? Then came the hard part. Who killed him? Jack was going to give his young sergeant the lead on this one. Rich could take the unmarked reserve car, go to civilian clothes, and play investigator. Jack resolved to guide him some but give him free rein to run the investigation. The county was growing.

With the growth came more tax revenues which yielded more funding for the sheriff's office. He reckoned soon he could expand by a couple of deputies.

Maybe an additional sergeant allowing Rich to become the office's first full-time investigator. And, cars for the additional badged staff.

"Okay, Jack. You are getting ahead of yourself. Sleep, man! There's a lot going on," he told himself. He glanced at Lily's halo of shiny dark red hair. The little black and white cat was curled up above her head. The two sleeping beauties were breathing in unison. Actually, they were lightly snoring in unison, but Lily preferred the term "breathing" instead.

The modern-day gunfighter smiled and closed his eyes. He was asleep soon after.

JACK, Rich, and Ray met at the office early the next morning. They sat around the conference table with mugs of strong coffee and discussed where they were.

"I should hear late this morning or maybe early afternoon from the lead criminalist on the case about the bullet used," the OSBI special agent reported.

"By now Zack has notified the next of kin. Do y'all want me to call him and arrange for you to go down and meet with them and the Arc management later today?" Jack asked.

Rich looked at Ray, who nodded almost imperceptively.

Jack pulled out his iPhone and went to the Phone icon, then selected Favorites.

"You on your third cup of coffee yet?" he asked when the ranger answered.

"Pouring it now. I went to Strauss' house myself. Those duties always suck for everybody. It was not appropriate to question the wife right then, so I told her I'd be back," Zack said.

"Would you mind if Rich and Ray rode with you?" Jack asked.

"Of course not. Your murder, my victim. We should work on this together. You're not coming?"

"Not today. I've given Rich the lead from Warrior County and we are working it jointly from this end with the OSBI. I'm sure I will see you more than once before this one is solved and all parties are in custody."

"While they are down here, we will drop by his place of business. I remembered why I had heard of Arc Enterprises. They are a tribal-owned outfit. They try to get the minority piece of government contracts, whether they are state or federal.

Whoever the contact is, probably the CEO, we'll press him to explain how it all works. Even under yesterday's bad circumstance, Jack, I can't see this being a domestic murder. So, it almost has to be his job or something else in Strauss' past."

"I wonder if they were in a competitive battle with another minority firm over some contract?" Jack asked.

"We'll find out later today. It's about three hours from there to here. When you boys think you'll arrive?"

Rich and Ray looked at their watches and conferred offline.

"Ranger, we'll see you about eleven," Ray said.

All parties knew eleven meant pushing it hard. Most of the run was Interstate, so it was not unreasonable to assume Western lawmen would drive it fast.

"I'll meet you in the Falls at eleven. Call me when you get close." Bodeway hung up and Jack handed Rich a slip of paper with the ranger's cell phone number. Rich put it in his iPhone.

24

"Ray, are you driving? We might not want to advertise a marked Oklahoma unit too much in Texas," Jack said.

"Yeah. I have the Explorer Interceptor you had. Did you trick it up? It's faster than normal ones. Which is saying a lot."

"It could have an unapproved chip somewhere near the ECU. Maybe. Possibly," Jack grinned.

"Ray, could you give Rich and me a minute or two with Rose on another unrelated matter?" Jack asked. The OSBI agent walked out as Jack asked his chief deputy to join them.

"Rose, I wanted to keep you in the loop. Rich and Ray are going to Wichita Falls to meet with Zack Bodeway. They are going to talk with the widow of the victim and someone high up in the victim's company.

"I'd like you to juggle things to get his district covered for a week or so. Maybe longer. You can count on me for part of the coverage whenever needed.

"Rich, wear plain clothes on this, okay? You can either go with a dress shirt and tie and Stetson like Zack or more like a big city detective in a suit. Your call.

"Rose, is the reserve Crown Vic still in good condition? Isn't it under a car cover in the back of the storage lot behind the building?" Jack asked.

"No. Before he retired, Clive and I decided the mileage was too high. We kept one of the smaller Impala-sized Police Caprices. Clive," she said referring to the longtime chief deputy, "thought it would be more contemporary looking. It also only had fifty thousand miles. We took the star and other identifying stuff off and had it painted dark blue. It's a great unmarked car.

"I didn't mention it because I figured Clive would," she said.

"Doesn't matter. Maybe he did. With the wedding, me being shot, and him retiring, things were crazy about then.

"Rose, if you would, have the garage we use get it ready for Rich to use on the case when he gets back from this run down to Texas."

THE TWO OKLAHOMA lawmen crossed the Red River into Texas two hours and fifteen minutes later. It had been a fast drive, averaging almost ninety, down I-44.

Rich called Zack Bodeway.

"You boys drive just like Texas lawmen," the ranger commented before giving directions to the Strauss residence.

Rich and Ray were quickly learning being compared to Texas anything was the ranger's way of complementing someone.

When they pulled up in front of the nice residence, Zack Bodeway was already sitting out front. He was in his truck talking on a cellphone. Rich commented to Ray the ranger was driving an unmarked Responder pursuit-certified model.

"No shock there," Ray noted.

Bodeway had not parked in front of the house. He parked in front of a neighbor's house near the edge of the Strauss property.

"Good practice. Parked at a bad angle for a shot from the house and close enough to retreat to the truck if needed. And, of course, not much of an announcement of his arrival for the occupants," Ray said. "Doesn't matter under these circumstances, but a good habit anytime," he added. Rich agreed as Ray pulled the mid-sized SUV in behind the ranger.

They let the ranger finish and get out first.

He was forty-five and six four in his boots. Bodeway wore a white shirt, conservative tie, off-white straw hat, and a brown gun belt with a .45 automatic on his right side. He was wearing Ray Bans and had brown hair and a neatly trimmed mustache.

"Damn, Ray! He looks like a poster Texas Ranger!" Rich said under his breath.

"And, Jack Lander's older brother," the OSBI agent responded.

"I'm guessing it would be Ray in the suit and there's Rich dressed kinda like me," Zack said as he extended a big hand.

"Yessir. I'm Rich Ammon. This is Special Agent Ray Colton."

"Glad to make y'all's acquaintance. Or re-make, Rich, since we have met before. I'm hoping the initial shock has abated for poor Mrs. Strauss today. I'll start off because she has met me. Y'all jump in as you wish. Just be gentle. This lady has had a helluva shock and we need to respect it. Let's go do it."

Zack rang the doorbell and a pretty woman in her mid-to-late thirties answered.

"Oh! Ranger. Come in."

She was dressed in a teal top and well-fitted blue jeans. She was barefoot in the house. Rich noticed her pedicure matched her top. Her long thick blonde hair was still wet. Either they had interrupted a blow dry or she did not care under the circumstances.

"Guys, this is Myra Strauss. Special Agent Ray Colton from the Oklahoma State Bureau of Investigation and Sergeant Rich Ammon from the Warrior County, Oklahoma Sheriff's Office. They are investigating your husband's shooting." Each proffered his hand as he was introduced.

"As I said yesterday, we have some routine questions we have to ask in any situation like this," Zack said.

"How are you doing? Do you have anybody staying with you doing this tough time?" Zack asked gently.

"My little sister is coming over. She might get here while you are still here. I am still trying to wrap my head around what happened. We always lamented not having kids. Now, I am glad we didn't. I can't explain this to me, much less children," she said.

"Myra, did Bill have any enemies you know about?" Zack asked.

"No. Not really. Everybody liked him. He was a deacon in the church and a coach for the local children's soccer team."

"Mrs. Strauss, will the funeral be at the church or at wherever he came from?" Ray asked.

"Oh, we are both from Wichita Falls. Born and raised. It will be here at the First Methodist about a mile from here. It's all so sudden! No date is set yet." Ray and Rich both wrote notes furiously. Rich knew Ray's question had been a ploy to find the name of the church and talk to the minister about his deacon. They would also speak with whoever was in charge of the soccer team.

"Ranger Bodeway, when will we get the body back so we can plan the funeral?"

"Myra, I am going to refer your question over to Sgt. Ammon. The death happened in his jurisdiction, so they will determine when the body is returned."

"Ma'am, the OSBI took your husband's remains to Oklahoma City for an autopsy. Sheriff Landers and I determined this was a murder, not a suicide at the scene.

Autopsies are pretty usual for murder victims. Ray, what do you think?"

"I have not spoken with our folks yet. We were leaving for here about the time they were leaving for OKC. I will let Ranger Bodeway, who is your primary contact, know as soon as I know something. Rich's sheriff may be the person who decides on the release. Warrior County is the primary investigating agency on this case. We are helping."

"Why an autopsy? He was shot! What more do you need to know?"

"Myra, it's standard in most murder cases. The more we know about the murder weapon, the distance and so forth, the better chance we have of a fast solution," Bodeway said. What he did not say was they already had the information available to study to determine the murder weapon. They knew how he died. Now they wanted to look for clues as to why. Had he had been in fights, had alcohol or drugs in his system, had a terminal disease? Things about him which might be a clue as to why somebody shot him in the head.

"Did Mr. Strauss seem worried or agitated in the past few days?" Rich asked.

"He was worried. He was competing for a minority add-on for a big contract. The other firm was under-handed, he said. He was much more nervous than I ever saw him in the almost twenty years I've known him."

"What was the name of the other firm?"

"I don't know. You will have to ask the people at Arc," she said.

"You said he was nervous. Do you think it was simply over the contract issue? Or was there anything else? Was everything fine between you two?"

"Everything was great with us? Why would you ask such a question, Agent?"

"It is a standard question we have to ask on every case like this, Ma'am. Nothing more," Ray said.

"Well, I resent it! It's like I am the suspect!"

"Mrs. Strauss, my question and the next one—where were you yesterday morning—and standard questions we always ask. These are elimination questions. Just like if the murder happened here, we would know your fingerprints would automatically be in your home, so we would take them to differentiate you from the real bad guy," Ray said quietly, but holding his ground.

"Ray is exactly right, Myra. These are standard elimination questions. If he had not asked, I would have. So please respond about your whereabouts yesterday morning, so we can move on," Zack said.

"I went to the gym. They have Pelotons. I try to work out on one of them every day."

"I just bought one," Rich said. "I love it! When do you work out?"

"Yesterday and most days around nine. I'm there for about an hour and a half and then come home for a shower. It's faster because the gym is only five minutes away."

Rich nodded at her in a participative manner and wrote unobtrusively as he smiled. Their list of places to verify was growing. If she was there when she said, she was eliminated as the shooter. She would not have had time to leave there and drive to the Oklahoma location and kill him.

The three lawmen looked up surprised as someone burst through the front door. They immediately dismissed the tearful blonde as a threat. She was Rich's age and gorgeous. She was dressed like Myra Strauss and favored her a lot, including the same beautiful natural blonde hair and tall fit shape.

"Gentlemen, this is my sister, Isabella Munro. Bella, these men are policemen investigating Bill's death. You know Zack."

The two introduced themselves. Isabella scrutinized them as she shook hands. None of the three knew she had dismissed the ranger as too old, the agent as too married according to his ring finger, and the sergeant just right.

She sat and they resumed their seats.

"Ms. Munro, we are largely doing our elimination questions here today. These are standard in each murder case and all three of our agencies, the Texas Rangers, the Warrior Sheriff's Office and the Oklahoma State Bureau of Investigation use the same protocol," Zack said.

"Ms. Munro, for our records and nothing more, where were you yesterday morning between the hours of eight and eleven?" Rich asked.

She looked at him nervously, her cheeks still tear-stained.

"Am I a suspect?"

"Nationally, something like thirty percent of murders where there are spouses or intimate partners involve one killing the other. So, we have to ask the question. But, as Ranger Bodeway said, these are elimination questions so we can move on to people who are serious suspects," Rich said.

"I went to work at my temping job. I have not found a position in my career field here at home in Wichita Falls since moving back from Tulsa a couple of months ago."

"Where would the job be?" he asked.

"Speedy Office Supply in town. I was there until around lunch time when Myra called me with the horrible news. Bill was the brother I never had. I'm going to miss him so much," she said emotionally. Rich wrote her answer down while still looking into her blue eyes. He had practice watching hands on everybody he interviewed. Especially car stops. Rich focused on eyes when the chance of a threat was virtually nonexistent. It was less off-putting. Being questioned by a police officer even made the innocent nervous.

"As we asked Mrs. Strauss, are you aware of anyone who would wish to harm your late brother-in-law?" Ray asked.

"No. He was a nice, non-controversial man. He got along with everybody."

"Did he ever mention anything about a big business competitive thing going on?" Zack asked.

"Not to me. He seemed up-tight over something but didn't seem to want to talk about it."

"About when did this start, Ms. Munro?" Rich asked.

"Maybe a month ago, I am not sure. But a month ago is a good approximation. And please call me Isabella or Bella. This 'Ms. Munro' stuff sounds like you are speaking to our mother." Rich just nodded. Not the time to get too chatty. Maybe after her alibi was validated.

"Anything else you all want to ask?" Zack queried the two lawmen.

"Since we are out of state, perhaps the two ladies' phone numbers would be helpful in case other questions arise," Ray said.

"Damn! I owe him a beer!" Rich thought to himself.

Both gave the numbers and the men stood and Zack said "Again, we are all sorry for your loss Myra and Bella." Rich and Ray nodded. Isabella locked eyes one more time with the handsome sheriff's sergeant and smiled.

As they walked out to their vehicles, Zack said "I have an appointment with the CEO of Arc Enterprises in thirty minutes. He is going to have a couple of his tribal council members sit in. I take it they are on his board of directors.

"It may be better if I take it alone and you two go by the church, gym, soccer field and office store. I suspect these guys are going to be tight-lipped and a group may be more daunting than one man.

"If you miss one due to time, let me know and I will cover it tomorrow," the ranger said.

"Sounds like a plan, Zack. Let's get on a conference call and compare notes tomorrow. Is ten in the morning okay? I suspect Jack will want to sit in, too," Rich suggested.

Ray and Rich found Myra had been at the gym when she said. On a whim, Rich asked a question and found Isabella worked out there also. Often with her brother-in-law. The manager would not say whether there was anything else beyond working out. Both lawmen agreed in the SUV later Isabella's tears and working out with Strauss may be significant. However, she could not have killed him. Her alibi about being at work was rock solid as was her sister's.

The field had two other soccer coaches still present. Both knew and liked Bill Strauss. They said he was great with the kids and his wife and her sister were often present at games and always at playoffs.

"I suspect what we have done today is exactly what we claimed we were doing, Rich. Eliminating the wife and her sister as suspect. Unless one of them hired a hitman."

"I guess if we get down to suspecting either of them

and a hitman, Zack can get a subpoena for bank records," Ray said.

"The real interesting material is what he will learn at Arc Enterprises about the competition. If enough money is involved for two small businesses, I could see a hit. Not necessarily by a pro. But we live out West. Everybody has a gun and knows how to use it.

"I just wonder what made him pull over and lower his window like he did. He must have misidentified the threat and pulled his own gun. Pulled it twelve hundred feet per second too late!" Rich said.

The two Oklahoma lawmen stopped at a chain restaurant off the Interstate for dinner on the way back. Ray chose the baked chicken dinner and Rich settled on a salad, steamed broccoli and blackened fish. The fish was good, despite not being local. There were not many Mahi-Mahi swimming around in Oklahoma.

"Rich, didn't the former sheriff introduce you to me by another name. Am I crazy?" Ray asked.

"No. The sheriff who hired me was a strange one. He was so threatened by Jack, he pushed him out. He figured he would cultivate me as his buddy and I would replace Jack. Yeah, like right out of college with only military experience."

"He was the guy who was in line to cash his check when a serial bank robber announced a robbery. He pulled a dinky little .380 in a busy lobby and died on the spot."

"Yep. He sure did. Anyway, my full name is Richard Lucas Ammon. I have been Rich all my life. The sheriff called me Lucas and expected everyone else to also. He was an absolute jerk. It took me a while to retrieve my own identity after him."

"He sure was a jerk, Rich. On a happier vein, the

victim's sister-in-law sure had eyes for you," Ray noted with a grin.

"I kinda thought so, but I tried to remain professional. It was tough. She is stunning, heck, they both are," Rich said

"So long as she is not part of a murder conspiracy, she would be fair game after the case is over. Especially since Lily Lander's nurse has moved on. I heard you and she were dating."

"We were. Both of us got too bogged down in our careers. I also think she got scared. We were pretty serious. Maybe those wedding bell jitters scared her," Rich said.

"Could have been what prompted her to take an out-of-town job she wouldn't have taken otherwise," Ray offered.

Rich shrugged. He really did not know.

Ray dropped Rich at the office around eleven in the evening.

He got back in the Police Responder pickup and drove to his apartment.

Rich pulled into a parking space next to his Mustang and went in. He had installed a "police vehicles only" sign and was shocked the apartment management had left the thing up.

He checked mail and paid some bills online before getting on the Peloton and working out for an intense thirty minutes.

Rich had youth, DNA, a good diet, and regular exercise on his side and looked like it. His boss was ten years older and looked as good. Jack was an example he planned on continuing to emulate.

He knew Jack was putting a lot of faith in him by giving him the lead on a major murder case. Rich planned to learn more from the sheriff and as much as he could about case procedures from both his OSBI agent friend and, especially, the famous ranger.

At ten the next morning, Rich had a Zoom meeting set up in the conference room and the ranger was in his ranch house library-gun room. Books, a set of longhorns on the wood paneled wall, and a rack of late 1800's lever action rifles added a true Western atmosphere on Zack's part.

"Zack, I don't know who your interior decorator is, but I'd like to hire her," the OSBI agent commented.

"Ray, thanks, but you're a hundred years late. My great-great grandmother was the decorator. She was a helluva woman, too."

"Guys, thanks for gathering this morning. I've been briefed by our two here. They will give an executive summary to the group and follow up with a joint detailed email to all of us," Jack said. "Ray or Rich, want to start us off?"

"Following the visit to the victim's home, Rich and I went to the sister's place of work. They verified her attendance which proves she could not have been in Warrior County shooting him. The same for Mrs. Strauss at the gym. The manager mentioned the sister and the victim frequently worked out together there. When pressed, he would not elaborate any further. All three of us, after visiting the house, agreed her tearstained cheeks and the working out neither sister mentioned was... interesting. We are not sure any conclusions should be drawn from it, but still we should keep the fact on the murder board," Ray said.

"We went to the soccer field and spoke with two other coaches separately. Both gave glowing reports on

Bill Strauss. Which pretty much completes Ray's and my report for now," Rich said.

"Okay, boys. Get out your pencils and sharpen them up, because I am going to ride a trail unknown to us... the process of government contracting. I learned a lot from the CEO of Arc and his senior tribal guys on the Arc board of directors. These guys are pissed. Killing their lead and only engineer with air quality experience set them way back in the process," Zack began.

"The process was like a government procurement. But it wasn't one. Let me elaborate.

"When the government wants a good or service, they put out a request for proposal, or RFP, under pretty tight circumstances. A portion of the money paid to the winner has to go to a minority company. It is usually around ten percent. I think it's referred to as an 8a set aside to a disadvantaged business.

"Most states and other local agencies have picked up on this type of process. It is fair and it keeps things simple, especially when the federal government is somewhere in the chain.

"The top of the particular pyramid here is the National Archives and Records Administration. It's generally referred to as NARA. They would have the General Services Administration, or GSA, locate or build them a facility. They have a number of records storage facilities around the country. I am not sure of the exact number, but it really doesn't matter. The one we care about is a facility being set up in the middle of nowhere in the Oklahoma panhandle.

"A major government contractor for these sorts of things won the contract to operate this facility under strict controls. The contractor is GRP Corporation out of Chicago. They won the contract some months ago.

They already had a track record of doing reputedly good jobs of running other sites for the government.

"These National Records Center facilities will protect archival records for a number of government agencies. They sit on records for twenty or so years and destroy most afterwards. Anything they deem still needed, they keep forever.

"The tens of millions of cubic feet of boxed records in these sites do not include anything that is sensitive or classified or evidential in nature. They are stored in the generating agency's sites which are usually near DC.

"This volume of records is mainly paper. Some of it has been converted to microfilm or microfiche, both of which will oxidize and deteriorate if not kept in controlled conditions.

"It is only recently government required archiving in digital format for some records.

Mainly we are talking about a helluva lot of papers, maps, drawings and photographs.

"Now, records in these paper-based formats have a host of inherent problems. They are flammable. What puts out fires in warehouses? Sprinkler systems. What do sprinklers do to paper records? Turn them into mush.

"Some of the technology to overcome this includes low oxygen storage. Low enough to not support combustion. But, humans need to be able to access and inspect these documents. Humans need a certain level of oxygen in the air they breathe. If it is around the level which does not support combustion, the exposure time is limited.

"There are some obvious options: oxygen cutoffs once fire is detected; limiting human participation with very expensive cataloging and retrieval and replacement systems. Using sprinklers to combat fire and just take a chance, was the most usual way in the past. Another option is having employees walk around with oxygen masks every time they are in the warehouse outside of controlled observation points. The options just go on and on. The good ones are expensive and the bad ones are really bad.

"This GRP Corporation put out an RFP to build and install a records protection system at this Oklahoma site. Remember GRP is a contractor. It is not the government.

"Arc Enterprises and Government Archival Services out of Tulsa are the two competitors we know about at this standpoint.

"The Arc guys claim the Tulsa company is BS. It was put together just to bargain for ten percent of a multi-million-dollar contract. We should research and visit it. Verifying when it was formed is a piece of cake.

"Arc thinks Government Archival Services is somehow behind Strauss' death.

Personally, I think killing your competitor in a major bidding war would be pretty stupid. But as we all know, the prospect of money breeds rampant stupidity.

Any questions?" Zack finished.

He looked around the conference room via his computer screen. Most were writing and nobody seemed astounded.

"A lot of good information. I agree with you it should be too easy to solve if an obvious competitor shot Strauss or had him shot. We definitely want to talk with the people at the Tulsa company, however.

"Do you want to come up for the visit, Zack?" the sheriff asked.

"I think it would be hard to justify. The murder is an Oklahoma crime. My participation is because the victim and his employer are on my turf. What I can do is see if the Arc people can give me names of contacts in Tulsa. I should have done it yesterday, but those guys were pretty tight lipped."

"Let me have Tac do a computer search on Government Archival Services first. I'll make sure you get a copy for your files. The company should be small enough for the right person to be obvious to us," Jack said.

"Okay. Let me know. I will hang tight here in Texas until I hear from y'all," Zack said, killing his connection.

Jack waited until the other two finished writing their notes from the ranger's input.

"What do you think?" he asked the two. He knew both were smart. He also knew neither had worked a murder case. Especially one which portended to be high profile. This was not a gangbanger or drug dealer killing one of his ilk. This was an engineer driving down the highway in a rural area. A man who appeared targeted, unless they had a random serial killer who would strike again.

Before the other two could answer, Jack hit them with another question which had been bothering him.

"Why do you think Strauss was in the area where he was killed? It is nowhere near a straight line from Wichita Falls to anywhere he would logically go. It's not even a straight line to Tulsa where his competitor is headquartered. It is not near nor on the way to the site where the warehouse would be."

He punched Zack's number into the conference room phone and left it on speaker.

"Hey. Quick question. Did the Arc folks suggest why Strauss might be in Warrior County? We cannot find a single logical reason. There was no town in the direction he was headed. Quanah is generally, but it is actually on a different road."

"No, they didn't say. George Sooktis is the CEO and my main contact. I'll call him right now," Zack promised.

They talked about possible shooter types and were interrupted twenty minutes later by the ranger's call back.

"They don't know, guys. I have a meeting I can't avoid. Maybe Ray can call Myra and Rich can call Isabella. She seems to like Rich." They could visualize the grin under the ranger's mustache as he said it. Rich reddened slightly.

"I'm sure they will do it well before your meeting is done," Jack said and hung up.

"I'll call Mrs. Strauss from the OSBI cubicle you just assigned me," Ray said, rising.

"I'll just call from here, then," Rich said.

He opened his book, slowly. He was waiting to see if the sheriff was going to listen in on the call. Jack arose and walked out with "Let me know what you find."

Rich dialed and she answered on the third ring on her cellphone.

"Isabella, it's Rich Ammon from yesterday."

"Oh, hi Rich. Any new information?" she responded.

"No. We are just sifting through a lot of potentials and one really obvious question came up none of us asked yesterday," he said.

"What is it?"

"Do you have any idea why Bill Strauss was in rural Warrior County, Oklahoma yesterday morning?"

"Not a clue. No pun intended," she giggled at the end.

"You should ask Myra. Maybe she would know."

"My pard from the OSBI is calling her now."

"Why call us separately?"

41

"We always try to talk with people separately. Folks are less constrained apart. Plus, I knew you would probably be at work."

"Yes. I came in for half a day. Then Myra and I are going over to the funeral home and starting to make final arrangements. We still don't know when we can tell them to pick Bill's body up and bring it home," she said starting to sob.

"You have been really struck by Bill's death. He must have been very important to you," Rich probed.

"He was. I still cannot believe I will never see his smile again. I did some real soul searching before I came home from Tulsa to Wichita Falls. He helped me through it. He was a bigger help than my sister. She basically said, 'tough it out!' He listened and commiserated with me like a father or big brother. I'll really miss him!"

Rich was curious about the Tulsa situation to which she alluded, but suspected it was not relevant to the case. Nonetheless he had to dot one more "i."

"Isabella, you mentioned Tulsa. Are you familiar with Government Archival Services there?"

"No. It sounds like what Bill was competing to do, but I never heard of them."

"It was his competitor."

"Oh. Do you think they are involved with his death?"

"We have to look at everybody with whom he interacted in the weeks leading up to his murder. They are just parts of a puzzle we have to put together to solve the crime. And, we will solve it, Isabella."

"Rich, I feel like we have clicked. From the first. Call me Bella. It's what the people I care the most about call me," she said. Her forwardness surprised him. However, he liked Isabella better than Bella.

"Bella is appropriate anyway," he said.

"Why, Rich?"

"Isn't it Italian for 'beautiful?'," he asked.

"It is."

"If it's okay, I may switch back and forth. I think Isabella is a great name," he said smiling at her through the phone.

"Will you be back down to Wichita Falls soon?" she asked. "Maybe we can have coffee or something?"

"Coffee or something would be nice. But after the case. It's never good to mix business with pleasure," he said.

"So true. I did once and it was a big mistake."

"Tulsa?" he asked.

"Tulsa. Maybe I'll tell you about it. After you solve Bill's murder, Rich."

"You have a deal. Perhaps you can tell me over dinner."

"You have a deal there, too. Are you heading up to Tulsa soon?"

"One of us probably will. I'm not sure where the case will take me first. For now, I am switching to plain clothes and getting an unmarked vehicle. Lots going on here in Warrior County. We may have the best sheriff anywhere. You, of course, have the best Texas Ranger," he said.

"I am familiar with Zack Bodeway's and Jack Lander's reputations. I even saw the movie about Jack and the female serial killer. Those two are the greatest gunfighters alive today."

"They are. Recently, Jack had been in the hospital in a coma. Just after he was released from the hospital, a group of dangerous prisoners escaped. He took out all of the federal prisoners alone and brought back the one state prisoner. A man he had put in prison."

"I know. I follow Oklahoma law enforcement more than you might expect. We'll save the rest of this discussion for dinner. Just hurry up and give Myra and me closure on Bill's death. And, me a date for the dinner, okay?"

"Okay, Isabella. I sure will. Later," he said and hung up.

"Moving fast here Rich," he said aloud to himself.

Ray walked in.

"Find out anything helpful?"

"She does not know anything about Government Archival Services."

"Neither does sister Myra. We do though. Tac just finished the workup on it and here is your set of four pages. One set has been scanned and emailed to Zack and Jack is reading his now."

Rich took his copy and read the summary quickly.

"So, Arc was right. This company seems to have been created just to go after the contract. They even picked an appropriate name."

He read on. Ray was waiting for the next paragraph to jump out at him.

"Ben McGonigle. Treasurer. Ten years with two served. Convicted of assault with a deadly weapon. Shot a coworker with a heavy caliber pistol. This is too good to be true. We need to talk with him. Really soon!"

As if by magic timing, the phone rang and the sheriff walked in.

"McGonigle. Are you on the way to Tulsa?" the distinctive and commanding voice of the Texas Ranger asked.

"Yep! With great haste," Jack said.

"You two want to handle it? Feel free to take the unmarked Chevy and save the state some gas money if you want," he added.

"Fine with me. I just need to put my investigative kit and patrol rifle in it. I'll leave my SUV in your locked area, Jack," Ray said as he headed out to his car.

Rich was already in his new uniform of the day. It was his normal jeans, boots and white Resistol sans uniform shirt or vest. His shirt was a white Oxford cloth button down. He wore his Sig Pro .357 semiautomatic in a high, close-in brown holster on a matching belt like his boss. And, the ranger. Brown rigs were scarce back East and in the mid-West. They were much more prevalent in the West and parts of the South.

He grabbed a dark wind breaker off the back of his chair and his briefcase and headed out the door. The jacket was more for coverage than weather.

"Be safe and good hunting, Rich" Jack said as the sergeant rushed past him. Being in charge had a lot of detriments. The worst was sending people to do what you would rather be doing yourself, Jack thought. He had to let Rich take ownership of this case. It was the only way he would learn and grow. Jack walked into Rose's office and updated his chief deputy.

He stood in the doorway and watched the dark Chevrolet pull out of the parking lot and accelerate to a safe, but fast speed on the way out of town. It was thirty miles before the two would pick up I-44, cross I-35, then get on the accelerator hard for the roughly hundred miles to Tulsa.

Ray was on his smart phone. He called his dispatch and told them where he was going then called his detective friend in Tulsa.

"Hey, it's me. I'm on the way up there to talk with an

ex-con who may end up being a murder suspect. Yeah. His name is Ben McGonigle and he works for a company there called Government Archival Services. We are maybe an hour and twenty minutes out if you want to meet us there. If you would, let TPD know we are on your turf. I have Warrior County sergeant Rich Ammon with me. This is related to the assassination style shooting a couple days ago of an engineer from Texas on a rural highway in Warrior County. Thanks, man! See you in a while."

Ray hung up and turned to Rich who had just spotted an Oklahoma Highway Patrol trooper on the median about a half mile in front of them.

Rich turned on the blue LEDs in his windshield, rear window and grille as they went by. The trooper waved his acknowledgement.

"I was just talking with Mark Akins. He is a really good detective. Great guy and a lot of experience. As you heard, he will meet us there. He's single so maybe we can take him to dinner to thank him for being involved."

"Absolutely," Rich said as he pulled to the left and flew past slower traffic. There was a line of traffic ahead in the right lanes. One Mercedes was hogging the left lane.

Rich pulled in behind him. The German car proceeded at eighty miles an hour. Rich turned his lights on. Nothing. He blipped the siren. No response. Air horn. Same.

"We have a clean shoulder. Hold on, I am going to use it."

Rich pulled over onto the paved shoulder, full lights and siren operating, and floored the Chevy. They flew past the Mercedes.

Ray had already written down the license number

and called the plate and car description into the highway patrol. He advised the operator had refused to acknowledge an emergency vehicle and move aside.

"There's a trooper about a mile ahead."

"When we see him or her, I will slow down with my lights on and bring the Mercedes to a crawl for the trooper," Rich said.

He boxed the Mercedes in and the state Dodge Charger hemi took it from there. Leaving the lights on, he increased back up to ninety and proceeded towards Tulsa. Once the highway was clear, he turned the lights off. As he approached the city, he dropped his speed down to the flow of traffic level.

The agent, a decade older and former patrolman, watched Rich. He was a really good fast driver. Ray knew his predecessor, Jack Landers had gone out on a bit of a limb promoting such a young deputy to sergeant. He had learned why in the last several days.

"MEMORIZED THE FACE OF BEN MCGONIGLE?" Ray asked.

"Pretty much. He's forty, six two and two twenty. Did some Golden Gloves boxing and was a Marine. I hope he is cooperative," Rich said.

"Well, there will be three of us. We can put him on the deck. I was a Marine too."

"Yeah? What did you do, Ray?"

"Force Recon. Afghanistan."

"Me, too," Rich said.

"Oh? With who?"

"Seventy-fifth Ranger Regiment."

"Then I'm thinking the two of us plus Mark will be

47

able to handle him if it comes to a confrontation," Ray said. Rich grinned back at him with a somewhat evil grin.

Rich pulled to the curb at the company, just off their property and behind a vehicle which looked very much like a LEO unmarked.

"Yep. Mark Akins himself," Ray said as he rolled out of the Chevy and greeted his friend.

"Mark, this is Rich Ammon. And, this photo is of our man, Ben McGonigle. Did time for ADW. Big Gyrene aged forty-four. We could have a tussle."

Mark shook with Rich and studied the sheet Ray handed him.

"This guy is very familiar to me," Mark said.

"He shot at a man over a gambling deal in an Indian casino parking lot some years ago. He ran. There was a bit of a manhunt. I remember because I was part of the manhunt and was one of the two guys who caught him. He put up a helluva fight.

If he sees me, my bet is he will rabbit out of here."

"Do you think it's worth having a marked unit from your department stand by on each corner?" Rich asked.

"Yes, I do. He's tough and he's fast. Let me call it in. We should stay here out of sight until we get a couple units in position." Mark sat back in his vehicle and picked up the radio. They waited for a few minutes and two black Tulsa police interceptor SUVs pulled up next to them.

"Thanks for showing up so fast. This is Ray from the OSBI down near OKC and Rich from Warrior County. Ben McGonigle is a person of interest in a murder down there. Remember about ten years ago when we chased him for a shooting and finally hooked him up?"

"Sure do. You were the one who got him, Mark. Clay

here and I were both there. We figured there would be shooting. Sure glad there wasn't," one of the officers Mark's age said.

"Here's the only photo we have of him. Would one of you pull in front of the Chevy and keep an eye out? Maybe Stan can go around back without going directly in front of the building and drive a couple blocks around and take position. Clay, wait until you see us go in the front and pull up a little. Let Stan know on the radio. I'll take my handheld, okay?" Mark said.

They gave Stan a couple minutes to back up and do a Y-turn. He took the long way around the building from where the firm rented office space and then called when he was in position.

The Tulsa detective, OSBI agent, and Rich walked into the building. There was a guard at a desk.

"Hi. We need to go to the Government Archival Services office. What floor is it on?" Mark asked.

"Do you have an appointment? I can call them if you don't and see if someone can see you," the guard said.

All three flashed their identification.

"We want to arrive quietly. So don't call up there and let them know we are here. I'm real serious about not warning them. Do you understand?"

"Ugh. Yeah. What's going on?" he asked.

"Not anything we can talk about right now. What is the office number?"

"Three oh two. It's on the right when you get out of the elevator."

There was no way the three were going to use an elevator. They found the steps and walked up three floors.

"I'd better wait out here and go in after you have him face to face. He knows me too well," Mark said.

He waited and Rich and Ray walked in.

"Hello. We are here to see Mr. McGonigle," Rich said.

The receptionist, a dour woman with heavy makeup asked "Do you have an appointment?"

"No, Ma'am. We are here on official business," Ray said showing her his badge and ID.

"Oh! What's he done now?"

"Maybe nothing. We just want some information from him."

"Okay, I'll call him."

"Do not call him. Just tell us where his office is," Rich said firmly.

"Third office down the hall on the right," she said. Ray walked to the door and opened it. Mark came with them but held back to avoid recognition.

The three walked down the hall towards the office. All the office doors were open.

As they passed the first office a big, bald man who looked like a barroom brawler, but dressed better bellowed out.

"Who the hell are you people?"

McGonigle sprinted out of the third door and ran towards an exit.

Mark yelled "Police. Stop!" and took off after him.

The big bald CEO charged out of the first office like a bull, hitting Ray and knocking him to the floor.

Rich took advantage of the man's awkward position after the collision and spun him around. He slammed him against the wall and twisted his wrist in a come-along hold. The man screamed out in a falsetto which did not match his size or anger.

"You just assaulted a state officer. You are real close to being handcuffed and charged." The man twisted away from the hold, spraining his wrist in the process.

He crouched to charge Rich. Rich, following the "punch soft areas, butt or elbow hard ones" mantra, gave him a devastating upper cut into the solar plexus. He went down hard.

"Ray, if you will cuff him, I will catch up with Mark."

"Here take the radio. It's on their tactical frequency. Let Stan and Clay know Mark is in foot pursuit. They will join and will put out a call for backup."

Rich caught the radio on the run and sprinted towards the exit door and down the steps three at a time.

"Tulsa units, your detective is in foot pursuit of suspect. We need some backup here!" Rich said into the radio.

Somebody, he thought it was Clay, said "Copy!"

When he got to the door, he hesitated. He could not see what was on the other side of the solid steel fire door. Rich drew his Sig and kicked the bar. The door flew open and he eased through ready to fire if necessary. Nobody was there. He saw Stan exit his vehicle and begin to run down the street away from the building. Obviously, he saw something or somebody. Rich was less than a hundred yards from the Chevrolet. He sprinted to it and hopped in. Activating only the lights, he accelerated around the corner and punched it in the direction Stan had run. He saw and heard Clay coming behind him.

"Stan, where are you?" Clay asked in the radio.

"Running after him. He's out of sight right now. Turn left onto Maple. You will see me.

Rich drifted the turn and accelerated. He saw Clay on his bumper and Stan about a block up running fast.

He screeched to a halt and the Tulsa officer running down the sidewalk jumped in, breathing hard.

Stan got on his handheld and vectored responding

units in. All of a sudden, they could see five or six black units with large white "POLICE" letters spanning the front and rear doors.

"I've caught my breath. Want to pull over and we can run some?" Stan asked, grinning.

"Your turf. You call it and I'm your huckleberry."

Rich pulled to the side and threw his jacket into the back seat. He had boots on and regretted his style choice immediately, but took off nonetheless.

After ten minutes the area was saturated with Tulsa police units.

"They are responding a helicopter to help us," Stan said.

Rich nodded as he scanned three hundred sixty degrees. It would not be unusual for an escapee to hide and end up behind them. They still did not know if McGonigle was armed.

The answer came suddenly as they heard two shots which sounded like they were a couple blocks away. They ran in the direction of the shooting.

Stan was on the radio asking who fired and if there was an injury.

A unit marked in and said, "The suspect just shoved a lady with grocery bags into a house and shot at me when I was going in the door. I'm okay."

A new voice came on the radio. Stan said it was their major, who was assuming the incident commander role.

"Unit speaking broadcast the address. Units in the area set up a perimeter around the address and hold. We have to treat this as a barricaded subject case now. I will respond SWAT and a negotiator. Air unit stay at a safe range but advise if you see activity at the address."

"Crap!" Rich said. "Now there's an innocent involved.

Hopefully, there are no kids in the house or old people." Stan nodded.

"Our SWAT is one of the best around. We were selected to go overseas with only one other US team for warrior competition. We also have won some state and local championships."

Rich was impressed with Stan's words and with the power a medium city police department had brought to bear so quickly. Within minutes he saw a mobile command post deployed and other agencies beginning to assemble. The dark Suburbans heralded the fast arrival of federal agents.

Because of his familiarity with the suspect, Mark went straight to the command post. He came out shortly and summoned Rich and Ray in to discuss the suspect being a person of interest in a Warrior County murder and the events leading up to the current situation.

"Sounds like you took every possible precaution and good tactics. You had uniform officers positioned out of sight, left the agent he knew guarding the outside of the door. Textbook. The bad luck was the boss yelling out warning McGonigle. Where is he right now?" the on-scene commander asked.

"Sergeant Ammon here subdued him and I cuffed him. I sent him back to your HQ to be held until I can arrest him formally for assaulting an officer and aiding and abetting. He may be an accomplice in the murder. We don't know yet. I'm thinking Rich Ammon and I should go back and see what we can learn from him now," Ray said. Mark and Rich nodded their agreement.

"Y'all own the murder case. I have this situation. We are setting up the comms now for the negotiator. I have a real good one, so we won't need a fed. Let me send a Tulsa detective with you. Go back and see if you can learn something from the boss we can use to negotiate with. I was involved with the original manhunt for McGonigle. He might have murdered someone in Warrior County. I wouldn't put it past him. Nor would I be shocked if he ran for a totally unrelated crime we don't know about either.

"Eric, come over here a minute. You know Mark well and may know OSBI agent Ray Colton. This is Sergeant Rich Ammon. Rich is an investigator with the Warrior County Sheriff's Office. He and Ray are investigating a murder where McGonigle is a person of interest. Go with them to HQ and help them question McGonigle's boss to see if we can learn why he ran and anything we could use to help make him give up peaceably. Lean on him hard. Every second he has a hostage, her situation worsens. And, we don't know yet if there is anyone else in the house."

The detective, agent and sergeant literally sprinted to their cars.

"Follow me," the detective said as he got in.

He energized his emergency lights and roared off, with Rich and Ray on his bumper all the way.

Detective Sergeant Eric Lawson radioed in to have the prisoner waiting for them in an interview room.

They arrived and were directed to the room. A sergeant gave them the man's name, address and a clean police report. No arrests anywhere other than traffic tickets.

His name was Harry Kronk.

"Mr. Kronk, I am Sergeant Rich Ammon with the Warrior County Sheriff's Office. This is OSBI Special Agent Ray Colton and next to him is Tulsa PD Detective Sergeant Eric Lawson.

"Your employee, Ben McGonigle, escaped because

you yelled when we passed your office. He is now barricaded in at a house where he took an innocent woman hostage. He shot at a Tulsa police officer first. This situation could end very badly. You are right in the very middle of it. We would like you to assist us. It may help you with the number of charges you are already facing," Rich said.

"You hit me!"

"I hit you after you knocked an OSBI agent down and wrestled out of my restraint hold. We are looking at McGonigle for murder. You may be an accomplice. You are damn lucky, I just subdued you in a manner from which you have already recovered. I had legal options from which you would not have recovered."

"I want a lawyer."

"You are welcome to your lawyer or a public defender. However, the situation with McGonigle and his hostage has escalated to a very dangerous one. If it takes a while for your lawyer to get here and you delay telling us something which could have peacefully ended the situation …. well, the people of Oklahoma will be mad. Really mad. I can assure you it will not help any of the charges you are facing," Eric Lawson said.

"How long to get a public defender?" Kronk asked.

Ray slipped out of the interview room door and came back in two minutes later.

"There's one in the building. His schedule is open and he has agreed to represent you. I gave him a short list of the charges you are facing and how much we needed your help. I stressed time is of the essence. He will be here in five minutes."

Lawson went out and returned with a cup of water for Kronk, who slurped it down nervously.

The public defender came in. He had on a new suit

and new haircut. He looked like he had finished law school and taken his bar exam yesterday. Maybe finished middle school yesterday.

He introduced himself.

"May I have five minutes with my client?" Attorney Pete Kline asked.

Lawson nodded.

"You will turn off the recorder and the microphones, right?" Kline asked.

"Of course."

The three officers left him alone with Kronk.

Kline tapped on the door seven minutes later as the plain clothes officers fidgeted in the hall. They knew every second counted in a hostage situation.

"In the interest of time, can we keep this interview related only to information about McGonigle which might help with regard to the hostage situation? Any charges or matters related to the murder can be discussed later."

Rich, Ray and Eric agreed.

Eric turned on the audio and video recording equipment and made the required statement about the time, place and persons in the interview.

He also asked "Mr. Kronk, will you confirm for the record you have been read and signed your Fifth Amendment rights under the Miranda Decision?"

Kronk acknowledged he had and the attorney stated his assent.

"Mr. Kronk, is there anything you can tell us which might help us bring the hostage situation to a rapid close?"

The attorney looked at his new client and nodded.

"Ben has a wife and a daughter. The wife is at home, probably stoned out of her gourd. The daughter is a good kid, despite her mother and father's issues. She is at school right now. He often leaves at about three to go pick her up."

"How old is the daughter," Rich asked.

"Older. She's a senior."

Eric looked at the other two.

"If you will get the daughter's name and school, I'll call the command post. The negotiator might want her there, if she is willing. She could be crucial in ending this thing with nobody being hurt," he said.

Ray obtained the information on Fiona McGonigle. He got the information on the wife, but in view of what they learned, suspected she would be of less use to them.

Eric rushed in.

"The negotiator wants her there ASAP! Mr. Kronk and Mr. Kline, thank you. Your help will be taken into account. Mr. Kline, will you agree for Mr. Kronk to remain in custody at least until the morning when we can all get back together?"

The lawyer and Kronk nodded and the three left the interview room. They advised the custody sergeant to return Kronk to his cell for an overnight stay. He wanted a charge, so Ray came up with obstructing justice.

"You know the way, so we'll be on your bumper again," Rich told Eric.

They went to Central High School and saw a sworn TPD campus officer immediately. As they jogged to the office, they explained to her why they were there.

The principal was out so they spoke with the vice principal. She looked up Fiona McGonigle and found she had failed a grade in elementary school and therefore was eighteen years old as a senior. Which meant as an adult, they did not have to get her mother to approve her participation in what they wanted. It was completely up to her.

The vice principal accompanied them to the classroom. They stood out of sight around a corner while she summoned the girl.

"Hi, Fiona. I am Detective Lawson. We need your help."

"It must be daddy. It always is."

"I am afraid he ran from some policemen who just wanted to talk with him. He shot at one and now has taken an innocent lady hostage. The negotiator on scene thinks your presence my help us bring this to a close with nobody being hurt. Will you help us?"

She stood there for a minute and then nodded affirmatively.

"How about a real fast ride in a police car? We need to get back as quickly as possible."

"Sure. My boyfriend always drives too fast. I am used to it," she said.

"Rich, you are used to driving fast in the country. How about Fiona and I follow you. I'll try to keep up," Eric said. Rich winked at him and he and Ray got in the dark Chevy and energized the LEDs.

Fiona slipped into the seat next to Eric.

"Fasten your seat and shoulder belt. You're going to need them!" Eric said.

They saw the campus TPD officer fly by in her marked unit, lights going. She went up three blocks to a large intersection and blocked it without bidding.

"There's a real pro!" Ray remarked as Rich drove the unmarked car through with full lights. Ray worked the siren toggles, using the yelp in the intersection, punctuated by the air horn. It got everyone's attention. Eric and his passenger followed them through at speed.

"Rich, we have two more big intersections and then a straight run on a four lane divided road as I remember," Ray said. Rich, watching traffic intently, nodded.

At each of the two intersections, Rich entered, blocked and allowed the TPD detective to power through. Then, he hit the throttle hard and passed him at speed.

On the four lane divided road, they picked up as much speed as prudence would allow.

"I guess my boyfriend only thinks he can drive fast," McGonigle's daughter commented.

Rich doused the siren as they got within several blocks of the hostage scene. Eric had advised them by cellphone nothing had changed.

They drove through the press and onlookers who were kept out by a line of TPD officers, then through a plethora of different uniforms and raid jackets to the command post.

Entering, Fiona McGonigle was introduced to the on-scene commander and his hostage negotiator.

"Miss, we really need to talk with your father. He just won't pick up the phone in the house. I'd like for you to ask him to pick it up when it rings. This microphone is connected with a powerful public address system. He will hear you whether he wants to or not."

With a quavering voice unfortunately heard by the media and the whole neighborhood, she did as bidden.

The negotiator dialed the home phone and McGonigle answered.

"Fiona?" he said.

The negotiator put the receiver in Fiona's hand. It was on speaker. The negotiator flipped a neon light within the command vehicle which was like a motor

59

G. WAYNE TILMAN

home. The light was "SILENCE" in bright red neon letters.

Fiona spoke with her father. The negotiator guided her on a white tablet which he hurriedly filled with notes by a black grease pencil.

She pleaded for her father to speak with the negotiator. Finally, he agreed.

"Ben, my name is Lee. My job here is to work as your partner to assure this matter is resolved quickly. And, with nobody, including you, hurt."

"If I give up, I'll go back to prison," McGonigle said.

"Ben, anything beats you committing a violent act with your daughter here. You don't want that, do you? She's doing everything she can to help you and me to bring this to a safe, happy conclusion."

They spoke for another ten minutes, often about irrelevant matters until the negotiator steered McGonigle back to where the negotiation continued.

Finally, McGonigle agreed to send his hostage out. After, he would walk out unarmed and with his hands raised.

The commander alerted the SWAT team and other officers what was going to happen and to hold their fire. SWAT had a green light in case everything went south and it was necessary to neutralize the hostage taker.

The woman came out slowly. Two SWAT operators appeared from nowhere and moved her behind the side corner of the house. It was the quickest protected location for her.

McGonigle walked out, hands held high. Four SWAT team members took him to the ground. They searched him thoroughly and cuffed him in the back. They helped him up and to the backseat of a patrol vehicle which left in the middle of a three-car caravan for TPD headquar-

60

ters. Another group of operators entered the house to recover the gun and assure no other person was inside.

The woman who had been such a brave hostage broke down in sobs and was reunited with her husband and their pastor.

Fiona McGonigle broke into tears and collapsed against the closest person. It was the sergeant from Warrior County. He patted her on the back as she soaked his white shirt.

When she broke away and left to see her father once he was booked, Rich turned to the commander, negotiator and SWAT leader. The latter had just reported to the command post.

"You gentlemen are consummate pros. I salute you. I am going to head to your interview rooms. You have an assault on a police officer and hostage taker. I have a murder suspect. He may be in a more cooperative mood now," Rich said.

They all shook hands, including Ray, Mark and Eric.

"I guess I have a press conference to make off the cuff. I suspect the chief and the mayor will, too," the major said.

The four whose visit to speak with McGonigle had prompted four hours of stress decompressed some as they drove downtown to interview him.

Rich called Jack on the phone and updated him.

"I agree. Though I doubt the choice will be ours anyway. I wish McGonigle and Kronk had different lawyers. Still and all, nobody got shot. Especially not us! So, I'm willing to step out for some better coffee than the machine here. Or, I suspect the pot in the detective squad room."

"Sound like words of wisdom. Let's tell Eric our plan. I am sure he will be in on McGonigle's first interview. Maybe he will text one of us when it's our turn at the trough," Rich said.

Not knowing the senior detective's location, Ray texted him their plans and request to be contacted when time to interview McGonigle.

The found a non-chain coffee and donut shop nearby and played cop with two donuts apiece and three cups of coffee.

Eric called them thirty minutes later. It seems attorney Pete Kline was on the ball. In view of two clients and one lawyer, with McGonigle, facing hours of interviews he had scheduled Rich and Ray's interview of Kronk first. Eric and Mark Akins from TPD would observe from outside. Rich and Ray would be given the same privilege on McGonigle before they questioned him themselves.

Rich took his last bite of a chocolate donut and finished his coffee. They were back in the hall where the interview rooms were within several minutes.

They did not have time to plan a questioning strategy. They chatted on the way over.

"The best questions are leading ones where you already know the answer, so we have to rely on them," Ray began as they walked.

"We know the structure of the request for proposal. Who's at the top, two of the minority firms who are bidders, and the general description of the design upon which they are bidding," Rich added.

"Right. I am not sure we need to play good cop, bad cop until we get in there and see how Kronk responds," Ray said. Rich nodded his agreement.

They entered the designated room. Kronk and his attorney were already seated.

Ray turned on the recorder and video and stated the time, location and persons present in the interview.

"Greetings gentlemen," Rich began.

"Thank you for the opportunity to use the information Mr. Kronk gave us and to reschedule our interview."

"Was the information helpful?" Kline asked.

"It was," Ray replied.

"What charges are pending for Mr. Kronk?" the attorney asked.

"The only charges at this point are resisting arrest. The reason we came to Mr. Kronk's company to begin with was as part of a murder investigation in my county earlier this week," Rich said.

"So, further charges may or may not be brought depending on the results of the murder investigation, of which your client Mr. McGonigle is a prime suspect," Ray said.

"Why do you think my clients or their company may be involved in a murder?" Kline asked.

"With all due respect, counselor, may I remind you we are here to ask the questions and you are here to counsel your client in answering them?" Rich said pleasantly but firmly.

"Go ahead then."

"Thank you. Mr. Kronk, how long has your company been in existence?" Ray asked.

"Four months, more or less," he said.

"Why was it initially formed?"

"I watch area RFPs for opportunities. I saw the one from GSC for fire control in an Oklahoma site and thought it was worth going after. I set up a minority firm with my wife having fifty-one percent ownership."

"Let the record show GSC stands for Government Services Corporation, a contractor in this case for the US Government," Ray said.

"It appears to be a small company with you as the CEO. Who was your engineer?" Rich asked.

"He is a retired air flow engineer I found. He was not in his office when you came yesterday. His name is Lloyd Emerson," Kronk said.

"What is Mr. McGonigle's function?" Rich asked.

"He was a general do-all. We wanted enough people to start a corporation but not so many we had to offer Workman's Comp Insurance."

"You say 'general do-all,' what did he actually do?" Ray asked.

"Not much of anything yet. He is my cousin and needed work after his stint in prison."

"Who else is competing for the minority portion of the GSC request for proposal?" Rich asked.

"The only one I know of is Arc down in Texas. Indian owned. Comanche or Cheyenne or something."

"Have you met any of the folks down there?" Ray said.

"I haven't. I had Ben contact their engineer and ask for a meeting. I thought maybe instead of competing, we could join forces. Half of a lot of money is still a lot of money."

"When was the meeting? And where?" Ray asked.

"It was Wednesday. They were going to meet half-way," Kronk said.

"Where?

"Southwest of Oklahoma City. I never knew the address. They were going to work it out by cell phone once both of them got in the area."

"What transpired in the meeting?" Rich asked.

"Apparently nothing. Ben showed up the next morning pissed off. Said the other guy, the engineer, had bagged him."

"So, he didn't show?"

"Yes."

"What was his name?" Ray asked, knowing they were getting to a crucial point.

"It was the guy who died. William Strauss."

"Why would you send McGonigle, a known criminal and troublemaker and risk your potential business deal? Why not send your own engineer or go yourself?

"I was trying to give him a chance. To show some trust," Kronk said.

"Had you ever had any contact with Strauss, related to the RFP or at any time?" Ray asked.

"Never. I don't know if Ben ever met him, killed him, or what. I sure didn't have anything to do with his death. Not at all!" Kronk said vehemently.

They were interrupted by Eric who requested they take a break for five minutes.

Rich announced the break and time on the recording then shut it off.

"A message just came in for you, Ray. It's some more ammunition, so to speak, for your questions," the TPD detective said.

Ray took the slip of paper from his criminalist. He read it and handed it to Rich.

"The caliber has been determined to be .357 Sig. As far as I know, there are no rifles or short carbines made for it. It is a semiauto caliber, so the empty case either ejected into the shooter's vehicle or was picked up. The latter is the mark of a pro.

"The US Secret Service has used a Sig in .357 Sig for years. They are phasing into Glocks in 9mm like the rest of the feds now. Our sheriff's department uses the Sig in .357 now. It mimics the .357 magnum revolver round and is snappier than the 9mm.

"I think the reason for the exit wound damage may be the caliber. This narrows our search down a lot. It is not a real popular caliber among citizens," Rich said.

"Eric, what caliber did your SWAT guys find in the house at the end of the barricaded subject incident?"

"A .38 revolver. Which is going to get him an ADW charge against a police officer and us also advising the ATF because he was a felon with a firearm."

"But not a .357," Rich reiterated. "We have to ask Kronk if he knows his cousin ever had one."

They went back in. Ray made the continuation announcement.

"Mr. Kronk, do you know if your cousin Mr. McGonigle ever owned a .357 Sig caliber handgun?" Ray asked.

"Not as far as I know. Is it like a .357 magnum?" he responded.

"Kinda, but only in semiautomatic pistols. Never chambered in a revolver as far as I am aware."

"Was he even allowed to have a gun?" Kronk asked.

"No. He was a convicted felon."

"Okay gentlemen, let's not get into any speculation here about charges for my other client. I don't want you guys mixing metaphors here," Kline said.

They spoke with Kronk for another thirty minutes, mainly getting a better understanding of the request for proposal and how they intended to handle the minority part if they won it.

"What charges do you envision for my client?" Kline asked.

"The only one we had, barring any unforeseen conspiracy to commit murder, was resisting arrest with force. Given agreement by the district attorney, and Mr. Kronk's cooperation today, we might be willing to not charge him. We would, of course, want you to provide paperwork saying he was detained appropriately and held overnight per counsel's agreement," Rich said.

"I believe I could see my way to preparing such a document," Kline said.

"Will you be involved in the interview of Mr. McGonigle?" he asked.

"Not the part about the barricaded subject. TPD will handle those matters. We will interview him about his whereabouts on the day of the murder and more details regarding his planned meeting with Mr. Strauss," Ray said.

They all stood. Rich and Ray nodded at Kronk and his lawyer and left the room.

"Our interview of McGonigle is scheduled for forty-five minutes if you want to grab a bite before watching from the outside of the two-way window," Eric said.

"Any idea when we will get to interview him about the murder? As you heard, he was supposed to be meeting our victim on the day of the murder. They were supposedly going to discuss the two firms doing a joint submission on the RFP," Ray said.

"I suspect it will be tomorrow. We will charge McGonigle with trying to shoot a TPD officer, fleeing, holding someone against their will, and the federals will charge him for being a felon in possession of a firearm. Are you going to charge Kronk with assaulting a state officer?" Eric asked.

"Probably not. He was pretty helpful. His information about the daughter may have kept people alive, Eric. I believed him about McGonigle and not knowing what he really did," Ray said. Rich nodded his agreement.

"We are going to hit him hard on why he ran when he knew you were there to speak with him. Was it because of the Strauss murder? Or was it something else he was guilty about? You may find it interesting," Eric said.

"We'll be there taking notes for our turn tomorrow. It's pretty interesting Kronk chose McGonigle to meet with Strauss, who was an engineer. Kronk had his own engineer. Why not send him to meet with Strauss?" Ray thought aloud.

"It bothers me, too. Kronk had to know McGonigle was conniving and probably untrustworthy. Why risk it? I thought his answer was a dumb business decision at best," Rich said.

"Eric, we told the lawyer, Kline, we would withhold charges if he would prepare a document acknowledging the overnight stay in the cell was his and his client's choice and no claims would be brought against us or the agencies involved, including yours, regarding his treatment. This was because he cooperated with every question and helped mitigate the hostage deal."

"Okay. I will make sure we get it before we spring Kronk and Kline leaves. Maybe before the McGonigle interview," Eric said.

"How late is the coffee shop down the street open?" Ray asked.

"It's closed now. It you drive, go three blocks further down. There is a halfway decent place to eat on the left. See you in about forty minutes?" Eric responded.

"Ten-four!" Ray said.

"You are showing your age with ten signals, pal!" Eric said. Ray saluted the detective and he and Rich hurried towards the exit.

They got in the Chevy and were seated in the restaurant minutes later.

"It's going to be a long night, I fear. Don't let me forget to warn my wife. We'd be smart to get a couple of rooms and not try to drive back home at midnight."

"I agree," Rich said. "Maybe we could find a Walmart or something and pick up clean socks and drawers and some toothbrushes, toothpaste, razor and all."

"Good thinking. We will check with Eric. He might know of a reasonable motel close by too, Rich."

On the way back, both investigators checked in with their bosses.

"So. You don't think there was any sort of conspiracy to kill Strauss?" Jack Landers asked.

"No, I don't. I hope tonight or our interview tomorrow will shed light on the planned meeting with Strauss and why McGonigle ran. He was real damn serious about not wanting to answer questions. I believe he did something. Ray and I just don't know exactly what it is yet, Jack."

"Okay. Use all your persuasive and, if necessary, threatening skills. Keep track of your expenses. I'll tell the chief you will be turning in a voucher. Be safe and let me know if there is a major breakthrough tonight."

"Roger wilco," he said to the former Coast Guardsman indicating Jack's last was "received and understood and Rich will comply."

They took their seats and donned earphones to listen to Eric and another detective, probably a more senior one, begin to interview McGonigle.

McGonigle was a hard case. Kline knew he had a tougher defense to mount with McGonigle than he would have with Kronk, had the latter been charged.

Kline had asked McGonigle under the blanket of attorney-client privilege if he had killed Strauss. McGonigle had said he had not, but his attorney was not so sure. The client was facing serious state charges and the federal gun charges. Those were cut and dry. He would serve time for them. He was a convicted felon who not only had a firearm under his control, he had fired it at a police officer in front of witnesses. The recovered revolver had his prints all over it.

Eric and his partner in the interview came in fast and hard. If McGonigle was shaken by their first salvos, he did not show it. Kline knew the best he could do was insure fairness and reduce incarceration as much as possible. But his client was going back to prison. There was no doubt about it.

"Tell us about your trip to Warrior County on Wednesday morning the tenth." The question was a fishing trip because they did not know the location of the meeting with Strauss. So, they used the location of the murder.

"I got there early and found a turn off. I called him and he didn't answer. I gave him a half hour and he never answered. He did not know where to show up. So, I drove towards MacKenzie and found a truck stop, had coffee and some toast and drove back to Tulsa."

"What time did you get to the truck stop?"

"Around ten or so, I guess. No later than ten. I still had plenty of time before they switched to the lunch menu," McGonigle said.

Rich asked Ray a question by note from their observation post outside the interview room. Ray took his earphones off and they spoke quietly without having to write notes back and forth.

"Did the medical examiner who did he autopsy have a conclusive time of death? I scanned the report for what I was looking for—the bullet—and didn't pay enough attention," Rich asked.

"Between nine-thirty and ten."

"Damn! Unless he drove as fast as Jack does, he has a pretty good alibi for not being the shooter. He would have to literally fly to get from the murder scene to a table at the truck stop when he says he was there. I hope he used a card. We will be able to track the time."

Rich stepped into the hall and called Jack. He was not in, but Rose Custalow, the chief deputy was.

"Rose, you know the truck stop where Jack and Lily broke up the bar fight a year and a half ago? Could you send a unit by there when the lunch shift is in tomorrow and see if Ben McGonigle had lunch there on Wednesday? I will let you know later if he used cash or a card. Thanks! Have a good night!"

At a break, Rich slipped a note to Eric to try to find out how he paid his lunch bill and told him he had requested a unit to verify the time from an alibi standpoint.

By ten PM, the interview had moved to McGonigle's reason to run when the sergeant and the OSBI agents came to interview him.

The TPD detectives pushed him hard, with constant interruptions by attorney Kline. At midnight, McGonigle asked to speak with his attorney in private. The meeting was granted.

Kline tapped on the one-way window when they were through. The two interviewers went in and restarted the interview with Kline being the first to speak.

"My client has a confession. We will offer it in exchange for the fleeing charge being dropped." Kline knew the fleeing charge would be the only negotiable one. Shooting at a police officer, taking a hostage and the federal gun charge were definite.

The two detectives knew they had McGonigle for some hard time. He was going to either confess to murder or some other crime serious enough to make him take the risks he did. They had little to lose giving up the fleeing. They knew the district attorney would agree.

"Alright. Pending almost certain approval from the district attorney, we will drop the fleeing charge in favor of Mr. McGonigle's confession," the senior detective, Lawson Payne, said.

McGonigle looked at his attorney, who nodded his go ahead. It was correctly presumed the TPD detectives had been briefed about the Oklahoma murder and the RFP.

"When Strauss stood me up, I had a wasted trip with nothing to show for it. The archive air deal was not looking good, which meant I was going to be out of work. Again.

"I wanted to get out of Warrior County. I've read about their gunfighter sheriff who shoots criminals instead of arresting them.

Once I cleared the county line, I saw a jewelry store. There was one old guy in it. I tied him up in the back and robbed it. He was fine when I left on Wednesday around noon."

"Mr. McGonigle, we will have to verify your confession. A couple of questions first. Where was it. Do you remember the name of it? Where did you put the items you stole?"

"I fenced a bunch of the stuff at Frenchy's Pawn outside of town here. The rest is in my garage."

"And, you stated you did not harm the proprietor?"

"Yep. I didn't hurt the old geezer at all."

"It is too late to verify your claim. We are going to charge you with the shooting at a police officer and taking a hostage, which will give us more than enough to hold you. We will ask the magistrate to not allow you to post bond. Under the circumstances, you are a danger to the public. This concludes our interview at twelve thirty AM," and repeated the participants and the date and location.

McGonigle was left to speak with his attorney.

The two detectives huddled with Rich and Ray.

"We won't know until we verify the time from the truck stop, but it kinda looks like he's not going to be Strauss' killer," Rich said.

"Guys, the jewelry store is in my district. I am totally unaware of it being robbed. I don't know the owner personally, but I am really worried about his safety right now!" Ray said.

He called his dispatch and asked that his supervisor be notified and to send some local police units to do a welfare check on the owner. "Guys, I have a really bad feeling about this!" Ray said.

All waited there until OSBI dispatch called back forty minutes later. Local police and rescue had to break in at the jewelry store. They found the old man tied in a chair in the stock room. He had been dead for several days. There were no overt wounds, but an autopsy would tell for sure. At the least, McGonigle was looking at felony manslaughter if not murder.

Ray was upset and decided to make the drive back home. He went with Rich while the latter looked for a hotel but could not find an available room. He took Ray to a rental and the OSBI agent rented a subcompact to drive home.

Rich picked up supplies at a pharmacy and parked in a dark corner of the police car area of the TPD lot after brushing his teeth inside the building. He pushed the driver's seat back as far as possible took off his boots and tried to sleep.

He saw a missed call as he put his iPhone on the seat. It was Isabella from only half an hour ago. After one. Going against his better judgement, he replied to her call with a text. "Hi. Sorry missed you. In Tulsa. Sleeping in car in PD lot. Rich"

His phone rang almost instantly after the text was delivered.

"Hi. How are you, Rich? Was just thinking about you. How is my old city? Hope I am not calling too late!" she said in a voice which was naturally sultry.

"No. There's no one to care even if it was too late. How are you?"

"Still trying to get my life in order after moving home from Tulsa. Still upset over Bill. Are you any closer to solving it?"

"I thought I had it done several times today. But, nothing so far."

"I saw a hostage crisis in Tulsa today. A deputy and OSBI went to call on a man and he ran. Do I know the deputy?"

"I'm afraid so, Bella. Everybody ended up safe and he's in custody. We will interview him tomorrow."

"About Bill's murder?" she asked.

"I have said too much already. You may have read the

hostage taker was part of the company which competed against Bill's. So, it's logical we are speaking with everybody concerned. Watch tomorrow's news. You will see he was involved with something else unrelated."

"Are you tired?" she asked.

"Yes, but more from stress than exercise. I have had several high speed runs in city traffic today. Fun in movies, nerve wracking in real life."

"You poor dear! Why are you sleeping in your car. At your height it must be miserable."

"Sleeping in a safe car beats several years in Afghanistan, with a rifle in my hand, Isabella. I'll take this any day."

"Several years. Wow. Army?"

"Yes. 75th Ranger Regiment."

"I know rangers are special. Will you tell me about it one day? Or, are you one who cannot or will not speak about your experience? If so, I understand. My father was that way about Vietnam."

"No, I'm comfortable speaking about anything I did which was not classified. I am very proud to be a ranger. And, to be a sergeant in an outstanding sheriff's department."

"Wouldn't you have made more money and maybe risen faster in a large police department?" she asked.

"Probably. I like the diversity of duties and the way we have to be self-sufficient. I have a great sheriff and couldn't be happier."

"I'm so glad, Rich! I have done a little research. I already knew about Sheriff Landers being such a gunfighter. I also found you were Oklahoma Officer of the Year last year. I am duly impressed."

"Thanks, but don't be. I was just doing my duty."

"Crawling into a destroyed mobile home after a

tornado and removing two old people? I'd say you went far above and beyond your duty."

"It was the right thing to do. I follow Davy Crockett. He said "Be sure you're right, then go ahead.""

"He was the frontiersman in the coonskin cap, right? Died at the Alamo."

"Exactly. He may have been the last man executed there. A lot of people don't know he was also a US Congressman before he went to Texas."

"You must be a history buff, Rich!"

"Yes. Western history especially. My college was pure Criminal Justice, so the history is just a hobby."

"I guess you are pretty familiar with Major Robert Rogers?"

"You are a constant surprise! Of course, I know the head of Roger's Rangers. We rangers trace our heritage back to them. Though Rogers himself fought against us as a loyalist in the Revolutionary War, many of his rangers were patriots."

"I can see we are going to have fun comparing historical notes," Isabella said.

"How do you know about Robert Rogers? Almost nobody now ever heard of him."

"BA. History of the American West at OU."

"My dream degree. You are quite a woman," he said before he realized what was coming out of his mouth.

"What a nice thing to say, Rich," Isabella said.

"It just kind of popped out."

"I like the way you state things. I bet you write beautiful police reports."

"Could be. Thanks."

"You have to be exhausted. I'd better let you try to get some rest folded up in your police car. Or truck. Or whatever they assigned you. Just hurry up and solve

Bill's murder. I'm keeping my fingers crossed for closure here in Wichita Falls. Also, for the conflict of interest to disappear so we can have dinner together. Okay?"

"I promise to do my best to make sure both things happen as speedily as possible, Isabella. Word of honor."

"Hugs and kisses. Good night Sergeant!" she hung up before he could respond.

Sergeant Richard Lucas Ammon realized two things in the next few minutes. A Caprice police interceptor was way too small for a man of his size to sleep in. And, he was moving very fast with Isabella Munro. And, it did not worry him anywhere near as much as it should.

Sleep finally came. So did morning. He put his boots on and put on the nylon raid jacket he had used as a blanket. He moved the blazer from the backseat to the trunk. It was six-thirty. He started the car and drove to the coffee shop close by. It was just opening, so he pulled into a parking space.

Rich found they had real breakfasts in addition to coffee and pastries. He had three medium poached eggs over corned beef hash and several cups of coffee.

He waited in the parking lot at the police building. He saw Ray arrive in the tiny rental and took him to return it.

RICH AND RAY were waiting outside the appointed interview room when two deputies brought a shackled Ben McGonigle over. Attorney Kline showed up immediately after, dapper and searched brief case in hand.

Eric and his fellow detective from last night were next to arrive. Both looked haggard and exhausted. Rich thought, all things considered, he was pretty presentable for someone who slept in his car. Ray chalked it up to the benefits of youth.

"Okay gentlemen, perhaps we should get together in a conference room and talk about today and where we stand with Mr. McGonigle," Detective Lieutenant Lawson Payne suggested.

They got cups of bad coffee and adjourned to a nearby room and sat down.

"Rich, how strong is Warrior County's murder case against McGonigle?" Payne asked.

"Not anywhere near as strong as I had hoped. I have a unit going to where he had breakfast to check on his claimed time. One of Ray's and my first questions to him will be whether he used a card or cash. A card would tie the time down nicely.

"If he was there as early as he claimed and assuming the medical examiner's time of death is pretty accurate, it seems unlikely he would be able to shoot Strauss and drive to the truck stop for breakfast. Which sends our case against him straight down the toilet. If one made a leap of logic and presumed the ME was way off and McGonigle went back to kill Strauss after eating, the whole jewelry store robbery gets in the way of my case.

"Ray's and my agreed upon goal today is to learn as much as we can about his trip to Warrior County and the negotiation for the records deal. If we get confirmation he was eating near MacKenzie at zero nine thirty, we may as well just pack up our tents and take the wagons home."

"I concur with everything my associate said," Ray added, "but remind you I will be deeply involved if not the lead on the jewelry robbery and death case. My supervisor and the Norman police department are trying to figure who's going to run it now.

"Makes sense to me, too," Eric and Lawson agreed.

"Our part this morning is to cover the bases from when he ran on you to when we took him into custody at the hostage scene. No more," Eric said.

"It strikes me McGonigle has no particular reason to cooperate with you two. He has easy guilty verdicts hanging over his head with the jewelry stuff, taking a hostage and shooting at a police officer. He's looking a long, hard time as it is. He is still on probation. And, he has the mandatory federal gun charge. Your time this morning may be short and in vain," Eric continued.

Rich and Ray checked their respective Sig and Glock pistols into storage lockers and went into the interview room. Kline nodded. McGonigle did not. He looked down at his hands on the table. His handcuffs had been removed.

Rich was not aware of whether he was wearing shackles around his ankles, but this was not the time to inquire.

Eric and Lawson were wearing earphones in the observation area.

Ray turned on the recording system and made the appropriate announcements about time, place and identity of all participants.

"Mr. McGonigle, Special Agent Colton and I are here this morning to ask you some questions about your participation in the submission of a response to a request for proposal for the air system for a federal records archive site. We will also ask you why you ran as we came down the hall to just speak with you. You appear to be one of the very last people to see William Strauss before he was shot to death. We will go into any contacts you had with him.

"At this point, we do not plan on questioning you

about what happened yesterday after you fled your office. Nor do we plan to question you about the jewelry store robbery you admitted last night to committing near Norman, Oklahoma on Wednesday afternoon.

"You should know my associate with the OSBI will have a leadership role in investigating the robbery and what happened to the owner. However, those matters will be reviewed in Norman at some future date.

Do you understand our plan today?" Rich said.

"No comment."

"Mr. McGonigle, will you confirm you have been read and signed your Fifth Amendment rights under the Miranda Decision?" Ray asked.

"No comment."

"Mr. Kline, will you confirm the rights have been given?"

"Yes. They were. Twice actually. The first time was just after his arrest following the incident yesterday and then again once he was thoroughly searched, finger-printed, and photographed here."

"Thank you, Mr. Kline," Ray said.

"Mr. McGonigle, did you at some time prior to this past Wednesday, speak on the phone with one William Strauss with Arc Enterprises in Wichita Falls, Texas?" Rich asked.

"No comment."

"Did you drive from Tulsa to Warrior County, Oklahoma last Wednesday for the purpose of meeting with William Strauss?" Rich asked.

"No comment."

"Did you actually meet with Mr. Strauss on Wednesday morning in Warrior County?"

"No comment."

Thirty questions later, the two had learned nothing due to lack of response. The man was unshakeable.

Eric knocked on the door and handed Rich a folded note.

It was the result of the verification of McGonigle's breakfast outside MacKenzie on Wednesday morning. Rose had gone over herself and found the waitress remembered McGonigle because he had hit on her and stiffed her with a 5% tip. The charge was put through on his card at ten AM. The waitress said she served him at least thirty minutes prior. She had seen him enter, shop around, and he disappeared for a while. She thought he was probably in the men's room. This verified he was highly unlikely to have been able to commit the murder of William Strauss.

Rich passed it to Ray. Ray read it with the same stone face Rich had. They knew the attorney was watching them for signs and both resolved not to give him one.

"Okay, Mr. McGonigle. One last question," Rich began.

"Did you, on Wednesday morning meet with William Strauss in Warrior County and shoot him to death?"

McGonigle paused for a second, then came over the table for Rich. Ray rolled out of the way and Rich stepped left and slammed both hands down on McGonigle's shoulders. It caught McGonigle off balance and he face planted on the table with the big sergeant on top of him.

Rich pinned him and grabbed his right hand. He twisted the wrist back, the lawman's hands squeezing several fingers apart.

McGonigle screamed at the pain. Eric entered and handcuffed him.

Ray made the announcement "The interview has

ended at ten forty-two AM with the suspect attacking Sergeant Ammon."

Several uniformed officers came in and took McGonigle into custody.

Rich focused a cold stare on the attorney.

"I didn't expect him to lose it," Kline said, withering under the look.

"I will see you at his trial and Special Agent Colton will also see you at the jewelry murder trial," Rich snarled.

"Are you going to charge him with the Strauss murder?" Kline asked.

Rich turned and walked out the door to retrieve his pistol without answering. Let him stew in his juices. He will find out soon enough no charges will be forthcoming on the Strauss murder.

Ray followed him, unlocked the locker and holstered his .45 Glock. Rich did the same and they left the keys in the locks for the next interviewers.

"Well, with all his passivity, I didn't see the over the table thing coming," Ray said.

"Just goes to show, you just never can tell," Rich said.

"I am going home, getting a shave and shower and sleeping for the rest of the day," he added.

They got into the Chevy and headed southwest towards the Warrior County Sheriff's Office for Ray to pick up his state car.

"Looks like I may have three murders to work on," Ray said.

"Looks like. I will start over on Strauss. You help when you can. You know I value your input, my friend. At least you have a confession on the old gent who died. The question is the charge. Negligent manslaughter? Some degree of murder during commission of a

G. WAYNE TILMAN

robbery? Bet the district attorney in the county outside of Norman will wrestle with McGonigle's man on it after a guilty finding," Rich said.

"I'm sure, Rich. This has been a weird one from the get go. Since McGonigle is no longer viable as a suspect, I have no idea where to look next."

"Tomorrow we should do a video call with Jack and Zack aboard. Maybe one of them can come up with a good thought. What about nine-thirty?" Rich said.

"Sounds fine. Maybe we can make it audible only and I'll do it from home. I am beat."

"Me, too."

When they got back to the county seat Ray recovered his SUV and left for home without going inside.

Rich checked in with Rose who took one look at him and told him to go home and get some sleep. She said she would arrange the conference call with Jack and the ranger for nine-thirty in the morning. He gave her a tired smile and walked out the door.

He had transferred his police gear to the Chevy, so instead of transferring it back to the truck, he drove the older sedan home.

Rich looked at the Peloton and shook his head. He opted for a hot shower ending with cold water instead. He crawled into bed and was asleep instantly.

He woke up thirsty at nine. After a drink of water, he wondered how Isabella was doing, so he called her.

She answered on the third ring.

"Hi, Sarge," she said comfortably like she had been calling people 'Sarge' all her life.

"Hi yourself. I just got back to MacKenzie and collapsed into bed after a shower. I woke up and thought about you, so…."

"Were you dreaming about me?"

84

"I may have been. I don't remember my dreams when I wake up," he responded.

"Good save, Rich! Anything new you can share?"

"My primary suspect's alibi was corroborated. It's ironclad. Back to the proverbial drawing board. I requested a conference call with our de facto task force for the morning. Otherwise, there's no news fit to print."

"I was hoping you had it solved so we could have dinner," she said. He was not sure whether her manner of speaking was coquettish or it was something she turned on and off. He really hoped it was the former. For him, at least.

"I was too, Isabella. Hang with me. I will solve it and we will have dinner as soon as possible."

"I guess your sense of propriety and ethics prohibits dinner before the case is solved?" she probed. Before he could answer, she added "because I'm still as suspect?" This time her voice had a serious hesitation.

"No, you were where you claimed to be. The reason is you are a victim. It would not look good and both the sheriff's office and I would be censored if it got out. Nothing more."

"I kind of thought so, but had to yank your chain a little bit," she giggled.

"You did. For sure."

"Is it okay to tease you?" she asked.

"Sure it is."

"I'm glad. I may be a good girl with a naughty side."

"And that's a bad thing?" he asked.

"Right answer! You go to the head of the class. Actually, you are the only one in the class."

"One on one sounds like a good ratio for learning," he said.

She hesitated and thought about it for a few seconds

and decided to agree and not explore whether it was a Freudian slip.

"What if you never find out who did it?" she asked.

"We will solve it. If we don't, you and I will be having regular dinners well before it hits cold case status."

"Breakfasts too?" she asked.

"Especially breakfasts."

"I am going to let you go back to sleep and dream about me some more. I always like to end on a win. Breakfast counts as a big win. Bye!" she blew a kiss and disconnected before he could respond.

Rich looked at the phone as if it might explain something to him. The phone was no help so he put it on the bedside table and rolled over. This time, he remembered what he dreamed about. It definitely included a curvaceous blonde in a leading role.

The next morning, Rich was up and on the exercise machine. He sent Isabella a text before he walked out of the door.

It was short and simple. "Remembered dream this morning. Beautiful blonde starred."

THE CONFERENCE CALL was more of an update by Rich and Ray to the sheriff and the ranger than it was a strategy session. Zack Bodeway offered to contact the procurement officer for the corporation which put out the RFP to see if he could learn whether there was a third or possibly fourth company seeking the minority set-aside. Jack suggested he also ask whether they were aware of any enemies which might stoop to cold blooded murder to slow or stop the completion of the site, or generally harm GSC for any reason.

"Does anyone else think we should dig deeper into the victim? On the surface, he's a well-liked deacon, a kid's athletic coach and a respected engineer. Can anyone be so perfect? Does he have a skeleton in a closet nobody knows about?" Rich asked.

"In absence of a better line of inquiry, perhaps Rich's line is one we should pursue," Jack Landers said.

They ended with Rich agreeing to look deeper into William Strauss. He did not say anything, but he had been fearful since the idea first appeared in his psyche it may harm his budding relationship with Isabella. He faced a law enforcement and a personal dilemma. His innate integrity pushed him to sit down with her face-to-face and flat out tell her what he was having to do.

"Hey, Rich. Drop by before you head back out, okay?" Jack asked.

"I've got the time now, boss. What's up?"

"I've been thinking and Rose is in agreement. We will have a couple additional slots for deputies open up shortly and Tac has worked out DHS and state funding to cover cars and equipment.

"What would you think about switching to an unmarked vehicle, keeping your district, but serving as our primary investigator? When you have a big case going like now, Rose will pull the two adjacent district deputies in to help cover your turf. Just like we are currently doing. It seems to be working okay. If we ended up with a crime wave around your district, as investigator you'd be on it anyway."

"That sounds real good, Jack. I'm up for it. I sure do like my F-150 Responder. Any chance of getting an unmarked version for both patrol and investigative work?" Rich asked.

"I have been thinking about trading my Expedition

on an unmarked Responder. Let's get two. We'll just get different colors," Jack said.

"You pick both colors and I'll take whichever you don't want," Rich offered.

"I was thinking dark blue or dark green. How about you?"

"I'll go lighter then. Maybe a tan or light gray?" Rich said.

"Rose is overseeing the orders with Tac. I'll put our requests in shortly. Who knows, there may be something in stock somewhere."

"Thanks for the trust you've put in me on the investigative job, Jack. I won't let you down."

"I am going to follow up with Isabella Munro, Strauss' sister-in-law. I plan to be upfront with her. She and the wife have alibis Ray and I validated. Isabella and I seem to have clicked. I want you to be aware of it."

"Zack said it was like Goldilocks and the Three Bears. She assessed the three of you and immediately decided you were her bowl of porridge—just right. It's a great compliment. Most women fall all over themselves when the fourth generation Texas Ranger is anywhere in their zip code."

Rich reddened but responded quickly.

"I cannot imagine Zack Bodeway even knowing a nursery rhyme!"

"Hell, boy, even a baby ranger's mama reads him nursery rhymes," Jack answered in a perfect Bodeway imitation. They both laughed heartily at their famous friend's expense.

"Go chase this fair lady, Rich. You got a raw deal on Eleanor Moffitt just up and moving away like she did. If you think this one's a keeper, go for it. As far as I'm concerned, any conflict of interest no longer exists."

Rich left, relieved he had told his boss about Isabella.

He decided to try to meet with Isabella in person. Using the unmarked vehicle would attract less attention from his peers in Texas and in other Oklahoma counties than driving down in a vehicle emblazoned with Warrior Sheriff.

Rich called Isabella from the car.

"I know you cannot talk right now, but I want to take you to dinner, talk about the case and your brother-in-law. If your schedule allowed, maybe we could go to the Museum of the Plains in Lawton? Tomorrow is Saturday, after all."

"You must have solved the case overnight," she responded surprised at the sudden change of heart.

"I am afraid not. I spoke with the sheriff and he approved me coming down. My primary theory behind the murder just evaporated. I need to know more about Bill Strauss to look for another avenue to explore," he said. "There has to be something or somebody in his past tied to his murder."

"When do you want to have dinner? I have to work until noon tomorrow," Isabella said.

"I know this is last minute. I would not do it to you this suddenly if it wasn't important. Could you meet me in Lawton tonight for dinner? We will work out the details for a possible visit to the museum."

"I can meet you for dinner. But, how about in Wichita Falls? I know a place you would like here. I have been to the museum many times, but still love it. We can plan at dinner instead of me making several trips up and down I-44."

"You make perfect sense. Name a time and give me the restaurant name and I'll be there."

She did and he agreed.

"I'll see you at eight then. Should I make reservations? It is a weekend," he said.

"Yes, probably. See you later," and she disconnected. He held the phone and smiled for a few seconds and then walked in and told Tac he would be out of range for calls tonight and part of tomorrow on an investigation, so have dispatch contact him by cell phone.

He had plenty of time to get to Wichita Falls without rushing.

Rich worked out at home, showered and packed a day backpack typical of a spec ops operator. It was flat dark earth in color and had MOLLE webbing to attach small accessories.

He dressed in sharply creased jeans and an Oxford cloth button down shirt. He put his big duty Sig in the pack and a smaller Sig 239 in .357 Sig caliber to match his issue pistol in an inside the waistband, or IWB, holster. He dropped a spare mag in his left pocket. He clipped his badge in its circular leather holder on his Western belt in front of the gun. Even in Oklahoma and Texas, he always wanted citizens to see the badge before the gun when he was out of uniform. It was hot out but he wanted some privacy for the badge and gun, so he added a Western vest.

Rich added a spritz of Bleu de Chanel men's cologne. It was not cowboy, but he found it appealed to most of his dates. Dates. Dates were sparse things since nurse Eleanor Moffitt had left for Houston six months ago. Come to think of it, he had not had too many before her either. "Am I too career-oriented?" he wondered.

He had been floored at Eleanor leaving. He really thought the two of them had something. They had a good time together for a year. Maybe a year was enough. Rich was not going to try to predict the woman tonight.

The sheriff's wife was the most beautiful woman he had ever seen. It was a unanimous opinion whenever Lily walked into a room. But Isabella was real close though. Real close.

As Rich passed Norman, Oklahoma, he suspected Ray was west of there investigating McGonigle's jewel heist. His friend had told him all but about ten percent had been recovered. The missing part was fenced to a disreputable pawn shop. Ray already had warrants on its owner.

He decided to call the OSBI agent.

"Hey. You figured out a charge other than robbery for our friend Ben McGonigle?"

"Naw, Rich. The prosecutor and I are going back and forth about it. I am assured, whatever the death charge is, old Ben is going to enjoy Oklahoma's best prison food for fifteen or twenty years then try out the federal system. And I'm not talking about Club Fed for him!"

"What's going on with the Strauss murder now we don't have any suspects?"

"I'm on the way down to Texas to do a deep dive into the victim. There's something we don't know in his past and it's important to the case."

"I agree. This means you will be seeing the gorgeous sister-in-law, I presume?"

"It does. I talked with Jack about it. Bodeway already told him she has the hots for me. I'm not quite as sure as the ranger is, but Jack says since she and her sister both had iron clad alibis, checked by none less than you and me, to go ahead and question her, date her, marry her, whatever."

"He didn't really say all those things, Rich. Did he?"

"Well, not all of them. But his drift was she's okay to

be buddies with and maybe we'll learn something as a result."

"I agree with him. On the personal side, Rich, ones like her are few and far between. My wife is a looker. I adore her. However, she goes to the beauty shop once a week and gets her damn big hair poofed all up and sprayed. It leaves a dent in the pillow, Rich."

This was too much for the sergeant who blew a mouthful of coffee he was drinking all over the dash of the Chevy and choked laughing.

It must have been contagious because his friend started and the two laughed until Rich had to pull over and fish some paper napkins out and clean the car.

"Now, Ray. I've seen some big-haired girls I thought looked good," Rich began.

"You're pulling my leg now. You know you are!"

"Well, maybe a little. I wonder if it could be part of a pre-nuptial? No big hair or the deal is off. Jack's neighbor is a lawyer. I'll ask her before this thing gets away from us. You are in it with me now."

Unable to immediately solve the Strauss murder, they chatted and joked for another fifty miles before Rich had to stop and get gas.

"I'll let you know what I find out," he promised the OSBI agent and rang off.

He pulled into Wichita Falls around seven and rode around. There were several motels with low density parking lots, so he figured he could find one after dinner.

Rich backed in at the restaurant. He already had eight o'clock reservations. It cooled off some, so he swapped the vest for a blazer. He knew to watch for a red Mustang convertible.

He heard some dual exhausts rumbling and saw a red

Mustang convertible pulling in. Isabella had not told him it was a new GT.

He stepped out of the police car and walked towards her. Rich opened the door for her and she got out with three inch heels and a skirt which stopped well above her knees.

She stood up and looked him over, then gave him a peck on the cheek. He was a little surprised it was so platonic but was well conditioned to not show tells.

"Hi, there." He stared at her under the parking lot lights.

"Isabella, you are striking. You just take my breath away."

"You're not too bad for a cowboy cop yourself. I'm famished. Let's eat."

She took his arm and they walked in garnering looks of approval. One look got a husband or boyfriend elbowed in the ribs.

"Reservations for Ammon," he said to the young hostess at the stand.

She looked it up and picked up two menus and two sets of silverware.

Rich would never look at a piece of silverware again without thinking about the stainless silverware knife sticking from Jack's then-girlfriend's heart on the floor of a café in Quanah. How Lily, the town's only doctor had been called. She and Jack were on their knees covered with blood. Jack needed the knife from his girl-friend's dead body for evidence. Lily had not been strong enough to pull it out, prints protected by a nitrile glove.

Jack had done it. Rich knew it had to have been the worst thing he ever did in his life.

He pulled himself out of the bleak place and smiled at Isabella who was looking at him concerned.

"I lost you there for a moment. Everything okay?" she asked.

"Yes. Fine. I just had a flashback regarding some silverware and a heart rendering case."

"Will you tell me about it?" she asked.

"Yes. But, it's sad. Let's hold it for another time. I want tonight to be happy."

"Me, too. We'll see how it goes," she said leaving him somewhere between confused and worried.

He held the chair for her and she sat down.

"You do clean up pretty good cowboy. Were you ever really a cowboy?" she asked.

"I was in high school. Not college. I went there after serving with the Rangers in Afghanistan," he said.

"What was your specialty?"

"Long range reconnaissance, sniping, snatches," he said.

"I meant rodeo."

"Oh. I was an all-around cowboy competitor, so I did it all. Bronc riding was probably my favorite. I grew up on a ranch in Texas."

"I guess I was not real clear, Rich. Does it bother you to talk about Afghanistan?"

"No. I don't have PTSD or anything. I lost some friends and gained some scars. It happens in war. Especially the hand-to-hand stuff rangers face. But it was my job. Just like the crap I see as a cop. My job. Somebody has to do it. What I learned in the rangers has transitioned me nicely into my current role. I think, anyhow."

"Where are your scars, Rich?" she asked, softening.

"Shrapnel on the left leg. Bullet through and through in the left shoulder. Knife gash right ribcage."

"So you got a couple of Purple Hearts?"

"No, one Purple Heart and two additional oak leaf clusters. Plus a Silver Star."

"A Silver Star is for heroism isn't it?"

"Yes."

"Will you tell me what prompted them to award it to you?"

"I went into a gulley where some other rangers were pinned down. They were wounded and taking heavy fire. I was lucky and helped get them out."

"Does a paper citation come with it?" she asked.

"It does."

"May I read it sometimes?"

"Sure."

They ordered. Both got brisket, corn on the cob and collard greens. Isabella asked about wine and Rich suggested she order the bottle of her choice. He said he knew it was red, white or pink and not much more. She picked a Shiraz.

"I was weird when you greeted me in the parking lot, wasn't I?" she asked.

"I wouldn't say weird. You didn't appear to be as happy to see me as I hoped. I guessed you'd tell me why when you were ready," he admitted.

"I'm ready. I have been fighting unrelated but strong emotions. You are involved with both. The first is obvious. Bill's murder. The second may or may not be as obvious. I became very interested in you very quickly. Quicker than I ever have before. So quick it scared the living hell out of me.

"My safety net was you not being able to go further because of the case. Then, today all of it changed. You were ready to have dinner and whatever might come after. You drove over two hours down here.

"You told me the best lead you had evaporated.

Which takes us into the second thing.

Did you come down because you are as interested in me as I am in you?

Or is it to get me to help you dig into Bill's past and maybe prove him to be a lesser person than Myra and I think he is...was? I was and am very confused and conflicted, Rich."

He looked at her for a long time. His look, blue eyes to matching blue eyes, was pensive but in no way secretive, aggressive or anything she could label as negative. The two words springing to her mind were "kind" and "honest." Lord, she hoped she was reading him right.

"Isabella, I don't blame you at all. I think we can clear up any confusion very quickly.

It was important for me to do this in person. Where you could read the look in my eyes and my body language.

"I'm not very good at conversations like this, so bear with me.

You are in my thoughts damn near most of the day and, as near as I can tell, all of the night. I had a girlfriend in Warrior County. She is an RN. She picked career over me and moved to Houston permanently. At the height of our relationship, I did not think about her anywhere near as much as I do you after mere days. I walk around smiling like I don't have good sense. It's all you Isabella. All you.

"I hope what we are developing really turns into something as wonderful as it looks like to me.

"Yes, my main lead has gone to hell. I have nothing. Yes, you may be able to help me ferret out something in your brother in law's past which will give us a new lead. Or you may not. I have no idea.

"I went to my boss and told him what I was going to

do. He already knew about us. Seems like the ranger and the sheriff have been gossiping like two old hens in the barnyard.

"Once he verified with me neither you nor your sister are suspects in any way, he dismissed the conflict of interest issue and said to see where our relationship might go."

"What were his exact words, if I might ask?"

"'If you think this one's a keeper, go for it.' I think I am verbatim."

"Am I a keeper?"

"Yes. We hardly know each other. I am convinced enough you are a 'keeper' to pursue you hard. So watch out."

"I'm ready for you. Give me your best, Rich."

The entrees came as she finished and they toasted themselves with the previously untouched Shiraz and began to eat.

"Isabella, tell me about yourself," Rich asked.

"I am a native of Wichita Falls, which I think you already knew. Myra's and my parents were wonderful people. Dad was a judge. Mom was a civic leader. I think in this social media age, she would be considered an' influencer'. They died seven months ago in a car crash. It was one of the reasons I gave up a job I loved in Tulsa to come home. Poor Myra. She has lost everyone she ever loved except me in the last seven months.

"Bill made a good living. So did Dad. A better one. He crafted a per stirpes, legacy to blood relatives only, trust. Don't get too excited, but both Myra and I don't really have to work ever again."

"I'll put it in the plus side of the 'keeper' tally sheet," Rich said.

"Myra and I have spent much of our time in the last

year dealing with the estate. The straightforward way Dad set it up made it easier for us, but there was still a lot of property to liquidate. Real property and tangible items both.

"You'll like this. He left a virtually unfired 1950's Colt Cobra snub nose revolver. He wore it under his judicial robes. I carry it with my Texas concealed license."

"Okay. A big one in the keeper's plus column. So big, I might just close the tally book and declare you an outright keeper, Isabella Munro. Oh! What's your middle name?"

"Maria. My mother was Italian."

"Hence your very Celtic looks," he said tongue in cheek.

"Oh, I think my surname is a pretty good clue."

"Aye, it is."

"What's your full name?"

"Richard Lucas Ammon. The family is Swiss, then moved to Bavaria. My line moved to Texas, where I was born. My father moved us up to Oklahoma because of cheaper ranchland there."

"Rich. You have not asked me about what I did in Tulsa. Is it because you already know?"

"No. I have no idea except you have been hesitant in broaching the subject. I was thinking bank robber, hit woman, or the like."

She smiled at his response.

"No. The polar opposite."

"How could it be? I thought the Pope was a male."

"Same first letter. I was a police officer with the Tulsa Police Department."

"I didn't see that one coming," Rich said.

"Does it change anything between us?"

"It does. It means I may not have to carry a backup

pistol because I'll know you are packing a Cobra. And actually have been trained in combat shooting."

"Don't worry. I plan to guard your cute little cowboy six."

"It's all yours to covet and guard," he smiled. From the look on his face, Isabella knew she could stop worrying. He was a keeper himself. Before the night was over, she learned keeper was a fishing term, but it did not decrease her ardor a whit.

They spent an hour getting to know one another. It was a genuine normal person date. No police business.

Rich had a feeling Isabella was leaving something out about Tulsa. She could have taken a family emergency leave when her parents died but chose to resign. He would not press the issue nor would he check with Eric at TPD to investigate further. She would tell him when she was ready. Or not. People have their reasons to keep secrets. Some of the reasons are even valid. He would give her the benefit doubt.

"What will you do for the half day I'm working? I know we are going to the museum after," Isabella asked.

"I was thinking of talking with your sister some more. I called Zack Bodeway, who seemed to know her pretty well when we met at her house the other day. I let Zack know I was on his turf and asking questions. He was good with it. He and Jack Landers have a sort of two-man brotherhood. Three, if you count Jack's famous Texas Ranger great uncle. Jack carries his ranger .45 and has put it to frequent use. You may be interested when an ex-con shot Jack at his wedding a bit over a year ago, the old ranger moved through the crowd with a Colt just like your Dad's in hand."

"Rich, it might grease the wheels a little bit if you and

I go over to Myra's and I give her my blessing on what you are doing. What do you think?" Isabella said.

"I think it's a great plan. Would she be up to a late visit tonight?"

Isabella flushed slightly and smiled as she answered.

"Oh, I think she would! She keeps asking me when my Oklahoma lawman was coming calling. She will be relieved to see you."

"We sure have a lot of cheerleaders in this romance we just started less than a week ago, don't we?" he said.

"It certainly appears we do. The good part is they are people who mean a lot to us and whose opinions we trust."

Rich nodded and temporarily got lost in the depths of her eyes.

"I better call her and let her know we are dropping by. Do you have a hotel here yet?"

"No, I scouted a couple. All the lots seem to have space, so I reckoned I could get a room at any of them."

"Stick with your story at Myra's. I have a better option we can discuss later."

Rich had a pretty good idea what her option was. It was fast, but he would see how it played out.

He paid the bill and they went out to their cars. This time, Isabella did not give him a peck on the cheek. Her kiss was long and passionate. He rated it as the best kiss he had ever had and told her so. She gave him another just like it to prove it was not beginner's luck.

She started the new GT and let the four hundred sixty horsepower burble as it warmed up. Rich smiled at the sound from the muscle car as he sat in the older police sedan. He would stay quiet about his Mustang. No need to share everything on the first date. He caught himself and backed his thinking up. Maybe he was being too rash. He would wait and see where the night went. Just maybe....

He followed her to the Strauss residence. It was only ten-thirty and the house was well-lit. They parked and went in.

Isabella hugged her older sister. Rich imagined the age difference was small. They could pass for twins, though Isabella, at five-ten, was an inch or two taller.

"Hi, Sweetie! Thanks for seeing us a little later than the normal visit," Isabella said.

"I just wanted to see how much you had nerve to tell me about this first date in front of Sergeant Ammon," Myra taunted.

"Well. We had a pretty open discussion at dinner, so I will be totally frank. We both agree there is something between us and we are going to let it develop. His conflict of interest concerns were dismissed by the sheriff which is one reason he surprised me with his call earlier today."

"Same day for dinner from three hours away? Pretty fast, I'd say!"

"It just worked out this way for both of us, though Isabella does have to work half a day tomorrow," Rich said.

"Which is why we came by tonight. The only lead just dissipated. Rich has to go back to square one. Which means looking deeply into Bill's life from adulthood until his murder. I was fearful it was the reason for the sped up relationship moves. I am now convinced it is not. There has to be something or someone we are not remembering or don't know about in his past. I truly believe the only way to get closure on Bill's passing is to pitch in and help," Isabella said.

"I fear you are right. Fear because it is painful to talk

about and because I might not like what we find out. But, the facts are the facts. There is nothing we can do about history except learn from it. In this case, learn who killed my husband and why."

"Myra, do you mind spending some time, perhaps an hour, with me before noon tomorrow?"

"How about eleven? We can meet at a natural foods place with an interesting restaurant counter." She asked his cell phone number and texted him the name and address.

"Natural foods would not be too hippie-dippy for you, would it?"

"No, not at all. I have a pretty healthy diet. Most of the time. It's tough to maintain, patrolling rural Oklahoma. That's going to change some. I am going to be the sheriff's primary investigator in addition to patrolling. This change is as of yesterday."

"You didn't mention the change!" Isabella exclaimed.

"We'd have gotten around to it. We just ran out of time.

Myra, do you have a resume for Bill? It would get a good roadmap for me to follow."

"There's the one he sent to Arc when he joined them six months ago. I will find it and bring you a copy tomorrow," she said.

"I want to provide the two of you with closure. My biggest worry would be a random killer who might strike again. My feeling is Bill was not threatened by the person or persons at first, then something changed it. He went off the road and drew his own pistol. He never fired it. I found it on the passenger side floor."

He saw Myra unconsciously shiver and stopped speaking to think about what line of commentary he wanted to pursue next.

"Rich, how about his truck? Was it damaged?" Isabella asked.

"No. The only damage was the front passenger window will have to be replaced, some body scratches, and you will have to get a service to clean and sanitize it. I can help you with both of those. Unofficially as a friend."

"Sanitize?" she asked.

"I was trying to be as delicate as possible. During your time with Tulsa PD, did you respond to any murder scenes?" he asked Isabella.

"Lots of fatal accidents, but no murders."

"Imagine the accidents and add the fingerprint powder and such from the forensic folks. It will take a professional specialist to clean it suitable for sale."

Myra was sitting there spaced out during the conversation. All of a sudden, she snapped out of it.

"Bill's gun? Did you say Bill's gun? My husband may have been the only man in Texas without a gun. He wasn't politically against them. They just made him nervous," she said.

"I did say it. There was a Smith & Wesson Shield 9mm with his prints on it. The RAM's console had a gun locker in it, which was opened. The only prints on it, or anywhere in the truck, were your husband's, Myra.

"The gun was not planted there. The criminalists with the OSBI tracked it down. He bought it two months ago in Wichita Falls at a small gun shop. He also purchased three boxes of full metal jacket practice ammo and two twenty round boxes of hollow point carry ammunition. The latter was the most popular brand and weight police ammunition in the country. It's what is in my Sig right now."

"Why on earth would he have armed himself two

months ago? And why didn't he tell me if there was danger?" Myra asked.

"This is exactly why I wanted to do a deep dive on the victim since we lost our only suspect with a motive. Think about things he might have said off the cuff. Ways he might have acted out of character starting about two months ago. Work on it tonight and we will talk about your memories tomorrow at eleven.

"This is going to make me go by the gun shop and talk to them. He might have said something about why he bought a gun. I'll go there before we have lunch and we can compare notes," Rich said.

"Damn! This is making me want to take tomorrow off and go with you, Rich!" Isabella said.

"I can feel those cop juices flowing. My conflict of interest may have ebbed, but yours hasn't. It's better for me to do it and us discuss it after," he said.

"Oh, okay."

"I hate to shorten our visit, but lots of things are on the agenda and I have a motel room to check on. Eleven tomorrow, Myra?" She nodded and smiled sadly.

Isabella and Rich walked out to their cars. She beeped the lock with her key fob and turned to him.

This time the kiss was full-contact, passionate and several minutes long. At the end of it, she said "I am in my parents large home. I made up a bedroom for you. This is a first date. I am not sure about what the rules are nowadays, but I think we should sleep in separate bedrooms tonight."

"How about pre-sleep?" he asked with a mischievous grin.

"I really don't know the pre-sleep rules. In fact, I am not familiar with the term. Did you just make it up?" she asked.

"Maybe."

"I guess we'll have to develop pre-sleep rules as we go then," she said as she fired up the Mustang GT.

He followed her across town to an upscale section and she pulled into an estate surrounded by a tall, black wrought iron fence. He noted she spun the muscle car around and backed in.

"Once a cop, always a cop" he thought as he followed suit.

She unlocked the door and rushed across the entry parlor to the alarm controls on a hallway wall. She entered the alarm code and checked the window of the control. No alarms since she had left. She knew it anyway. She would have received a call from the monitoring company.

"Mi casa es tu casa," she welcomed him.

"Let me show you around, then perhaps one more drink for the evening."

The house was what he expected of a longtime Texas judge. He thought it was a shame to sell it. He was pretty positive it was owned outright. This was not a house for a single person nor even a couple. It was a house for a wealthy, entertaining family.

Rich went out to the car and got his bag. He also brought in his patrol rifle, good neighborhood or not.

They sat close to each other on a burnished leather sofa in a library filled with volumes. Her father's desk was in one corner as there were several large oils on the walls. It was a man's room. It needed some longhorns hanging on the wall and maybe a rifle or five to fully be a Texas man's room, but he kept the thought to himself.

"So. Where were we?" she asked, somewhat coquettishly.

"At the point where I was getting ready to kiss you again."

"Well don't let me stop you." So he did not.

Fifteen minutes later, she put her hand on his and said "Let's save the rest for a few days and anticipate it. I think anticipation would be quite enjoyable, don't you?"

"I doubt if it would be as enjoyable as not waiting," he observed.

AS HE WAS wont to do, retired ranger Bud Carey was in his recliner asleep in front of the big screen television. On it, some movie armorer had provided John Wayne an 1892 Winchester for a scene in 1867, just after the War Between the States.

"Who would know?" the armorer probably thought to himself. "He's the Duke. What else matters?"

It would have mattered a great deal to old ranger had he not been snoring in his recliner chair.

Over in the main ranch house, an original two-bedroom settler's cabin, the sheriff and his gynecologist wife and their small black and white cat were quiet too.

It was eleven-thirty at night and both had been up since well before dawn.

Jack Landers had tended to his horse Remington and to both of Lily's mares earlier.

He was coffee'd out for the day and an almost empty bottle of Diet Dr. Pepper sat beside him. The auburn haired beauty slept with her head on his shoulder and the tiny cat was asleep on top of her. It was a comfortable scene of domestic tranquility Jack did not wish to disturb.

It ended up to not be his decision. His iPhone rang

and he answered before it rang a second time, seeing it was his dispatch.

"Yeah, what do you have?"

"Sheriff, we have another highway shooting. This time it is on County Road 271, about five miles from your ranch. I have notified the Chief Deputy. Rich is still out of the area. Bob Rogan is running on it now."

"Is the victim DOA? Or do we know?"

"It appears the victim is dead per the truck driver who called it in."

"What's Bob's approximate ETA? And is the truck driver going to wait for us?"

"Fifteen minutes and yes."

"Call the OHP and see if they can cordon off 271 from here to its end. I'll be there in less than ten minutes."

He was already dressed, so he slipped on boots, his gun belt, and tactical vest. Grabbing his hat and keys, he bent over and kissed the sleeping Lily and went out the door.

It was midnight in rural Oklahoma. Few but the odd truck driver would be on the roads. Then he remembered it was Friday. Now, almost Saturday. Maybe some revelers would be about. Nonetheless, he had room to open the Expedition up.

He energized the LEDs and ran it like a Western sheriff.

Nine minutes later, Jack saw an eighteen wheeler pulled over. Like with Strauss, a pickup was pulled off the road.

Jack pulled in with his hood angling out and walked to the truck. As before, a male subject had been shot in the head with something powerful. Powerful enough to make a mess but not to the extent of the Strauss murder.

This time, both front windows were up and both had bullet holes. Through and through wound. He already knew it from the evidence between the wound and the passenger window.

"When did you come up on this?" he asked the truck driver.

"Oh, 'bout twenty minutes ago."

"Did you see anybody? Another vehicle?"

"I didn't see anybody here. But I had a little white foreign car meet me just before I got here. He was hauling ass, I'll tell you! He musta turned off if you didn't see him."

"One occupant? Male or female?" Jack asked.

"Yep, one. Couldn't tell sex."

"Hold on while I put this out."

He pulled the handheld from his hip pocket.

"Warrior-1"

"Go ahead, Sheriff."

"Request the OHP and Bob run County 58 south from 271. If they could start from opposite ends, it would be good. Look for a white subcompact. Foreign. Occupied one time. Gender unknown, over?"

"Roger, Sheriff. I am putting it out via simulcast now."

"After the simulcast, advise OSBI Special Agent Ray Colton. Also request he start a criminalistics team to this location."

"On it, boss."

Jack sent a quick text to Rich.

"At scene of another rural road shooting. Looks very similar so far. Finish with Strauss wife in morning and head back."

Jack put road flares out on the east and west lanes.

He walked around the scene, looking for car tracks,

empty shell casings, brake marks on the paved road, even damage suggesting the victim had been run off the road.

Despite a high lumen tactical flashlight, he did not spot anything useful. Jack took a roll of yellow tape and cordoned off the several years old Tacoma pickup and the area around it.

The compact pickup was off the road. It had hit a stump hard enough to inflate the driver's side air bag.

Jack popped some road flares in front and behind to give himself and the criminalists in a couple hours a safe work haven.

Deputy Bob Rogan who had the adjacent district and was covering part of Rich's district also, arrived and Jack assigned him to carefully look around the pickup for any possible shooter positions and for brass.

Jack aimed his light in the truck. As near as he could tell, the victim had been hit in the rear side of the neck. The bullet probably severed the spinal cord, killing him instantly. It had entered through the closed driver window, was a pass-through wound and exited the passenger window. The scene in the car was much cleaner than the previous shooting which had happened within several miles.

He knew he could not perform his approximation of the bullet path and where it ended up like he and Rich had before. The bullet clearly had gone into thick woods and they were pitch dark. Even with heavy spot lights, it would be easier to track the bullet in daylight tomorrow.

Jack aimed his light in the cab of the truck. It appeared initially the bullet had travelled a parallel path as if shot from a similar height vehicle beside the truck. He knew all of this was subject to verification and study by the criminalists, or CSI's as they were called by many agencies.

He did not see a firearm on the floor. It also appeared the victim's head was only slightly turned to the left. Either he drove by the shooter stopped on the other side, or the shooter surprised him by passing unexpectedly. But the victim was certainly not looking full face at the person who killed him.

Jack felt something was not quite right about this killing compared to the other one. Was it the beginning of a serial spree? His gut said no. Either totally unrelated or a copycat killer. Which, in and of itself, could spawn more murders.

He wanted to talk with a psychologist or psychiatrist about the difference in the ways serial murderers and their copycats thought. And how their profiles differed. He wanted Rich in on the conversation also. It would be a good step on his investigative learning curve.

"Jack, I don't see anything helpful here. Of course, it's dark as a cave. Tomorrow might be more fruitful," Deputy Bob Rogan said.

"I had the same experience, Bob. But, we'll never get a chance to review this crime scene with it being as fresh as it is right now.

"I'd like for you to go over and get a formal statement and contact information from the driver who found and reported this. Once done, you can let him go."

"Will do, boss."

Once the driver had been released, Jack asked the deputy to stand by the scene. The criminalists and Ray Colton were still at least an hour out.

Jack needed coffee and suspected Bob did, too.

"How do you want coffee and do you want bagels or donuts?" Jack asked Rogan.

"Black and donuts. Any kind and about three. Let me give you some money."

"No money required. Hold down the fort and I'll make a quick run to the truck stop and be right back."

Knowing the criminalists and Ray had been awakened to respond in the wee hours, Jack got a cardboard half gallon jug of coffee and a couple dozen mixed donuts and bagels. He was back in twenty minutes and found Bob still alone.

They drank coffee and ate donuts and waited, speculating on what happened. Without prompting, Rogan came up with the same conclusions Jack had.

At three o'clock, Ray pulled in. The criminalist van was ten minutes behind him.

Ray walked over and looked in the window of the Tacoma.

"Same MO?" he asked.

"Maybe. But, it doesn't seem right," Jack said.

"Anything on the vic?"

"Yes, a wallet, with ID, credit cards, and a hundred dollars in cash. There is also an older cell phone of the flip phone variety. There is no emergency contact number and not photos of a potential wife or kids. On first glance, he looks to be single.

"The truck driver met a small white car going fast just before he came upon the scene here. I had OHP and my deputy look for it with no joy," Jack said.

He pointed out the differences between this shooting and the other one to the OSBI agent before the criminalists got there. It was better to let them apply their procedures and come up with their conclusions based on measurements and evidence.

They watched as the criminalists set up large lights and carried their equipment cases out.

"I spoke with the truck driver who found him. Neither he, nor my deputy nor I touched the handle, window or door on the driver's side. I opened the passenger door with nitrile gloves to check for signs of life and to retrieve his wallet. I know it's better for you or an ME to get it, but I wanted to know who this person was and whether he was in my county from the standpoint of notifying next of kin."

The lead criminologist was the woman who had given him a ride back to his county after one of the times he had been shot. It had been her first day on the job.

"From just a first glance, it looks different from the one earlier in the week. Something about it feels more random. Evidence or an autopsy could change my mind though," she said. Jack nodded his agreement.

"Please advise Ray and me ASAP when you find the bullet. I'm thinking it is not going to be a different caliber."

"Okay, Jack. I'll call or text you both."

He walked back to Ray and his deputy.

"I'm going to go home and clean up so I can go to work. Bob, I'll have your relief in the district come straight here so you can go get some rest.

Ray, you got it from here? I will make sure Rich gets engaged on this as soon as he gets back from Wichita Falls. I told him to come back after talking with Mrs. Strauss."

"Did he say anything about talking with Ms. Strauss?" Ray asked.

"No, but I'm sure he did. There's coffee, donuts and bagels over by Bob's SUV. I'm outta here folks. Be safe."

JACK ARRIVED home and saw his great uncle sitting outside enjoying the pastoral scene enhanced by Jack's small herd of buffalo grazing on a distant pasture as the sun came up.

"Hiya, Uncle Bud. You got the pre-dawn buffalo watch duty today?" he asked.

"I do, boy. It's fine duty to have. By the time I was growing up on the Cinco Peso, the bison were gone. Killed off because the government knew they were an important part of the plains Indian's sustenance. People piss and moan about everything. Why not about the way we treated the people whose land we stole?"

"People do whine a lot. Some of it is righteous, some is just plain whining. I get real tired of the latter," Jack said.

"I heard you go blasting out a bit past midnight. Ain't no regular hours when you got a badge hanging on your shirt."

"Nope. Another shooting. How about this? Get in the Expedition with me and let's go back to the scene. I'd sure like your feelings about what happened. The OSBI team is there doing forensics, but we can still stand back and feel the scene."

"I taught you about feeling a scene a long time ago Jack. I'm glad you still do it. Sometimes your gut trumps forensics. Not all the time, but enough to keep it a viable practice. Let me get my gear on. Give me five minutes," the old ranger said.

Jack went in the house. Lily and the cat were still in bed. Jasmine looked up and did her normal good morning "rrreep." And, promptly went back to sleep. Lily didn't even rrreep, so Jack left her a note beside the bed.

He didn't have time to clean up, so a hit of deodorant and he dragged a toothbrush over his teeth.

Looking in the mirror as he spit tooth paste into the sink, he realized he was going to have hat hair all day. To

G. WAYNE TILMAN

hell with it. He put the white straw Resistol cowboy hat back on and walked through the main room. He met Bud at the truck and assisted him in. Jack folded the walker and put it in the back seat.

"I'm ready to roll, boy," the ranger said and Jack floored the throttle.

They got to the scene quickly. It was still barely touching on dawn.

Ray, Bob, and the two criminalists were there. They could see the tripod and laser set up to track the path of the bullet from the gun to wherever it landed. They would wait until strong daylight to use the laser.

It would also be safer than bumbling through prime rattler country in the dark.

"Uncle Bud, I hate poisonous snakes. And I don't have much love for the rest of them either."

"You may have mentioned your dislike to me over the three and a half decades I've known you. Especially after the big rattler almost got you as a boy."

"I never saw anybody draw and fire as fast as you did with this .45" as he patted the stag gripped gun on his hip.

"Didn't have much choice. I wasn't gonna bring a snake bit boy back to the Yellow Rose. I'd have been deader than the snake," Bud said, referring to Jack's mother. The Yellow Rose, as Bud called her from her childhood was still a strikingly beautiful blonde in her late fifties.

"And, of course the one you shot from a rearing horse who fell over and put you in a coma did not help your love of reptiles either."

"Nossir. It did not."

"Who is this fella?" Bud asked.

"His name is Henry Lang. He is from near Norman as near as we know now."

The old ranger stood back from the scene and studied it, leaning against his walker for support. He studied with eyes which had seen hundreds of crime scenes from murder to rustling from horseback instead of trucks like now.

"Boy, let's us walk back down the road a ways. This shooting didn't happen here. It happened down there," he said pointing from the direction from which they had come.

All of the lawmen followed the old man as he pushed his walker along the highway. He would stop and look around and sniff the air. An untutored viewer would have thought it theatrics. Jack knew different.

In the old West, there had been outstanding trackers. Trackers of men, dangerous men. They had names like Bass Reeves and Heck Thomas. Then, in Texas, the Bodeway generations of Texas Rangers. And, a bit later, Bud Carey.

"Boy, shine your light over here," Bud pointed. The area lit, Bud Carey walked over and stood studying the earth beside the road.

"He was shot here. See where his track left the road erratically and the wheel was jerked right back? Then came back into the dirt? Make sure the forensic folks take a sample of the scraped paint from the side of his truck. That was not from brush as he was shot and ran off the road. It was from where the shooter pulled up beside him, shot him and the victim swerved off and back and sideswiped the shooter's vehicle.

"I doubt there'd be casings here. If he shot an automatic across the length of his vehicle, they would have fallen in his floor or on his seat. If a revolver, they would have stayed in the gun until he reloaded. You can walk it in the daylight to look for other evidence. But, don't expect to find brass casings.

"Maybe a cigarette butt," he said as he lit a Seneca, his match hand automatically shielding the flame from nonexistent wind.

"Or maybe a candy wrapper or beer can. Especially if it was a beginner or a crime of passion. A pro would not leave a damn thing to help you. You can bet on it."

A sheriff, an experienced state investigator, and a deputy stood quietly thinking. The old man had taught them what he had learned over more years than their combined law enforcement experience. They knew the paint scrape on the Tacoma would be a highly instructive clue now.

They also knew each had slipped into the trap of making assumptions without studying and thinking. Things, like scratches on a vehicle, were not always as they appeared.

They went back and advised the forensics techs to study the long, deep scratches on the driver's side of the truck and collect paint samples. As they walked around the truck together, they realized what they had not learned in the dark. The scratches on the passenger side were not as deep or long. Those scratches were on the side which actually had brush to scrape paint as the truck ran past them. It was obvious now.

Jack silently kicked himself. He should have known better. At least he was smart enough to bring in the A team in the form of Bud Carey. He would, although with some embarrassment, tell this story to Zack Bodeway. If anyone alive would appreciate it, the other ranger would.

The techs were doing their thing. He called Lily and

asked if she wanted to meet him and Uncle Bud at a diner for breakfast. Though sleepy, her voice was a sweet as always. "How can one man be so blessed," he thought as he hung up and told his great uncle they were going to eat with his second favorite female in the entire world. The old ranger's smile was priceless.

THE NOTIFICATION of an incoming text at midnight had awakened Rich Ammon. He could not immediately reach his cell phone due to a five foot ten blonde draped over him on the leather sofa. Trim, she was muscular and heavier than she looked. He got his arm out and leaned hard.

The text was from the sheriff. Another roadside shooting. The first two words popping into Rich's mind were "serial killer." Damn!

He read the rest of the message and responded he would see the sheriff in the office by mid-afternoon.

"What is it?" Isabella tried to ask coherently.

"Another shooting. Sounds similar to Bill's. This is not good."

"Do you have to go?"

"Not until after I talk with your sister. I'm afraid we will have to take a rain check on the museum."

"I was dreaming," she said.

"Was it a sweet dream, Isabella?"

"Umhmm. I don't want it to stop. We have to go to the bedroom."

"As in one bedroom?" Rich asked.

"As in one bedroom. C'mon before I wake up," she mumbled getting up and leaving a trail of clothes all the way upstairs.

They slept after an hour or so.

Rich got up at six and went downstairs to the kitchen wearing his jeans. They were about all he could readily locate

He found coffee, eggs, bacon and English muffins far easier than his clothes.

Coffee first. Bacon second.

He did not hear the barefooted woman approach until the last minute and spun around. She grabbed him and kissed him.

"I like a man who makes me coffee. I'm pretty sure I could love one who adds bacon and eggs."

He grinned at her and poured a mug of steaming coffee for her.

She had on his LL Bean Oxford cloth button down from yesterday. Nothing else. She had not deemed it necessary to button it. Rich did not argue the point with her.

"How do you want your eggs?"

"However you like yours," she smiled.

They had a quiet breakfast. Their resolutions had evaporated last night and, it appeared to each the other was glad they did.

"When are you going to speak with Myra? I can't focus on the early part of last night."

"She wants to meet for a vegan or similar breakfast at eleven," he said.

"What will you do until then? You have four hours to go three miles."

"I am just blissfully existing right now. I have not given serious thought to anything other than suggesting you call in sick."

"Staying here with you for the next four hours would be my first choice. However, the shop is under staffed

118

and needs me. You asked for a raincheck on the museum. How about giving me a raincheck on the four hours?" she asked.

"Would an unlimited account be too much?"

"Probably not. It's a bit early, but I'm thinking unlimited might work out."

"Me, too."

"Why don't you hang around here until you need to leave? I'll show you how to set the alarm."

"Okay. Thanks. I will. Should we talk about last night?" he asked.

"If you want to grade it, I'd say it's off the scale and no need to talk about it. If you want to say it was a mistake with the way you are looking at me …. well, I'd be astounded."

"Good points, Isabella. Just asking in case you wanted to talk. I'm the strong and silent type. I don't need to."

"You are strong and silent. You are also as gentle as a puppy or kitten. Do you think I may bring out the very best in you? I know we haven't known each other very long."

"No. I don't think you do. I know you bring out the best in me," he said emphasizing the word "know."

"Good. Don't you forget it either. Especially around my beautiful sister."

"One, I have all the sister I can handle right now. Two, she's a grieving widow. It would not be right to do more than smile politely at her."

"Right on both counts. But, she is a complex person. I always suspected they had an open marriage. I would not put her above hitting on you, you long legged keeper you."

"Isabella, if they had other partners, it could be

related to the case. Would she be open to me about it or defensive?" Rich asked.

"I don't know. I really don't. We talk about everything. Just not their lifestyle. I don't know if she is ashamed about it or what. This is a small area. Now our parents, especially Daddy the Judge are gone, she may be a little more open. I'd be curious about your findings."

No matter how his feelings were developing for the woman standing inches from him, there was no way Rich was going to discuss anything her sister said in a police interview with him. It simply would not be appropriate.

Accordingly, he just smiled at her and let her make of it what she would.

They ate the breakfast and cleaned the kitchen, leaving only the coffee and bacon aromas behind.

In a home with four bathrooms, they shared one and showered. He shaved while she blew her hair dry at a double sink.

Rich dressed in his Warrior Sheriff golf shirt, jeans, and would wear his blazer to cover the embroidered badge on the chest of the shirt. Isabella circled him, brushed his jacket with her hand and slapped him on the butt in approval. Or, so she said.

She was dressed informally but business-like for the shop. He walked her down to the Mustang GT.

"I take it you also have a personal vehicle. I bet it's a pickup truck!"

"Nope. It's not. I won't tell you. I will surprise you on the next trip."

"Surprise? You drive your maiden aunt's Dodge Stratus?"

"I actually had a Dodge as my first county car. But, it was a little bigger than a Stratus."

"Hemi Charger, huh?" she probed.

"Exactly. The sheriff and his wife were riding on their ranch. A rattler spooked his horse and he shot it. They were on a rise and the horse lost its balance and went over. Jack hit his head on a rock and ended up in a coma for days.

I was closest when Lily called 911. She said where they were required a four-wheel drive. I damn well was going to get to my friend first. I did, but it totaled the Charger in the process. Lily reported I left the ground for over ten feet jumping a hill close to the scene."

"Did you get into trouble?" she asked.

"No. The chief deputy and, later the sheriff, both said they would have done the same to get to me. We have one tight group Isabella. I hope you get a chance to meet them soon."

She kissed him and climbed down into the pony car.

"Once you set the alarm, you can lock the main lock from inside without a key. Call me from the road. I could possibly be missing you by then."

"Possibly?" he grinned.

She blew him a kiss and pulled out the drive slowly. She turned onto the road and roared off, the relieved exhaust almost hiding the sound of the tires squealing.

"Texas girls," he said aloud to himself. "No other women drive as fast or can wear jeans as well. It's in their DNA."

Rich went into the house and sat on last night's memorable leather sofa. He took out his phone and looked on Safari for information about key terms to watch for in speaking with someone about the "lifestyle," or swinging, as it used to be called.

It was not a subject he had interest in beyond his case. As always it was important to have advanced familiarity with as many interview topics as possible. He did have a personal interest because this was the sister of someone in which he found himself deeply fascinated. If she was a part of the lifestyle, did it impact Isabella more than she admitted?

He spent some time on the phone with Jack about the new murder. He then called Ray about the same subject and had to skirt around his prior evening and current morning to get to the reason for his call. His new friend was clearly living vicariously through Rich.

He still had an hour to kill before driving over to the restaurant. Rich went out to the trunk of the unmarked Chevy and got a spray can of his favorite gun oil out of a kit bag. He unloaded the smaller Sig and field stripped and cleaned it.

Rich looked at his watch and then performed the same on his larger duty pistol.

By the time he cleaned the gun oil off his hands, packed and loaded the car he had just enough time to arrive at the restaurant. He was a little concerned about the interview in such a public place. Particularly if it went very far afield with Isabella's suspicion.

He cruised the block and noted a park not far away. The perfect place to talk openly.

Rich parked and walked in, his blazer hiding the sheriff emblem embroidered on the golf shirt as well as hiding his gun and the badge clipped on his belt.

"Hi, Myra," he greeted Myra Strauss. It amazed him how much the two sisters favored one another. They were both gorgeous. She was far more so than she appeared under the distress of their first meeting.

"Hello, Rich. I hope you like vegan food."

"Anything's fine with me. You cannot imagine some of the local fare I had in Afghanistan.

"Looking at the special arrangement here, why don't we keep the conversation here social and walk over to the park after we eat and speak more openly about the case and what you may have in your folder," he said.

"Good idea."

He looked at the menu and chose a salad and a vegetable juice. She did the same. It was surprisingly good, he thought. He knew he would be starving before long though.

Myra tried to subtly find out about his date with her sister. He was not sure whether she was being protective, nosy, or had some other agenda.

"We had a delightful dinner and chatted for a long time. I got a call before the night ended and had to cancel today's afternoon trip to the Museum of the Plains.

"There was another highway shooting. I was called back to Warrior County following our talk today."

"Was the shooting just like Bill's?" she asked.

"There are similarities. When I spoke with the sheriff it was far too soon to conclude much. By the time I get back this afternoon, the CSI people should have some answers for us. The sheriff would not even venture a guess to me. It appears I will take lead on this case too."

"So, you won't see Bella for a while?" Myra asked, changing to a more comfortable subject.

"Oh, I will see her just as soon as I possibly can. Who would not want to keep company with the Munro sisters?" he said with a smile.

She beamed at her inclusion.

"If the situation was different, there might be some competition, Rich."

"I'm flattered. Thank you," he said.

Once she knew he had a time constraint, she focused on getting through the meal and over to the park.

Once there, they sat on a bench away from any potential listener. He had a full view of people who might walk close enough to hear.

"I feel like we are having a clandestine rendezvous," she ventured.

"We are, kinda. We have to discuss things which are only our business and not for other's ears, Myra."

"I found Bill's latest resume and printed you a copy," she said handing it to him.

As he scanned it, he asked "Did anything jump out at you as being relevant to the case?"

"No. Not on the resume. But I found some old Army papers. I knew he was in the Army, but not much more. He was an officer. A first lieutenant. He already had his engineering degree and used it during his military service."

"What got your attention there?"

"Well …. he turned in another officer. He was selling information to a company trying to bid on a contact with the military."

"What happened?"

"The other man got court martialed and was sent to prison at the military part of Ft. Leavenworth. He received fifteen years." She said.

"Fifteen years tells me he was selling some pretty heavy duty secret plans, even if not to a foreign government.

When was this, Myra?"

"Are you ready? Fifteen years and one month ago!" she said.

"Wow. Was the prisoner's name there? I can get release information on civilians from Leavenworth. The military information not so much."

"Yes! Major Allen Willis! There's even a booking

photo of him fifteen years ago. I don't know how Bill ever got it. Maybe this Willis threatened him or something."

Rich took the booking form and photographed it with his phone.

"Does the place where Isabella works have scanning capability?" he asked, not knowing whether they just sold office supplies or also had services such as scanning, mailing, printing and the like.

"I am pretty sure they do. Bill was preparing some documents and needed to send them somewhere. I'm sure he got them scanned there."

"When we get finished, I will go over and get this scanned. I'd like to have Tac at the office working on it while I am driving back this afternoon.

"Myra, how about other places he has worked. I obviously have not had the chance to study his resume. But do you know of any work disagreements or clashes of any type?"

"No. He was a calm, peacemaker sort of a man. I am confident if you contact each of them, you will hear the same thing."

"Okay. Let's move into the personal and sometimes uncomfortable arena now," he said, noting the worried look on her face.

"What is it about your and Bill's relationship you are not telling me? You get nervous every time it gets personal. What's there, Myra?"

"Will you share anything I tell you with Bella?" she asked, making Rich think Isabella might be involved.

"No. I will not. If the information might be harmful to her life, maybe. However, I would talk with you first. Your and Bill's personal life? No. It would be a breach of ethics and I won't do it.

So. How was your and Bill's personal life? Happy? Did you argue? Any sort of abuse on either side? A third person?"

He noticed she reddened at the last. He just waited silently, looking at her with a pleasant smile. She squirmed a little. He did not know if it was discomfort or she was teasing him. These two sisters were something. They could turn the heat on and off at will.

Finally, she cleared her throat.

"You promise?" He nodded.

"Bill and I were on the edge of the lifestyle. Are you familiar with the term?" she asked.

"I know it is the new term for swinging. I don't know much about what happens, except for the obvious. I admit I'll be amazed if you tell me it exists in provincial Wichita Falls."

"If it does, I would fall over in shock myself. We went a bit over a hundred miles to a club to do our thing, so to speak."

"What you two did and with whom and how many could have a real bearing on the case, Myra. Are names and contact information available? I would think folks might keep those things pretty private."

"Many do. Many do not because they are constantly looking for new partners and having their names and reputations out there helps," she said.

"Are there magazines? I assume there probably are websites."

"We didn't use anything like websites. Not private enough. There are some chat sites we used to communicate once we made a connection." She wrote two encrypted site names down and handed the slip of paper to him.

"What happened at your club? Orgies?" he asked.

"Oh, heavens no! You are thinking of California in the 1970's. The club was a place where people of a like mind socialized with drinks and snacks and, if there was some interest, contact information was exchanged for later use. It was just a side room reserved at a restaurant, like for the Rotary or something."

"I see," he said, though he really did not. "How many people did you make further contact with and over what period of time?" he asked.

"Let me set the stage a little better, Rich. At least according to our experience. Others, even at the same group, may have other experiences.

"For couples, we mainly looked for one female. Maybe two would be a consideration, but we never got beyond one. Couples we found out, seldom looked for a swapping couple or for one or two men," Myra said.

"It seems like, at least in your case, it was slanted more towards the man's interests. Him and one or more women?" Rich asked.

"It would seem so until you factor female fantasies in. The only ones I can relate to are my own. And my sister's. Girls talk."

He really wanted to pursue this line of inquiry but had to restrain himself.

"You are not asking, but you really, really want to know about Bella's don't you?" she asked in a low smoky tone.

"I need to keep our focus on things which may be directly related to the case and why someone would decide to shoot your husband. Unless Isabella's part in your interests directly affected the case, we don't have to go there," he said.

"Can you handle it if I go into more details?" she asked in the same voice.

"Yes," he said fearing she was getting ready to assume control of the interview with him being unready to retrieve it.

She went into soft swaps and hard swaps and other terms he had read during his fast Internet journey into the lifestyle. She elaborated in detail about her own fantasies and needs and how the lifestyle fulfilled them. At least in this version, Isabella did not exist.

"Myra, this is all interesting. It's new to me. I really appreciate your candor and will protect your privacy. This woman Monica you have mentioned several times... it strikes me it might be more comfortable for her if you were to set up a meeting and probably even sit in on it," he said, adding "I realize it is a long drive for you."

"Her name is Monica Kennedy and she is up in Norman, Oklahoma. Let me call her and arrange everything. I get my nosy arranging talents from my mother. Mama was Mrs. Social Butterfly around these parts. I will describe you and it will guarantee a meeting," she finished with and smiled at him. She had turned the interview into a game and won it with her shared fantasies and intimacies. Both of them knew it.

She followed him, he thought somewhat possessively, to the shop where her sister worked and went in with him.

"We have found a possible break in the case!" she announced to Isabella and most people within a block of the shop. The current and past officers she was addressing winced at the loud, open disclosure.

Isabella scanned the arrest sheet with the details and mug shot of Major Allen Willis. She praised Rich for preparing the attachment as a scan rather than the screen shot on his phone as he originally considered.

"It will be much clearer for the recipient to take details needed to run inquiries on a variety of police and public systems," she said.

Myra stood beside Rich her hip pressed against his. She surely had dropped out of the grieving widow persona, Rich thought as he sidestepped a couple inches to the left. He had a feeling the sisters were going to have a heart to heart discussion once they found a private spot together.

He thanked and insisted on paying Isabella. She gave him a long hug and kiss for his change. Rich would normally have been suspicious the length of the embrace was for her sister's benefit. However, he had quickly learned Isabella Munro took hugging and kissing as very serious endeavors.

He turned to Myra to thank her and got embraced immediately. Luckily no kiss was tendered. Otherwise, there may have been an assault in the store with him in the middle of it.

"I'll be in touch as soon as I know something. Thanks to both of you for everything," he said as he retreated to the door.

"And thanks for making me the delicious breakfast," Isabella said sweetly, totally destroying the myth about him in a motel room. He caught a flash of Myra's eyes as he opened the door of the Chevy. Time to get out of Dodge. Fast.

RICH CALLED THE SHERIFF.

"Hey, Jack. Got a few minutes?" he asked.

"Sure. What did you find out in Wichita Springs?"

"Two pretty interesting things.

Bill Strauss, as an Army officer, turned in a major for selling information to corporate interests. Apparently, no foreign governments were involved, just companies who contracted with the government. The guy, Major Allen Willis was court martialed and sentenced to fifteen years at the military section of Leavenworth."

"When? And where is he now?"

"Fifteen years served and released one month ago. I have Tac trying to track his current whereabouts down. The timing has to be more than mere coincidence. We now have another suspect on our hands."

"Excellent, Rich! I'll make sure Tac knows how important this is. What's the other thing?"

"Do you know the term 'lifestyle?' and I mean the colloquialism, not like lifestyles of the rich and famous."

"I know what it refers to, but not much more," Jack answered.

"Well, it appears Bill and Myra Strauss were involved in the lifestyle. Myra said it was a low level involvement with one woman. I am setting up a meeting with her now. She is north of where they lived. Actually, in Norman."

"Interesting. Did she just volunteer this tidbit of information?"

"No. Isabella told me. So, I eased into it without giving up the source when I interviewed Myra.

"Do you think she might have been involved in it?"

"The lifestyle stuff? I don't think so. Her body language was signaling disapproval. There is a lot of sibling rivalry between those two. They generally keep it below the surface, but it comes out at interesting times. The words possessive, territorial, and competitive come to mind," Rich said.

"As your friend, not your boss, watch your ass. These two sound dangerous."

"Think they'd shoot or knife me?"

"No. I think they'd play you like a fish and have you for dinner though."

"I mentioned to you in passing about Isabella Munro having been a patrol officer with Tulsa PD. She resigned instead of taking some sort of family leave when their parents were killed in a car crash last year. It strikes me as a bit odd, but I would hate to have it get back to her if I checked with one of the guys up there I know from the Ben McGonigle matter," Rich said.

"I am sure someone else could check the facts and keep you out of it. It might also be interesting to know the details on the car crash. You had told me the father was a district judge. They tend to have a lot of enemies. Usually on both sides of the law.

I bet our ranger friend knows all about it," Jack said.

"He may know more than you suspect, Jack. Zack Bodeway apparently dated Myra Strauss before she married the victim."

"Whoa! This thing has more tentacles than a Portuguese Man of War on steroids. I will ease into it with Zack.

Do you think the woman in Norman may be a suspect? Jack asked."

"At this point, I don't know who's a suspect. Major Allen Willis going to prison because of Strauss and getting out just before the murder looks pretty good. This Monica Kennedy may know something. What if people move around in the lifestyle circle for fun and not attachments, but then somebody wants to get attached? What if the somebody is a little whacked out? At least we are getting questions, Jack. I'm hoping they will lead to answers."

"Me too. The press is starting to ask questions here. I am waiting for the term 'serial killer' to come up very soon. I really don't think it is a serial killer. I think we either have two unrelated murders or we have a copycat. Unfortunately, the latter can become a serial killer. But I will be surprised if it does."

"I will be back in an hour and a half. Want me to go straight to the scene?"

"No, come here and I will go with you. Uncle Bud made some pretty astute observations last night. He showed us the shooting happened down the road from where the pickup came to rest. It would still be good to walk the scene in daylight and talk through it.

"While you are heading home, I will call Zack and will poke around Tulsa PD and find out a little about your new friend."

"Okay, boss. See you soon," Rich said and rang off. Jack called a friend at TPD and got the background on Isabella Munro's career there and her leaving.

Rich saw a large Interstate truck stop and convenience store ahead, so he pulled off and filled the tank of the unmarked car. He walked in and got a large coffee to go and resumed the run north on the Interstate then west to MacKenzie and the office.

Jack Landers walked down the street and got a ham sandwich and Diet Dr. Pepper for a late lunch. He looked at his watch. Rich should be rolling in soon.

He stopped at Tac's workstation on the way in. The communications deputy was busily at work on a spread-sheet for the vehicle inventory.

"Just what I was going to ask you about. What's the

situation with the two new F150 Responders and the Interceptor SUV for the new deputy slot?" he asked.

"All three on the way. Luckily the two pickups—yours and Rich's—are already in state. They are fully equipped as to crash bar, siren and killer light package, gun rack and more. As near as I can tell, we just have to program the radio, add the tonneau on the short bed, and hand you guys the keys. I'd say you will be driving them by the end of the week."

"Good news, Tac! Since we don't have a deputy for the new slot, there's less rush on the SUV. Did you and the chief deputy decide to trade my Expedition or the sedan Rich is using? We will need one as a backup unit."

"We decided to trade yours. It's a lot more valuable and we thought it inappropriate to pass down a vehicle lots of folks associate with the sheriff himself."

"Oh! What are the colors?" he asked.

"Yours is dark green and Rich's is kind of an off white. If you decide to mark yours, you may want to swap with him. The emblems and all may fade into the dark green."

"Great. Thanks for jumping on this, Tac.

On another matter, I understand you have been trying to get a location on Major Allen Willis. Any luck?"

"No, sir. The Army is not cooperating very well on him."

"Bring me the paperwork. I will make a phone call or two," Jack said.

Rich walked into the lobby.

"Hiya, Helen," he greeted the business manager and mother confessor to the office.

"Hey, cowboy. Think the other cowboy is waiting for you," she said nodding towards Jack and Tac.

"Good news, Rich. You have an off white Responder and should be in it before the week is over. You can impress your new girlfriend on your next trip down," Jack said.

"I dunno, Jack. Not girlfriend. More a person of possible romantic interest. Not a done deal."

"I might have some news to sway you over. We can talk on the way to the crime scene," Jack said disappointing both Helen and Tac who were eager to hear the rest of Jack's story.

Rich turned to Tac.

"Thanks for rushing the truck through. Anything on the whereabouts of our major?"

"No and I think the boss will brief you on him along the way as well as briefing you on your new squeeze it sounds like." Tac was a handsome young man and could work his superhero grin almost as well as the sheriff from whom he learned it.

"You ready?" Jack asked.

"Let me drop off the jacket. I don't need to hide my bonafides like I do down in Texas."

"Unless you are with Bodeway. With him you can waltz right into the capitol wearing your cowboy hat, gun and boxer shorts."

"No doubt. Okay, I am ready."

They walked out and got into the Expedition.

"Let's get the non-clue stuff over first," Jack said.

"Miss Isabella was a second level patrol officer at TPD. It appeared she was on a fast track to make detective. She had over two years under her belt. Smart. Everybody liked her."

"So why did she up and quit as soon as her parents were killed?"

"Their death was almost a convenience to hide her real reason. She and her sergeant had started dating. It was getting serious and getting in the way of the job for both of them. The whole romance was kept on the downlow. Virtually nobody knew about it but the brass was aware. Both had made disclosures about dating a fellow officer. The two split up at management's suggestion and it became very awkward. There was not another slot for her in a different patrol district, so she quit. There was no harassment. Nothing negative. Everybody was on her side. Except the sergeant's wife who is a detective there. She would have been Isabella's boss should she have moved into a detective slot."

"Interesting. I guess I cannot hold it against her. People fall for people. Often the wrong people. It looks like it happened there and she took the high road," Rich said.

"Given this, Jack, my only remaining concern is the competitiveness between the two sisters. I felt like I was in the middle of it for no reason yesterday. No reason at all."

"You have good judgement. Just use it."

"On another subject, the Army is digging in against telling us anything about Willis. I am going to call the Army prison barracks or whatever they call it at Leavenworth when we get back. I am sure a rural sheriff in Oklahoma is not going to wow them very much.

"If it does not work—and I doubt it will—I am going to reach out to the agent who is now filling Mary Lee Chang's former position and see if the feds can get the information. Her name is Supervisory Special Agent Cheryl Louder. She came by and did a courtesy call on me a couple months after Mary Lee was killed."

Rich knew Chang was the agent who had been killed by a serial bank robber on Main Street in MacKenzie. A robber who made the fatal mistake of trying to outdraw Jack Landers in a Dodge City style walk down.

Jack had done the Mozambique Drill. Two in the center of mass, one between the eyes. It was fairly standard procedure for many, if not most, law enforcement agencies.

"Don't pull on Superman's cape or draw on my boss," Rich thought to himself. While Jack had left the double-single action Sig as the office's official issue handgun, he had told Rich no semiauto was faster for the first shot than a 1911. Rich noticed the famous Texas Ranger carried one also. Maybe he needed to reconsider. He asked Jack.

"Jack, I have been giving some consideration to switching over to a 1911 for my official handgun. What do I need to do?"

"Get one. I can help you with choices, though very few are bad. They are all basically the same with the widest variance being price. The price usually has to do with hand fitting, smoothing of the feed ramp between magazine and barrel, and the name on the gun. Shoot the hell out of it before you tell me you are ready to qualify with it. Maybe take a specialty 1911 course. There are some world famous ones. Then, when you are comfortable, I will run you though our standard qualification. I will watch for comfort, handling and compare your 1911 score against your last several qualifications. It you convince me you're ready, I'll tell you I agree.

"I believe it is still the finest fighting handgun ever made. Yes, the Sigs, the Glocks, and other striker fired guns are more popular and hold more cartridges. But on the latter, I have only reloaded once in a firefight and the shooting was already over and I was doing it tactically," Jack said.

"Yours is the slightly shorter Commander length with the four and a quarter inch barrel instead of five inches, right?" Rich asked.

"Right. I didn't pick mine as you know. It was Uncle Bud's. He carried it in the rangers most of his career. I saw him draw and kill a man with it when I was a teen at a rodeo. I never saw anybody move so fast as he did. He presented it to me when I finished the academy. I was blown away. I grew up shooting it with him. Now, I carry it every day."

"And, you've used it quite effectively a number of times."

"Yes, Rich. I have been real lucky," he said softly and with modesty.

They arrived at the latest shooting scene. It was cleaned up. The Tacoma pickup was gone and the criminalists with it. They walked the scene so Rich could get a feel for it.

Jack explained he had learned walking a scene a couple times from his great uncle and how important he had grown to learn it was. How you should try to visualize where everything happened. Where the participants were. And why, if you saw the scene at night, it was important to come back and walk it again in daylight. He pointed out the clues which immediately told the old ranger where the action shooting had taken place instead of where the truck had stopped.

"What key things are we waiting to hear from the OSBI?" Rich asked.

"What the paint samples taken from the door tell us where the shooter's vehicle sideswiped the Tacoma. Which should get us closer to knowing where the shot was fired.

"Unfortunately, it now appears, thanks to Uncle Bud,

the shooting happened while they were both moving. They could not use the laser trick to track the resting place of the bullet because it could have been in the woods for a hundred yards along the road. So, we don't have it to tell us caliber or anything. The closest we will come is autopsy. Since you were out of town, I asked Rose to go over to OKC for it later today. The ME can at least give us an estimation from the skull entry and exit wounds."

"Do you have a gut feeling, Jack?"

"I do. I might be dead wrong, but I think it was in the .38 range. It appeared to me at night the entry and exit wounds were about the same size. It would take a cartridge at least as powerful as a 9mm to penetrate a window, a head, and another window. The entry and exit looked to be close to the same diameter. So, if it did not mushroom, it was likely a hardball instead of a hollow point. It could have been a .357 Sig like the other, or a .40. It did not appear to be a big enough hole for a .45. Again, I could be wrong, just guessing in the dark."

"Along the non-hollow point thinking, could it have been a hard lead revolver round. Maybe a .357 magnum but not in hollow point?" Rich asked.

"Absolutely. Probably even a hyped up .38 Special lead would not have penetrated like it did. And, any larger revolver round would have left a bigger hole.

"We are doing what we have to. We are Monday morning quarterbacking. I guess we have to have faith in the ME. I don't know who is doing the autopsy. I have to assume they are good. Just remember without a bullet to study, all he has is hole diameter to go by. I daresay you and I know more about firearms and different bullets than he or she does," Jack said.

"Your notes said the truck driver saw a small white

vehicle in the area and you had Bob and the OHP look for it. You have not mentioned it, so it did not pan out?" Rich asked.

"Right. I also doubt the OSBI folks are going to tell us it was white paint in the collision damage on the side of the Tacoma either.

"If there was a driver and a shooter and they side-swiped the Tacoma intentionally, I think a subcompact might have gotten the worse end of the deal. A Tacoma is not a Silverado or other full sized truck almost three tons of steel. It is, however, a lot beefier than a subcompact. The little car should have skidded and left tire prints on the pavement. There were short, slight ones on the highway beside where the Tacoma went off then on then off the paved road.

"We still should have had evidence of the accident on the part of the smaller car. Maybe trim bits on the road or something.

"All of which leads me be to believe the shooter's vehicle was larger and the trucker's 'small white car' was unrelated," Jack said.

"Once we get the information from the paint scraping, I will check with auto rentals and paint shops within a hundred mile radius to see if someone turned in or repaired a vehicle today with the color paint OSBI reports to us," Rich said. Jack nodded his agreement.

"Jack, if the ME says measurements point to a bullet diameter of .357, we could have a .357 Sig like killed Strauss, a .357 magnum, a .38 special, or the one we have not considered yet."

"Which have we not considered?" Jack asked.

"A powerful cartridge mainly in the 1911 we were just talking about. It was popular in the gangster period in the 1930's and is still real popular in Mexico."

".38 Super! You are right. I never thought of .38 Super. It's powerful enough to do all the penetration. It's also not a caliber a casual shooter would likely have or be good with. Rich, you might be on to something here!" Jack said, getting excited.

CHAPTER THREE

THEN THE RADIO SOUNDED.

"Warrior-1"

"Warrior-1 go!" Jack answered into the mic.

"We have another bar fight at the same place Lily shot into the ceiling. Reported to be five or six guys and they are breaking beer bottles for weapons. I don't have anybody closer, but you are a two-man unit right now."

"Mark us en route Code-3. We have an ETA of maybe eight minutes."

Rich reached over and hit the lights as Jack did a Y turn and floored the accelerator. A lot of drunks or an innocent visitor for lunch could get cut badly and maybe bleed out before they arrived so speed was paramount.

Rich left the siren off as Jack drove fast and well. They began to encounter traffic and Rich worked the siren package, going from wail to the high pitched alert to the air horn as appropriate to the traffic and signals.

Some civilians, two couples and one family, were rushing out as they pulled into the lot and slid to a stop.

They ran into the danger the others were running from. As always.

"Anybody hurt?" Jack asked a family with a pre-teen boy and girl.

"Yeah, a couple of biker types are cut up. It has gone from five guys to around ten. I had to get my family away from this mess! There's another family trapped in a corner booth inside."

As Jack barreled forward, Rich said "Sir, we'd appreciate it if you'd wait here in your vehicle. You may be the only sober person we can get the story from after we calm things down."

"The two of you are outnumbered five to one. You better wait for backup."

"No time, sir. We have to stop it now," Rich yelled over his shoulder as he cleared the door just behind the sheriff.

The two stood side by side, hands loosely down near their handguns.

"You want to yell at them, sergeant?" Jack asked.

"Sheriff's Office. Cut the fighting out. Right now!" the younger man ordered in a loud commanding tone. An order which was totally ignored.

"I hate drunks," Jack said. "I wish we could fire into the ceiling like Lily did. But it's not accepted police procedure. Get your expandable baton extended. We gotta wade into this mess," Jack said.

Both flicked their batons open and moved in.

"Separate! Anybody holding a broken bottle will be considered armed and dangerous. And will be shot!" Jack yelled.

A big drunk lurched towards Rich with an upraised broken beer bottle.

Rich violated the target area rules for baton use and

hit him on the wrist hard enough to break it. He knew he might have to explain it later, but the man was attacking an officer with intent to kill. He could have legally justified shooting him.

The man screamed and dropped the bottle. The next swing of the baton was in an approved area on his leg and he went down.

Two biker types were on either side of Jack and trying to pin him. A third wrestled the baton away.

Jack brought his leg up with his shin connecting with the third man's groin, twisted left and head-butted the man holding him there. The left man let go, allowing the sheriff to step back and kick the right man behind the knee from a rear angle. The kicked leg folded up and he hit the floor

Three more came in towards them.

"Gun time," Jack said, but Rich was already drawing. A front man drew a wicked hunting knife from under his shirt and was well within the "twenty-one foot danger of cutting death range." His eyes were locked on the sheriff, who had put his three friends down without breaking a sweat. Like most untrained knife fighters, he was flashing the blade from side to side and holding it wrong. But, he was moving in fast towards Jack.

Rich shot him twice in the center of mass and once in the forehead, just as he had been taught. The man fell dead and the bar room fell silent.

Jack swept the room with his .45. The crowd moved away from the two lawmen like the surf rolling back off a beach.

Rich knelt, gun still pointed at the crowd, and felt for the pulse he knew was not going to be there. It was not. The man was dead on scene.

The sergeant moved eight feet from the sheriff. They

angled so they had visual control of the room and their backs.

Jack yelled to the bartender.

"Call 911 and get an ambulance rolling. Do it now!" He watched as the employee complied.

They heard distant sirens. The cavalry was coming. but the fight was over.

Chief Deputy Rose Custalow was first on scene. She came in with her twelve gauge at high ready, followed by a trooper and a game warden. Tac, upon receiving the call from the bartender, had simulcasted a "Shots Fired. Officers involved" call to all law enforcement agencies in the tri-county region.

Fifteen minutes later, EMTs had checked the dead man and were patching up six drunks with glass cuts.

The family man they had spoken with as he was ushering his family to safety and locked them in the car and returned with his son's aluminum baseball bat in case he could help. He witnessed the man coming at Jack with a knife to cut him and Rich having to shoot him. He gave his statement to Rose as Jack and Rich triaged the fighters into groups of ones actually cutting people and threatening the two lawmen, and members of the crowd whose only crime was public drunkenness. The third leg of the triage was the group receiving first aid.

Within twenty minutes, deputies, Ray from the OSBI, more troopers and the sheriff of an adjacent county were on scene.

As the state law enforcement officers, Ray and an OHP lieutenant put together a shooting board and asked the adjacent county sheriff to chair it. It had an assortment of Oklahoma peace officers. They heard statements from Jack who said he had been in fear for his life, Rich who said he had to elevate to deadly force for immediate fear his boss would sustain a serious or fatal wound. The bartender and the civilian who had come back to help both stated the man approaching the sheriff looked to them like he wanted to cut him badly or kill him. Ray took possession of Rich's duty Sig to record the ammunition used and to compare a bullet from it with the ones which killed the subject in the bar. While the shooting review board would issue a finding signed by all and delivered to the sheriff and the county prosecutor, they assured Rich his shooting was righteous.

Sheriff White from the next county over, took him aside and said "Son, you may as well get a lawyer. Some damn relative of the fella you shot is going to sue you. Always happens."

Since the review board represented the most senior law officers there and Rose was present though not on the board, they all met to discuss what, if anything needed to be done. All concurred to arrest the fighters and release the others with stern warnings.

"You up to bringing them to the Lord?" Jack asked Rich.

"Sure. Can I be tough?"

"You better be!" The sheriff from the next county over was listening from afar and got a big smile on his face. *These damn Warrior boys don't mess around*, he thought.

Jack and Rose watched as the former Airborne Ranger read the riot act to about fifteen men, right in their faces.

"Making Rich a sergeant was a good thing. Making him our investigator was too, Jack" Rose said quietly.

"It was, Rose. As I remember it was you who suggested the former." She smiled.

Since none of the injured required hospitalization,

the wounded group was included with the fighters and were arrested. There were plenty of cars with blue lights to provide transportation to the regional jail.

As Jack, Rose, and Rich walked out the door, Rose said, "Boss, I am sorry I missed the autopsy in OKC today. I heard the call when I was pulling onto Main and figured I needed to be here."

"Rose, you made the right decision. You always do. The only thing we really care about was the caliber of the gun used on him. And, maybe whether he was an addict or has anything interesting on a tox screen. Like drugs to make him drowsy," Jack said.

"If you would, talk with the ME and see about the diameter of the entrance and exit holes. They looked pretty similar to me, though I was guesstimating in the dark. See if he can rush the autopsy report," Jack said.

Jack and Rich got in the Expedition and returned. "Oh, Jack. Give me a minute for a phone call," Rich said and walked quickly back to the squad room and called the Fraternal Order of Police chapter office and requested a FOP defense attorney to contact him about the shooting.

He walked into Jack's office, where the sheriff and chief deputy were.

"Sheriff White suggested I get an attorney for a probably upcoming suit by the family of the man I shot in the bar."

"I was going to suggest the same thing."

The two got back in the Expedition and returned to the crime scene. They spoke seriously along the way.

"How are you doing? We don't have the on-call psychologists or psychiatrists large departments have, but I am happy to retain one or arrange a chaplain for you to speak with," Jack said.

"No thanks, Jack. This is my first police shooting, but I had a lot of them in Afghanistan. Some at a thousand yards as a sniper, some at smell the garlic on their breath distances. The closest call was one coming at me with a big ass knife. A kukri. I did a double tap then too. Just with my M4 carbine and not my Beretta."

"Habit with the double tap? Or did you think the rifle was just not enough for one shot at close range?"

"Both. To me, the 5.56 is just a military version of an old varmint caliber like .222 of the same bullet diameter. It's a damn .22 for the Lord's sake! I don't have a lot of faith in it."

"Yet you carry one in your truck every day," Jack grinned.

"Because my sheriff issued it and expects me to."

"What would you carry instead of that and in addition to your shotgun?"

"A lot bigger diameter bullet. We are rural enough we could justify a .308, but I'm not sure we need the recoil for patrol use by people who won't train with it like SWAT or a soldier or Marine.

"With a .300 Blackout we could convert our existing rifles by just replacing barrels. It would be the cheapest.

"Cheaper yet would be to allow personal guns within specific parameters. I have a .30-30 deer rifle like the one you carry. I'd pick it any day over my AR."

"You've given some thought to this, Rich," Jack said.

"I have. I'm not sure anyone else with us has. I hope our folks have not bought into the media crap about "those deadly, highly powerful AR assault rifles." Statements like those are based in ignorance or to promote the speaker's agenda, Jack. Again, we are talking about .22 caliber rifles. Nothing like the serious .30-06's our grandfathers carried in WWII."

"You want to put your 1894 Winchester in the rack of your new truck, go ahead. Keep the issue rifle and ammo in the bed storage for backup. I won't make you qualify with it. Just do it without advertising. If someone in the office questions it, tell 'em I approved it. I will tell the chief deputy. She's pretty darn cool and may want to do it herself. I know she puts away a deer or two each fall. Per her wonderful heritage, you can be sure she uses all of it. I'd bet you lunch she either uses a .30-30 or a shotgun with slugs."

Rich grinned.

"She uses a Marlin .30-30. We talked about hunting over lunch a few months ago. And you are right. Our Rose is cool as all get out," Rich said.

Jack pulled in to where the truck on the last shooting had come to rest.

He showed Rich the brush which had scratched the passenger side and that there was nothing but road on the driver side. Certainly nothing to cause deep gouges.

They walked down the two-lane road to the stretch where Bud Carey was confident the shooting occurred.

"See where the Tacoma swerved on and off the road here? See the shorter tire marks beside? Bud says this is where the sideswiping occurred. We both think it was a result of the victim, upon being hit, losing control and in his swerving sideswiped the shooter's car. Unless a shooter was a pro and used a stolen car to dump later, there is no logical reason to shoot someone in the head and then do a version of a PIT maneuver to run them off the road. A dead man is going to run off the road without you having to wreck your getaway vehicle, right?" Jack asked.

"Right. I can see why the criminalists would have had an impossible job locating the bullet. It could have been fired anywhere along this stretch. The faster the victim was going, the longer the search distance," Rich said.

"When are you scheduled to meet with the third player in the Strauss threesome?"

"Dinner time tonight in Norman. She said she knows a quiet restaurant where we can speak openly," Rich said.

"Sounds like a trap and you're the target."

"Probably. I'll be careful. Not to worry. The widow Strauss will be with me."

"Oh, boy. You could be in for it. Let me know in the morning. I'll be fascinated to find out what you learn. My recommendation is stay in a public place in full sight of a lot of people."

"I agree and I'll let you know what I find out."

On the way back, Rose Custalow called on Jack's cell phone.

"Jack, I just heard from the ME. He measured the entry wound at .36 inches and the exit at .38 inches. He says it had to be a 9mm, .357, or one of the .38's. A .22 or .32 would not make a hole that much larger than their diameter or have the penetration. Anything in the 40's would make a larger hole in and out. The tox screen was clear of anything but a few prescriptions for Type II diabetes and some cholesterol issues consistent with the autopsy findings. No abuse of prescription drugs, no use of illegal drugs. Just a middle-age guy with a middle age body."

"Thanks, Rose. Rich is here with me. We are on the way back. Your information supports our theory it was a +P 9mm, .357 magnum or Sig, or .38 Super. The first and second could have been fired in a handgun or carbine. Not the .357 Sig or .38 Super as far as either of us know."

"I can't help you there, Jack. I never even heard of .38 Super."

"Hey, I just told Rich he can use his .30-30 as his patrol rifle like I do. You can do the same if you want. We'll just do it on the down low and let deputies step forward if they want to also."

"Thanks, Jack. I might give it some thought. If we have three of us carrying .30-30's, I'd better pick up some extra boxes of ammo for the office," she said.

"Good idea. If you haven't eaten, meet us at the café in about ten minutes. If there is a remote table available, we can bring you up to date on the cases and the next steps. It wouldn't hurt to have another set of eyes and ears on it."

"I haven't and it's navy bean soup day. I'll go now and try to get us a rear table so we can talk," she said.

"We'll go straight there then and park out front instead of stopping at the office. See you soon," Jack said.

"Man, they have great bean soup," Rich said. "But no way. Not with me meeting those two women down in Norman tonight."

"Prudent," Jack grinned.

They parked the Expedition in front of the café and found Rose at a rear corner table where they could converse privately.

They brought her up to speed before two bowls of homemade bean soup and one salad had been delivered.

"To shoot through a vehicle window when driving past, probably with a pistol, is pretty tough at any speed. It's a helluva trick at highway speed. I have to assume the shooter was going fast enough to pass this guy," Rose speculated.

"Yeah. I'm thinking the same thing," Jack said.

"This was a professional type shot. The Strauss

murder strikes me as being more stationary. Strauss had drawn his pistol from a console or glove box. Something alarmed him. He sure didn't do it after being shot through the side of the head with a high velocity round. He might have been slowing or even stopped with the shooter next to him," Rich said.

"Well, I am still hungry after this piddly salad, but I have to go by my apartment and get clean clothes on for my big interview down in Norman tonight," he added.

"Wish I could be a fly on the wall," Rose said. Jack nodded emphatically.

"And I wish either of you could do it instead of me." He left before other observations could be made and paid for the lunches on the way out.

He could turn around his shower and change in ten minutes. The trip to Norman was not anywhere near as long as to Wichita Falls.

Rich stopped in at a gun shop in town and looked in the counter where the new and used handguns were shown. They had a used 1911 Commander like Jack's.

"Has your gunsmith gone through it?" he asked the owner, who he had known for several years.

"Both of us did. It is older and smooth as silk. Broken in, not broken down. I liked this one so much I shot it a good fifty times. Nary a blip. The fella who traded it threw in a total of four magazines. Two original Colt and two premium Wilson's.

"Rich, I'll give you an automatic ten percent police discount off the tag price."

Rich was handling it, working the slide, hitting the mag release to make sure the magazine dropped clear on its own, and checking the sights. It felt good in his hand and he said so.

He said "I'll take it," already reaching for his credit

card as the owner slid the federal background check form across the counter.

With an Oklahoma concealed carry license, he was able to leave thirty minutes later with his new purchase. All he needed now was a lot of practice ammo, some carry ammo. Ammo was available but the supply and prices were not as good as several years ago. The Warrior Sheriff's Office did not issue any 45 ACP's so he was on his own finding cartridges. Planning ahead, he already had a carved palomino color holster and two-magazine carrier to match his belt

He took a quick shower and even shaved. He knew presenting himself at his best was more than just profes-sionalism. He wore his normal dress up outfit, a blue blazer, creased jeans with boots and a white shirt open at the neck. The only outwards indication of his employ-ment was a sheriff's star lapel pin in the jacket. Under-neath the jacket was lots of indication.

Just before he went out his door, his cell phone rang.

"Rich, it's me. Myra Strauss. I am so sorry. I have eaten something and gotten food poisoning. Since we had the same lunch, I hope you haven't had the same thing!"

"No, Myra, so far I'm fine."

"It must be a touch of something then. You would have it by now if it was lunch. I started throwing up and more around mid-afternoon. I waited to call you because I thought it would go through my system. It sure felt like it should have.

"Anyway, can you meet Monica alone? I am so sorry to ask you to. I have something very important to tell you."

"Sure. It sounds like you need to stay at home. I'm

heading down to Norman now. What is it you want to tell me?"

"Monica apparently has no idea Bill is dead. I thought it would be better to tell her at our meeting," Myra said.

"Um …. okay. Odd. It was covered by all of the media."

"I am afraid the only thing Monica pays attention to is her libido."

Before he could respond, he heard an "Oooh!" and what sounded like a barefoot person running, feet slapping tile. Then, a retching sound which gave credibility to her claimed gastrointestinal issues. He went ahead and hung up. He had heard more than he wanted.

Rich made it to the restaurant early as planned. He wanted to size up Monica Kennedy from afar before they met. He knew her description. Thirty-eight, black hair and blue eyes and per Myra, a "killer body."

Well, okay," he thought.

It was well into dusk. The entrance was well lit and he waited there.

He went in to the hostess stand and got a fairly remote table held for two, saying he would wait for the second party at the front and escort her in.

Ten minutes after the appointed time, he saw a small white vehicle tear into the parking lot.

He thought it was a Fiat 500. A medium height woman in her thirties got out, without regard to the very mini skirt she wore. She had dark hair and matched Myra's description of Monica.

She walked towards the door looking side to side. He stepped out and she spotted him and smiled.

"Monica?" She smiled and nodded vigorously.

He handed her his badge case with the gold star and his official ID with photo.

She examined it in the light and looked him up and down. He felt a little like a side of beef hanging in a butcher shop.

"A sergeant, huh? You must be a detective," she said has she handed back his badge case.

"I am. Come on in. I have a table for us."

She took his arm and walked in as if this was a date.

He seated her, not unusual in their part of the world and one of the social niceties Rich revered.

"You are just like Myra described you!" she said, obviously pleased.

"Big, gawky and looks like a cop?" he responded.

"Like central castings choice for a handsome cowboy or Western lawman for a blockbuster."

"Thank you. I have been both a cowboy and a lawman. I'm glad you see handsome. I don't when I shave."

"How about me?" she asked.

"You look as lovely as Myra said. I recognized you as soon as I saw you get out of the white Fiat 500."

"Oh. You saw me get out? Perhaps I should have been more ladylike."

He smiled and did not answer. It was going to be difficult to conduct an interview with her. He was determined to not add fuel to the flames.

"Perhaps we can order and then chat about the official stuff while we wait for the dinner to come?" he asked.

"I hope you are able to expense this," she said.

"No. We don't conduct interviews at dinner. This was my choice. Don't give it a thought."

"I have eaten here with Myra and Bill. The beef is superb. If you like steaks, this is the place. I was thinking of a petite filet myself."

"Sounds good. I am starving from just a small salad for lunch. I bet they have a filet mignon which is not petite," Rich said.

The server came and asked about drinks.

"Can we have wine? A red since we're having beef."

"You can. Just remember you are driving. I am technically on duty, so I will watch you have wine."

"Are you sure? Who would know?"

"I'm sure. It's not something we cheat on."

She ordered a glass of Merlot and he got an ice tea.

"You know Myra. What do you think of Bill?" she asked, seemingly sincere.

"Monica, did Myra tell you why I wanted to meet with you?"

"She said it was a police matter and you were really hot."

"It is a very serious police matter and it involves Bill," he said.

"He's such a mild, pleasant but uninteresting man. What could he possibly have done?"

"I am afraid I have bad news for you."

"You do? Involving Bill the engineer?"

"Bill was murdered almost a week ago in my county. Which is why I am speaking with everyone I can who knew him."

She was struck and seemed to freeze in place. Her eyes widened and she stared at him. No tears. Just surprise. He presumed from her comments she thought of him in a very neutral way.

Finally, she spoke, choosing her words carefully.

"Why was he murdered? How?" she asked.

"The why is what I have been tasked to find out. The how was he was shot as he drove down a rural highway in Warrior County around nine in the morning."

"Do you know who shot him?"

"We are building a profile. The person is an accomplished marksman. Probably with a handgun. We think it was a .357 Sig or .38 Super caliber."

She almost imperceptively flinched when he said the caliber.

"The poor thing. He did not deserve to be shot! I am sure Myra is beside herself. They did not have a very romantic marriage, but he was good to her and put up with her…lifestyle desires and adventures."

"And, Monica, they involved you I take it?" Rich asked.

"I'm not in trouble am I?" she asked worried now.

"Not as far as I am concerned. What consenting adults do with other consenting adults without exchanging money does not break any laws of which I am aware.

Should you be in trouble?" he probed.

"No, no. Not at all. Talking about stuff like this makes me very nervous."

"Just discussing the weather with a cop makes most people nervous.

Monica, tell me about how you interacted with Myra and Bill. Who contacted whom first?"

"There are meetings in a meeting room at this restaurant. I saw new people come in. She was gorgeous and he was acceptable. We ended up having drinks. I saw she was into it. He seemed to be going along to make her happy."

"Will you elaborate on what happened with the three of you?" he asked.

"Are you getting into this, too?"

"I have to develop a picture of every aspect I can about

Bill Strauss. Sometimes building profiles can be uncomfortable. It's just part of what I have to do to solve crimes. Especially heinous murders like this one, Monica."

"Okay. Let me know if I upset your tender sensibilities." He smiled and nodded to encourage her.

"I think she wanted to see Bill and me together. So, we did it. Bill was obviously not into it and never finished. The first night was a failure from a hooking up standpoint."

"What happened then?" he asked.

"Bill was embarrassed and got dressed and went out. This was at a nice motel. I don't know where he went. The lobby? Their car? Who knows? Anyway, Myra had been really excited. Now she was so disappointed. I consoled her and we realized we had a chemistry so we acted on it. Do you want details? I will be glad to tell you everything."

"No. Thank you. I am really just trying to get at why he was shot. You may certainly maintain your privacy on those details."

"What if I might like to tell them to you?" she asked.

"I have two murders and a million clues to evaluate. I think if you went on it would make my concentration on those clues tougher."

"Oh, I knew you would like them!" He smiled pleasantly and did not respond to her comment.

"Monica, did they hook up with another person or couple?" he asked.

"I don't know of any, why?"

"I am trying to see who might be jealous enough to kill him."

She paled and took a long sip of Merlot.

"Can you name anybody in your group who did not

like Bill, who wanted him out of the way so they could move on Myra? Anybody who was jealous?"

"Jealousy does not fit in what we do," she said.

"People are people. They have emotions and egos. I suspect even folks who follow your lifestyle fall in love with people. Or out of love with them. What do you think??

"I think it's a blind alley. They were newbies. It has to be something else."

"Let's switch and talk about you. Tell me where are you are from? What you do for a living? If you have ever been married?" he asked.

"I was born outside of Oklahoma City. I went to school there and college right here."

"What was your major?" he interrupted.

"A bachelor's and master's in library studies. I am the research librarian at a city library. Yes, I am married but we are separated currently."

"Why did you separate? I'd think you would be the catch of a life" he said playing her ego intentionally.

"I am really into the lifestyle. It's who I am. My husband thinks its trashy. So, I kicked him out a month ago.

"Were the Strauss's the primary people with whom you interacted?

"I had others. But Myra was my steady person for the last four or five months."

"Did your husband know them?"

"No. He might have known their names. I am very open. Meeting them would have been traumatic for him. He has PTSD."

"What gave him PTSD?" Rich asked.

"Bosnia. He was over there. He was not actually in

combat. He was a mechanic. But, what he saw and felt screwed him up."

"Indeed. What's his name?"

"Roland, but people call him Rolly. I think it's stupid."

"Is he medically retired or does he work?"

"He has a small disability payment every month but he works full time."

"Good for him. What kind of work does he do?"

"He's a combat marksmanship instructor locally at the county range."

"That's the kind of thing I would do if I wasn't what I am," Rich said trying to build common ground, though she did not seem too interested in her husband.

"Were you in Bosnia too?" she asked.

"I was all over the place, Monica. Mostly I was in Afghanistan."

"What did you do there?"

"I was with the 75th Ranger Regiment. I did all sorts of things, most of which I cannot talk about."

"Yeah, yeah, or you'd have to kill me. I've heard it all before."

He was sitting against the wall in a relatively dark corner so he slipped his jacket off though his pistol and badge would have shown to anyone looking closely. Rolling up his right sleeve, he showed her a tattoo. It was the 75th Ranger Regiment scroll with *Sua Sponte* written below.

"I guess you wouldn't have gone to the pain to get it if you weren't really a ranger. What does the Latin mean?"

"'Of his own accord', but back to a more interesting subject," Rich said.

"Does Roland compete?"

"He does. Kind of long range metal pistol targets."

"Interesting. I never competed. I always thought it would be fun."

"It's his life. I could be, but the Monica bus has left the station," she said, showing what he read to be real emotion for the first time. He thought she actually loved her husband.

"I am sorry you two had to go through the breakup over the lifestyle. Do you ever think you'll get back together as a couple?" Rich asked.

"No. I am going to keep doing my thing until I am so old nobody wants me. I am destined to be alone, except for one night stands," she said. He read she was now begging for sympathy. He had to be supportive but noncommittal. He reached over and patted her hand and then withdrew his.

He was saved by the arrival of the server with some of the best food he'd had in a long time. Rich did not plan to come back to a meeting in the backroom with Myra or Monica but he might come back soon for a steak. He shared the latter but did not mention it would probably be with Isabella.

"If you need a dining companion, call me," she said, getting more back to what he reckoned was her norm.

"Of course. Have you ever been up and over to Warrior County?" he asked and she choked on a piece of steak. She recovered before he had to do a Heimlich maneuver on her.

She gulped down the second glass of wine.

"What's a town over there?" she asked, her throat hoarse.

"The county seat is MacKenzie. There is another town at the far end of the county. It's called Quanah."

"Like the Indian chief," she said.

"Exactly."

"What do you think Bill was doing way up there?" she asked suddenly.

"I don't know, Monica. Can you think of any reason he might travel there?"

"Who me? Of course not. I hardly knew the man," she said.

Keeping an expressionless face, he thought *"You slept with him. So, you somewhat knew him."*

"Does Roland travel around to teach and go to matches?" he asked.

"Why all the interest in Roland? He's even less interesting than Bill was," she said.

"This is just two new friends getting to know one another now."

"I like the sound of getting to know one another."

"Maybe Myra won't have food poisoning next time," he ventured.

"We don't need Myra unless it would add to your enjoyment."

"She sounded really sick when she called me and begged off our dinner tonight."

"I think she is sick because you favor her sister over her."

"They are both lovely women. When I met them less than a week ago, Myra was a grieving widow and Isabella was not."

"I think, Rich, the grieving is over and a little action would do her good. She's actually very good at ….. oh, well."

"Have you met Isabella?" Rich asked.

"Yes, I did not like her. She seemed pretty judgmental."

"Judgmental? About what, Monica?"

"Her sister's and my relationship and lifestyle in general."

"Was she aware Bill had been involved?"

"Heavens no. She would have been devastated. He was the brother she never had."

"I see." He put his credit card on top of the check and motioned for the server who was extending an inordinate amount of privacy. It made sense given the regular meetings there. She probably recognized Monica as a regular, too.

"We could have ended this evening on a more exciting note," Monica said.

"Yes. There are certain rules in my business. Mixing business and pleasure is a big one. It's after twelve. I spent over three hours for a half hour interview. It's not something I usually do."

"Oh, live dangerously," she said.

"I killed a man coming at the sheriff with a knife eleven hours ago. I think I live dangerously enough, don't you?"

"You are pulling my leg, right?"

"Check the news. I suspect it's all over it. 'Gunfighting sheriff now has a clone.' Not my favorite headline."

"Doesn't killing someone make your PTSD act up?"

"I don't have PTSD. So, no."

He signed the check and put his card away. He tore up the customer copy and deposited the small pieces on his bread dish. She knew he was not expensing a very expensive dinner. Maybe there was hope yet.

"Let me walk you close enough to your car to know you got away safely. I really have to come back in and hit the restroom real fast before I start the drive back."

They walked out and she embraced him. He gave her

a hug and kissed her on top of the head. He watched her walk to the small Fiat. A small white car. He wondered if it was the one the truck driver who found Bill Strauss saw?

She got in with even less decorum than when she arrived and sent him a smoking hot smile as she did it. Monica started the little car and spun it around, tires squealing, and took off. Once she was out of sight, he got in the Chevy and drove back to Warrior County. Coming back in for the restroom was a ruse to not prolong time at her car. He did not want to get involved any deeper with her. Her animal magnetism was over the top, but she made the small hairs on the back of his neck scream "trouble."

HE WENT into the office the next morning. There was no information yet from the criminalists about the vehicle from which the paint scrapings were taken from Bill Strauss' truck.

He sat at the computer and began doing a background check on Roland Kennedy. He looked up the information on the gun range where he worked and printed it all out for his folder. He found a drunk and disorderly arrest just after Kennedy got out of the Army.

Rich made a second copy of the National Criminal Information Center, or NCIC, sheet and folded it over with the picture prominent and the relevant information on the reverse. He hung this photo up on the murder board. He logged into a law enforcement only service and found out Roland Kennedy owned a dark gray Chevrolet Silverado. Rather, the bank owned it and it appeared Kennedy's credit history was not good.

The next foray onto the Internet was the site for the lifestyle club in Norman. A small number of people posted their photos and particulars. He was not surprised one was Monica Kennedy. He printed her photo and bio and put it on the board beside her husband's.

He checked out social media sites for both Kennedy's. Both posted around the time Strauss was shot.

He made note of the times of the postings. They were not alibis because they could have been posted from anywhere with Wi-Fi access, including a vehicle with the service. Like OnStar on a Chevy pickup.

Just before lunch, Tac called Rich from the front.

"Hey, buddy. I have a call to transfer to you from your lady criminalist friend."

"Thanks, Tac. Send her through."

"Hi, it's Rich."

"Hi Rich. We submitted the paint sample from the second murder victim's trucks to PDQ for paint data queries. We got the answer. It was a two year old Chevrolet or GMC pickup dark gray in color. It could have been full size or the Colorado/Canyon size smaller ones. Does the result help your case?"

"You bet it does! My newest suspect drives a dark gray Silverado."

"Sounds like visit time! I just passed the results to Ray also. He'll probably be calling you."

"Thanks. Lunch on me next time you are over this way," Rich said and hung up.

As soon as Ray called, he would try to set up a Zoom briefing session with the usual suspects.

A few minutes later, the sheriff walked in grinning. He placed a sheet of paper in front of Rich.

"Your copy Rich. I'd still speak with the FOP attorney

in case the decedent's family sues. If he includes us, our counsel will also cover you."

Rich quickly read the document. It was the results of the shooting commission conclusion. Bottom line, it was deemed appropriate use of deadly force and the matter was over from an investigative standpoint.

"Whew, Jack. I knew it was justified. But I am glad it's official.

By the way, I picked up a used Colt 1911. It's smooth and I will get used to it and prep so we can have our little qualification session soon.

"Once I hear from Ray in a minute, we are going to try to set up a quick Zoom meeting. We have a new suspect as of last night's interview and the paint results on Henry Lang's Tacoma. And, I believe we have the little white car. However, there is a real twist," Rich said.

"Maybe putting you in this investigator role was a good choice."

"I hope so." He hesitated, then continued "I will go into whatever details you want from the interview last night. She was candid to a fault. Or, I can encapsulate it for the Zoom."

"Let her rip however you want. Isabella involved?"

"No, Jack. It appears not at all. The sister, Myra the wife, has a tight alibi too. The only way she could be involved would be if she hired someone. I doubt it, but if we find a need to delve into a hired killing, following the money on a wealthy woman who never did anything like it before should be pretty easy."

"You say wealthy. It doesn't sound like Strauss was wealthy. His wife does not work, does she?" Jack asked.

"No, but the two daughters inherited the estate of a longtime Texas judge. I saw the house. I would consider it a mansion, with its black iron fence around it. Isabella told me it has six bedrooms."

"Just remember rich people often keep some amount of wealth in untraceable form. Krugerrands, Maple Leaf's, and other gold coins. Quite frankly, I am enough of a prepper I would too. If I had the money," Jack said.

"Good point. Unless we are all missing something with the two women, I still don't think they are behind it. On Strauss, we have the recently released guy he snitched on in the Army and a new one you are about to hear about. One whose circumstantial evidence is even stronger than former Major Allen Willis."

"Sounds like a good briefing. I look forward to it. I have an update on the Army angle to report too," Jack said as he walked back to his office.

Ray called and they set the meeting for three o'clock, pending availability of the ranger. Rich called him. He was not at his ranch where he usually did the Zoom meetings. He said he was at a sheriff's office, excused himself for a minute and came back saying he could do it there.

The meeting commenced at three with the four men and Rose participating.

"Thanks everybody. We have some developments, so Ray and I thought a quick meeting would be in order," Rich began.

"First, I would like to ask Rose to tell us about the forensic information from the autopsy of the latest victim. Rose?" Rich asked.

"Hi, everyone. As you all know, I could not attend the autopsy in Oklahoma City because of a bar fight here which ended in a righteous officer involved shooting."

"Whoa," Bodeway interrupted. "I don't know what

you are talking about. Did my boy Jack have to shoot someone else?"

"No, he was taking care of three bikers when another came at him from only a short distance away. Rich had to neutralize him to prevent the sheriff from being stabbed or slashed," Rose said.

"I hope you did a Mozambique or failure drill boy!" he said to Rich.

"As perfectly executed one was ever done. We had enough senior people and witnesses on scene to have a shooting board, He was cleared and the prosecutor and sheriff," Jack did a joke curtsey for the computer camera," both approved the finding of justified."

"In that case, you better give the boy a fine Christmas present this year!"

"He's getting two. A new unmarked Responder pursuit truck and the permission to carry a 1911 on duty," Jack said.

"So, there will now be a third person who dresses and carries appropriately."

"You all know we identified the bullet used on Strauss as a .357 Sig. We were unable to recover the one used on Henry Lang. The ME measured the entry and exit wounds and determined it to be a full metal jacket .38 or .357. We are going with the probability it's another .357 Sig or a .38 Super. Which means it could be Strauss' shooter."

"Jack, do you want to tell us about suspect, former Major Allen Willis?" Rich said

"Okay. This is from material Myra Strauss found in her husband's files. As a first lieutenant, he blew the whistle on his major. The major was selling inside information on a project to one of the competing contractors. We cannot find out what the information was. Our assumption is it must have been pretty significant because the court martial handed him fifteen years at Leavenworth. He served all fifteen and was released one month ago.

"I contacted the Army and they stonewalled me. I have reached out to Supervisory Special Agent Cheryl Louder at the FBI to try to get us some information. We just found this out a day or two ago, so I am not sure when or if she will get the information."

"Ray, will you tell us about the paint sample findings on from the damage on Henry Lang's truck?" Rich asked.

"Yes. First let me mention we did the forensic work on the two cell phones we have. Neither had any suspicious numbers in or out. Nor did they have suspicious texts. Both had apps for the same encrypted message site. No way we can break it. About every federal agency has tried and failed. The apps have millions of users and most are just regular folk who are tired of hacking and eavesdropping.

"We did a PDQ or Paint Data Query and found Lang's Tacoma was involved in a sideswipe accident with a two-year-old GM pickup. Dark gray in color. Either a Chevy or GMC. Same paint choices. We cannot tell the body size. Could be full size or smaller."

"Now, whoa down here boys. It sounds like y'all are talking about your second, Oklahoma only, murder," the ranger said.

"Zack, we are. I should have warned you at the opening. My part will tie this together and surprise everybody."

"Then let's jump ahead to your part. I need to see the relationships here. It appears things have taken a big turn in the trail," Zack Bodeway said.

Jack nodded at Rich, who had planned on reporting

last. Bodeway's efforts on finding out about the accident in which Judge Munro and his wife died would have to wait

"Okay. This and the conclusions we might draw from it are only minutes old. I still have not put everything in its proper place on the murder board yet.

"I interviewed one Monica Kennedy in Norman last night. I was referred to her by Myra Strauss. The Strauss' were part of a lifestyle group. What we used to call swingers. Both ladies claim Ms. Kennedy was the only outside partner in this three-way endeavor.

In their first get together, the woman agreed to pair Strauss with Kennedy with Myra Strauss as an onlooker. Strauss was not happy with the situation and left in the middle of his interaction with Monica Kennedy. He waited in the hotel lobby, parking lot or somewhere. The two women proceeded.

"It seems they got together several subsequent times to, as Ms. Kennedy described it, 'explore different avenues of their sexual interests.'

"Strauss had bowed out. Kennedy is married to a man named Roland Kennedy. He also did not approve of his wife's proclivities and she kicked him out. He had developed PTSD while serving in in Bosnia. For whatever it is worth given the source, she described him to me as being unstable.

"His job is tactical pistol instructor and pistol competitor in several tactical shooting venues. Let his talent soak in for a moment. It gets weirder.

"I was pursuing this line of inquiry related to the murder of Bill Strauss, not Henry Lang.

"However, Roland Kennedy drives a two-year-old dark gray Chevrolet Silverado pickup truck.

"The truck driver who found Lang reported

meeting a small white car with one person in it not long before he came upon Lang's Tacoma. We put out a BOLO on it and nothing came of it. So, we dismissed it as unrelated. We may have been premature.

"Monica Kennedy drives a tiny white Mini.

Circumstantially, we have to look at them as persons of interest in the Lang murder instead of the Strauss murder," Rich finished.

There was silence for several seconds, then the ranger spoke.

"Well, it gets curiouser and curiouser. At your request, I looked into the accident where Judge Munro and his wife died.

"Salient facts were either badly missed in the investigation or intentionally withheld.

The DPS trooper's original hand written accident notes were in the file. Possibly as an oversight. They stated, but did not make a big deal over, paint from a different vehicle was on the right rear panel of the judge's Mercedes S model.

"No mention of it or another vehicle being involved appears in the final computer records of the investigation. I think the judge and his wife were forced off the road at a juncture guaranteeing a severe accident.

I think a type of PIT maneuver was used.

And, I think the two were murdered in cold blood."

There was a much longer period of silence as the rest of the participants absorbed what the ranger said.

"Since I have not been as deeply involved as the rest of you, let me summarize where we are on these two cases, okay?" Rose Custalow said.

"The Texas Rangers will likely open a murder case on the death of the judge and his wife. They are the in-laws of victim one. The original case was either incompetently investigated or more likely criminally altered.

"There is an Army case where the convict who served fifteen years as a result of victim one—our joint victim—whistleblowing on him. He was released a month before the two murders and is MIA right now. The Army won't help. Jack has reached out to the feds.

"The judge's daughter who is the victim's wife, Myra, is a swinger. Her swinging partner's husband could be the suspect in either victim one's murder, or more likely from evidence, victim two's murder. Or, maybe both. The swinging partner with victim one's wife, drives a car like the missing one seen at victim two's murder scene. Her husband, the new victim two suspect, drives a truck matching paint samples taken from victim two's Tacoma.

"Did I miss anything?"

"No, Rose. I think you have admirably summed up everything we either know or think we know," the ranger said.

"Here in Texas, I will bring this to Austin, and cause a shit storm the likes of which has never been seen. My smartest move would be to retire and take up underwater basket weaving," he said.

"Zack. I honestly always wanted to be you. Until now," Jack said.

"But first let's develop a strategy," Rich said.

"Zack, there is not much we can do up here to help you. Because of the parts value on a new big Mercedes, you might be able to locate the judge's car in a local parts yard. How many could there be in Wichita Falls?

"I suspect your waking hours will be filled with this new case. We'll support you however we can. When you develop a suspect for the wreck, we'd sure like to look at him for the Strauss murder.

"In Oklahoma, we need to bring Major Allen Willis and Roland Kennedy in. There is a good chance they are connected by a weird twist of fate and no more. There's also a good chance one of them is a murderer. Maybe both.

"I think Ray and I should bring Monica Kennedy into an interview room, Mirandize her, and have a very serious chat.

"We may also have a third murder suspect in the Strauss case. The person who killed the judge and his wife if Zack's suspicion proves true."

"I concur, Rich," Jack said, "and if there are no more questions or ideas, we all have a lot of work to do, so I suggest we adjourn and get to it."

He left for his office and Rich immediately called the OSBI agent.

"I thought it might be better to talk to Roland Kennedy first. Maybe find out what we can from him. Whether he has been up to Warrior or not and definitely inspect his truck. What do you think?" Rich asked.

"Good idea, Rich. I believe time might be of the essence here. Let me swing by and pick you up and we'll go straight to the range. If he's typical in his job, he will be armed with a loaded pistol. I think we have to go very carefully with him."

"Me, too. See ya when you get here."

He walked into Jack's doorway. Jack was meeting with the chief deputy and looked up.

"Headed to the range with Ray to talk with Kennedy. Depending on a lot of things, we might bring him back here for questioning."

Jack nodded, reached into his top drawer and took out a Taser pistol. He handed it to his sergeant and said, "be safe."

The range was on the Warrior County side of Norman. Having a state officer investigating there was no need for a courtesy call to the sheriff there or Norman PD.

Rich handed Ray another copy of the sheet he had prepared on Roland Kennedy. It had a clear facial and body shot from his Facebook page.

It had a plate and VIN on it for Kennedy's truck. They looked for it before going in. The parking lot was medium and packed. They considered the crowded lot a good a good thing, because it made them less likely to arouse suspicion looking around.

They found the truck quickly. The passenger side had a long scrape matching the one on Lang's Tacoma. It looked like Kennedy was going to have to take a ride.

They went to the office and found the manager.

"I am Special Agent Ray Colton from the OSBI," Ray said holding out his credential pack with badge and ID.

"This is Sergeant Rich Ammon from the Warrior County Sheriff's Office. We are here to take your employee Roland Kennedy into custody. You have a busy day with lots of people here and he is presumably armed. We want to do this the safest way possible and keep anybody, including him, from getting hurt."

"What has he done?" the manager asked.

"We want to speak with him about a shooting in Warrior a few days ago," Rich said.

"Rolly is a little squirrely. But, I don't think he would shoot anybody."

"We have some pretty good evidence he did. Can you summon him into your office by a speaker system? Try to keep it business and we may be able to avoid a standoff or him running."

"Rolly, come to the manager's office for a phone call," he broadcast.

"As he approaches, motion him in as you leave and say 'you can take it on the desk phone,'" Rich said.

As the manager stood at the door waiting, Ray whispered to Rich. They were hidden from the outside by standing on either side of the door. "I don't like the positioning. Too easy for a crossfire. We have to be careful."

They heard boot steps and saw the manager was getting twitchy.

"You can take it at my desk," the manager said on cue and walked past him out the door.

Ray said "OSBI, Kennedy!" with his badge and ID out.

Rich saw Kennedy's right hand drop for his gun. Rich shot him in the back with the X26 Taser and Kennedy folded up and hit the floor. Ray reached for him and protected his head as he hit the deck.

On the floor, Rich removed the fishhook-like prong and slipped the Glock pistol out of his holster. A further check prompted the removal of two knives and two loaded magazines. Nothing unusual for a tactical pistol instructor. Also, nothing either lawman wanted to deal with like they almost had. Ray cuffed him from behind.

The manager walked in and looked down.

"Do y'all use suppressors? I did not hear a shot."

"Taser. The fool tried to pull his gun. Which was some kind of stupid," Rich said.

"Do you know the guy up in Warrior who just had to shoot a fella in a bar room?"

"Yeah. Real well," Rich responded as he continued removing everything form Kennedy's pockets. He unlaced Kennedy's boots and checked for weapons in them.

"I hear the biker guy was about to knife the gunfighter sheriff up there."

"He was."

"Why didn't the sheriff shoot him?"

"He was busy fighting three other guys."

"I disremember the name of the deputy," the man said.

"It is Sergeant Rich Ammon," Ray said.

The manager paused for a minute and realized it was the man he had been speaking with about the shooting.

"Sorry. I didn't know it was you."

"That's okay. I'm sorry I had to do it.

Kennedy was moving around now. The two helped him into a chair for a few minutes.

"You need some water?" Rich asked.

"Yeah. Why did you shoot me with something?"

"Because when the agent identified himself, you tried to draw on him. I was afraid if I shot you several times at close range they may be through and throughs and accidentally hit my partner. So, I used a Taser on you."

The man scowled at him, so he added "Besides it's cheaper to use the Taser. High quality hollow points are getting so expensive."

Kennedy's eyes widened a bit and the manager mumbled from outside the door "you got that right!"

Ray held the cup of water he had gotten from a dispenser to Kennedy's lips and the suspect drank it.

"You want to try to stand up yet?"

"Yeah. Am I being arrested?

"Yep. You probably weren't going to be until you got stupid and tried to assault a police officer with a deadly weapon. You are lucky you aren't being zipped into a body bag right now," Rich told him.

Rich started walking him out to Ray's SUV. Ray was

obtaining a statement and contact information from the manager and thanking him.

"You and the sergeant are pretty tough, aren't you?" he said with apparent sincerity.

"We've both got tough jobs," Ray responded and shook his hand.

Probably thirty students and target shooters were lined up with curiosity.

Rich had not intended a perp walk but had it anyway as he walked their tactical shooting instructor to the police SUV for a trip to the sheriff's office.

He hooked the prisoner in. With the seat belt-shoulder harness and his hands cuffed in the back, he was not going anywhere.

Ray called his control and advised their mileage and prisoner aboard and destination.

"And, please call Warrior County and tell them I am underway with their sergeant and a suspect in the murder of Henry Lang," Ray ended.

Kennedy turned to Rich and said "I was scared for my life," sullenly.

"Look, Kennedy. This is not one of your classes where you teach people what to say to the police following having to shoot somebody. You would have drawn on and killed a man in a suit identifying himself with a badge and ID. Capital murder of a police officer. If I hadn't had not brought the Taser, I would have killed you dead. Right then. Right there. This is not some BS fantasy for pseudo special operators or holster sniffers. This is for real.

"So, you need to spend the next forty-five or so minutes until we get to my office thinking about whether you need a lawyer and whether you are going to tell us the truth.

"Think about it. You got picked up a few days after the death of Henry Lang. We did not invent you out of our imaginations. Some solid evidence directed us to your doorstep. You lie and we will know it.

"I might have Tased you, but the guy in the front driving is who you want to worry about. I sure as hell would not want him to interrogate me on a murder charge!"

"I...." Kennedy began, but Rich held up his index finger in the classic sign to wait and not say anything.

"If you want to confess, nod your head and we will pull over, read you your rights under the Miranda decision, and begin recording. Otherwise, hold your tongue until we get the Miranda and lawyer part done and all have some coffee," Rich said.

Kennedy looked out of the side window and sulked.

They arrived at the Warrior County Sheriff's Office and walked him in. He had already been thoroughly searched, so they just took his belt, watch and boots and gave him a cup of water and put him in a cell.

Jack watched.

"What do you think?" he asked Rich and Ray.

"His truck has a scrape down the passenger side. It appears to have gray paint in it and fits the damage on the driver's side of Henry Lang's Tacoma.

"I have a team going down with a flatbed wrecker to get his truck and take it back to our lab for a side-by-side and paint chip comparison. They may do an initial look here on the way.

"He was wearing a Glock 9mm with hardball in it. I will bet when we get a warrant to search his place a .357 Sig or .38 Super will show up. Maybe a .357 magnum, but he doesn't seem like a wheel gun type of guy. In his mind, he's Mr. Tactical. I think his self-image will trip him up in questioning," Ray said.

"How about his mental status? Do you think his PTSD will get him diverted from either questioning or immediate prosecution?" Jack asked.

"Maybe. But, I wouldn't think so. I talked with him some. Not stuff which would be impacted by him not yet having been read his rights. I saw more inflated ego than mental condition. A shrink might see it differently. I have a question, or some advice, to ask you. Do you think we bring in Monica, the estranged wife, now or see if he implicates her? Possibly having him in custody looking at murder one may be enough to make her open up," Rich asked.

"Man. You have posed a tough one. It could make her open up. Or clam up. There is always the chance her small white car is not the one the truck driver saw and she knows nothing.

"To me, it's a coin flip guys. I'm not waffling on you. I could debate it either way," Jack said.

"How about this, Ray? Let's charge him with resisting arrest with force. Maybe Jack or Rose can handle the attorney or public offender angle while we get a warrant and search his place. While we are in Norman, we can go pick her up. Ray, feel free to comment."

"If Jack's up with it, so am I. Seems like about all we can do," Ray said.

"I'm okay with it, Rich. Rose is in the office. I will assign the lawyer or public offender part to her," Jack said. "I'll advise her now. Having him stew in his juices in a cell for a little while may be a good strategy. It should also give you two a chance to interview him with a better fact base after you search his place.

"You better read him his rights and get the Miranda

agreement signed. Then, tell him you are going to do a warrant search and ask him for the combination to his gun safe and any gun locker at his place of employment. Tell him you will specify in the search warrant any locked conveyance will be forcibly opened otherwise. Ray, do you have anyone on staff or on call who can open a high-grade gun safe without a combination?"

"I do. We'll take her if he won't give us the combination.

A stop at the cell was fruitless. Kennedy refused to give combinations. They advised him failing to do so may cause his safe to be damaged in the warrant search. He merely shrugged

"Okay, let's move. Your Explorer again?" Rich asked. Ray nodded and they walked out the door. Ray was already on the phone to his headquarters. Norman was in a different court circuit from Warrior and he needed an agent from headquarters to meet them in Norman at the Cleveland County Court for the judge of proper jurisdiction.

"YOU KNOW, Ray, it's a lot easier on television. The cops just say 'let's get a warrant and 'boom' they have it and are on their way," Rich noted.

"It is. I have to deal with it a lot because my territory is in several circuits. Some territories have multiple agents. I have one of the rural ones. Actually, they are the majority."

They arrived and met with OSBI Special Agent Lee Parks who ushered them in and introduced them to the proper magistrate.

Before they left, the criminalist with the locksmith

experience met them and would follow in her own vehicle.

They were in and out in a record thirty minutes and the search privileges included the residences of Roland Kennedy, his estranged wife, Monica, and the gun club.

They went to the gun club first. The same manager was still on duty.

"You guys arrest Rolly yet?" he asked.

"We put resisting arrest on him to hold him. We will question him after we finish our homework. You are stop one for the homework. We need to search his locker."

"Looking for anything specific?" he asked.

"We are interested in a .357 Sig or .38 Super firearm first and foremost. You never know what other interesting things might pop up though," Rich said.

"I suspect you will find a Glock 32 in .357 Sig. He likes it better than the same sized Glock 19 he was wearing when you took him in custody. The ammo is a lot hotter and a lot harder to get. He uses it for one phase of the competition he does on our shooting team. Winning matches is good advertising."

"I take it he shoots hardball in competition?" Rich asked.

"I doubt if he owns anything but hardball for it. Hollow points are tough to find."

"I know. I carry a Sig in .357, but I am switching over to .45 Auto." The man nodded and his expression suggested he thought it a wise decision.

"I have duplicate keys for employee lockers, so if the lady with you has shape charges in her Pelican case, she won't need them," he said.

"Oh darn! I came all the way over hoping to blow something up!" she said jokingly. At least Rich thought she was joking. He was not totally sure, however. He did like her. They would see her showcase her craft at Kennedy's apartment.

The manager unlocked locker number seventeen and they removed a Glock 32 and five fifty round boxes of Fiocchi 124 grain ammunition. There were extra shooting glasses, electronic earmuffs, a couple of competition nylon shirts with the range's name on them and one porn magazine.

They booked and bagged all in evidence bags. The criminologist would take them back to the lab for the ones working the two Warrior cases.

They went about four miles to Kennedy's apartment. It was in a rent-controlled complex. The arrival of an obvious police SUV and accompanying van attracted considerable attention, even mid-afternoon on a weekday.

The three found the resident manager with some difficulty and showed her the search warrant. She balked at opening the door and Betsy, the criminologist explained in tougher language than either Ray or Rich might have used, why she had no choice.

The manager walked them to the apartment and unlocked the door.

"We'll lock it when we leave. You can go now sweetie," Betsy told her.

"Betsy, I like you more every minute," Rich said.

"Cowboy, I could almost be your cougar girl. Except I'm probably too old. I like you too. I know all about your sheriff. We worked together when he was in Ray's slot. Now in the last few days, I am hearing more about you. Warrior County seems to grow them tall and deadly. My kind of boys!"

Rich gave her a carefully practiced "Aw, shucks,

Ma'am" cowboy grin and she bought it hook line and sinker.

"Okay, before you two start a mutual admiration society, let's get in and search this place," Ray suggested.

"Don't be jealous, Ray honey. I still love you, too," came a reply which shut him up.

They found a Liberty gun safe in the living room.

"Crap! It's a good one. This will take a while and I may have to go out to the van and get some more stuff," Betsy said, obviously relishing the challenge before her.

It took her a while, but eventually she opened the large safe.

They booked a Ruger AR 15, a Remington 870 pump shotgun and then took out a Springfield 1911 in .38 Super. Among the ammunition was a box of Aguila .38 Super full metal jacket.

"Bonanza. Now we have two pistols, either of which might be the Lang murder weapon and one of which we have a bullet to compare for the Strauss killing.

"Betsy, once we finish checking these things in, we'll carry them down and put them in your van. Can you reset the combination to one of our choice?" Ray asked.

"Sure. What's your birthday? Perfect! Two digits in order for each your month, day, and year."

"Got it. Thanks! Now, one more stop. I don't know what Kennedy's estranged wife Monica's hours are at the library. I guess I have to call her and tell her we need to speak. Just so you know, Betsy, I questioned her over dinner the other night. It had been set up by Myra, Strauss' widow. She got sick at the last minute and I had to wing it. The Strauss' and Monica are part of a lifestyle group. Do you know what it means?" Rich asked.

"Honey, I could tell you things which would turn

your hair white. Of course I know what it means," she said, beaming at him.

"Anyway, since I was a man who seemed to be breathing, she found me appealing. I have no idea how she is going to react. She flinched when I asked her about the caliber of her husband's pistols. She flinched again when I asked her if she has ever been in Warrior County. I don't know how up you are on this case, but the truck driver who found Lang saw a small white car in the area. My deputy and the OHP were unable to locate it. Monica drives a small, white Fiat."

"I can tell this one is going to be fun," Betsy commented.

"I fear very emotional," Rich responded.

"You're a gunfighter, new friend. You can do this."

"Thugs I can handle. Women .... not so much."

"Yeah, right. Betsy have you ever seen his girl-friends?" Ray asked.

"I have not. Maybe we will in a few minutes?" she responded, grinning evilly.

"If she is, it's 100% one-sided," Rich said.

"Methinks he dost protesteth too much," Betsy said, deliberately paraphrasing from Hamlet to suit her meaning.

"The instruments of darkness tell us truths," he responded without needing to misquote, having been Hamlet in his high school play.

"Wow! Even from Hamlet! I am impressed, cowboy!" she said.

He did the grin again as they got in their respective vehicles.

They decided to drive to her apartment and call her from the curb there. Rich tried the library first. Whoever answered said she would be there for a few minutes longer before leaving for the day and transferred the call.

"Research desk, Monica Kennedy."

"Monica, it's Rich Ammon."

"Oh, hi Rich! It's good to hear from you. In town for another dinner?"

"In town, but on business with my OSBI agent partner. Would you meet us at your apartment so we could clear some things up?" he asked.

She hesitated.

"Am I in trouble?"

"I don't think so. Our questions are mainly about Roland."

"Is he in trouble?" she asked.

"He's in custody at the Warrior County Sheriff's Office."

"Oh! What did he do?"

"We went to talk to him and he got stupid so we had to take him into custody. We still have not talked to him. My chief deputy is working with him to see if he wants a public defender before he speaks with us."

"Okay, Rich. You say you have someone with you?"

"Yes, Monica. I have Special Agent Ray Colton and Criminologist Betsy Brown, also from the OSBI."

"Will you have to come in? It's a mess," she said.

"It would be tough for four of us to talk in a car, so yes. Don't worry about the mess. You should see my place." He immediately regretted the last thing out of his mouth and a sideways glance showed Ray grinning and shaking his head.

"Okay. I can be there in just a few minutes." She hung up.

"Maybe one of us should have gone to the library to

watch her come out. What if she takes off on us?" Rich wondered aloud.

"It would suggest she's guilty of something. We could locate her with one simulcast BOLO," Ray said. Rich was internally wrestling with himself. He liked Monica. He had no interest in a relationship with her but hated to see her stressed and scared. He knew she was both right now.

Several minutes later, Monica came roaring up in with her little hot hatch. She got out and was wearing slacks and a nice blouse. Her hair was in a ponytail and she looked like a pretty suburban housewife. Certainly not like the woman with whom Rich had dinner.

The two investigators and Betsy got out and greeted her pleasantly. Rich gave her his best and most sincere smile. He was not faking it a bit.

"Thanks for meeting us so promptly, Monica. This is Special Agent Ray Colton and this is Criminologist Betsy Brown." Monica extended her hand and shook with all of them, Rich included.

"C'mon in. I can make some coffee if you want?" she asked.

"Coffee is always welcome, Ms. Kennedy," Ray said affably.

"Sit down in the living room. It's the most useless room in the apartment. I never use it. You might be the first folks who have."

Monica disappeared. Betsy walked in to help her. Actually, she went in to watch her to make sure she did not get one of her husband's guns or duck out the back door.

Betsy had been in her job for years and was good at it. She was particularly good at bonding with victims. It sounded to her like this woman, ten years younger than Betsy herself, was a victim.

As they chatted, she could feel Monica's nervousness decrease.

They walked back out carrying a coffee urn, cups, sugar and cream.

"Rich, I like Betsy. I'm glad you brought her along. She calmed me down. Will you tell me about Roland? He's not hurt is he?"

"No. Maybe a little sore. He tried to draw his gun on Ray. I had to Taser him. Ray caught him as he fell so he wouldn't hit his head. He's fine now."

"Is he charged with anything?" she asked.

"For now, only resisting arrest."

"How can I help? Post bond for Roland?"

"There are a couple ways. First, you can give us permission to search your apartment in case Roland put any evidence here, possibly without your knowledge."

"You are welcome to search. I have nothing to hide. There are some adult toys I guess I need to warn you about."

"If it would make you more comfortable, you could point them out to me instead of these two men," Betsy said.

"Oh, I would not be embarrassed but I will do as you suggest."

"May I have your phone and the PIN? We always have to look at phones," Betsy said and Monica logged in and handed it to her without hesitation.

She told Betsy where to look for those items and Betsy commenced the search while the two investigators spoke with Monica.

It struck Rich this was going too well. Too well

always made him nervous. Had he misread Monica badly? He really expected fear, tears and a lot of drama.

"What else, Rich?"

"This is a good opportunity to fill in some things you may have forgotten when we spoke at the restaurant. Or some things you didn't want to tell me then."

"What kind of things?" she asked.

"You flinched when I mentioned caliber of pistols. Why?"

"I don't know. I just did."

"You also were uncomfortable when I asked you if you had ever been to Warrior County."

"Okay. I have been to Warrior County. Maybe five or six days ago."

"Please talk about your trip up. Where you went and why."

"Rich thought I was seeing a man with our group. He got really worked up about it. He arranged to meet the man up there."

"How did he arrange it?" Rich asked as Ray took notes.

"They used an encrypted message app. It's the one we all use in our group."

"Okay, then what happened?" Rich asked.

"Roland was really out of sorts. I was afraid he might hurt the man. He had forgotten I still had the tracker on for his cell phone. I knew when he was leaving from his apartment, so I tracked him up in my car."

"Before we go any further, what was the name of the man?" Ray asked.

"His name is Hank Lang."

"Do you know what kind of car Hank drives, Monica?" Rich asked, treading lightly.

"It's a truck. A Toyota I think."

"Did you find Roland and or this Hank fellow?"

"No. I got caught up in traffic here. By the time I got to the intersection where they were supposed to meet at a pull-off, Roland was already heading back this way."

"What did you do then?"

"I turned around and came home. I had called in sick, so I made it a home….er, spa day."

"Hank Lang. Did you ever hook up with him?" Rich asked softly.

"Will it upset you if I did?" she asked.

"No, Monica. You are part of a group. Apparently, Hank was too, right?"

"He was."

"Then, it would be expected."

"Okay, I did. He is great. He doesn't look like much. But, he is nice and funny and gentle. Hank initially thought we were just an adult dating group. From his standpoint, it's how he uses it. As far as I know, I am his only date.

He is a real find. I don't know what I did wrong."

"What do you mean?" Ray asked.

"He never called me back. I even sent an encrypted DM to him from work today. No answer. Why? We seemed great together."

"Monica, this is where I ask you to sit down and tell you I have bad news. But, you are already seated," Rich began.

"Did Roland kill him?" she screamed.

"He was shot the day you went to Warrior County. It is beginning to look like Roland is the shooter."

"That bastard! See if I put up his bail! Hank was a nice man who never hurt anybody."

At this point, she put her head on her chest and began to sob.

On television, somebody always got the sobbing person a glass of water. Rich never knew why. Your great uncle was mauled by a grizzly. What the hell good would a glass of water do? Since he did not know the answer, it is exactly what he did. He got her a glass of water. She slurped it down gladly and gave him a tearful look of appreciation. Yet one more mystery added to his life.

The next question was on thinner ice. In court, a wife could not be compelled to testify against her husband in a criminal case and vice versa. Monica and Roland were legally still married. Both Rich and Ray were experienced patrol officers, but only had a year in Ray's case and a week in Rich's as investigators. Could they ask her to tell on her husband?

Rich had been serious when he quoted Davy Crockett's "Be sure you are right, then go ahead" motto to Isabella.

Rich was not sure he was right this time, but he charged ahead anyway.

"Monica, Bill Strauss was shot the same way, with the same size bullet, in the same place, a few days earlier. Did Roland shoot him?"

"Wasn't he at work? He had to take off to go to Warrior."

"The manager at the range does not remember. I asked him today. Roland is paid by the class. He is not a salaried employee. The manager only remembers days there were no classes scheduled the week the two shootings occurred. Roland did not take off. He just was not working," Ray said.

Monica sat there letting the enormity of what her husband could have done sink in.

Betsy walked in and caught Ray's eye and motioned him over.

"This is a small apartment. I tossed it thoroughly. I cannot find anything related to either murder. There might be something on the app they use, but they must delete a lot, because there was nothing on either victim's phone or either of the Kennedy's. Nothing."

Ray motioned Rich over.

"The only thing we have is corroboration of her being in Warrior on the day of Lang's death. Unless you think she shot him or helped Roland in a way we have not figured out, I don't think we have enough to charge her on anything.

"I think she is not criminally involved in any of this. I see why you felt badly about having to take her through this. She strikes me as a nice, pretty and somewhat lonely lady," Ray said.

"I know I'm not an investigator, but those are my feelings exactly," Betsy said.

"Mine, too. Let's say our good-byes and head out," Rich said and the other two nodded agreement.

"Monica, thanks for all of your cooperation today. We are all done here. I don't think we made a too much mess for you to have to clean up.

I'm really sorry you have had to go through this in the past few weeks. I hope everything gets better for you. I really do."

He put his Resistol on and they left. They each knew they had professionally fulfilled their jobs with her. All three walked away with a hollow feeling in the pits of their stomachs, however. Despite her sexual proclivities, she was but another victim in this series of events.

Betsy diverted back to her lab. Ray and Rich drove back to Warrior County.

Rich called Rose to check on Roland Kennedy's decision regarding his fifth amendment rights and whether he wanted an attorney to be appointed.

"I read him his rights in front of Jack. He had already decided not to answer questions without a public defender and signed the Miranda form. I checked and we did not have a criminal public defender available. There was one available elsewhere in the circuit, so he was appointed. I have heard of him. He's a hot shot in his own practice.

Kennedy lucked out. He's getting experienced defense most people pay a lot for.

They are going to meet here at nine in the morning. Once the public defender meets him and is satisfied, you and Ray can interview him, so let Ray know."

"Thanks, Rose. I'll call Ray now. See you in the morning."

Rich got home and found he did not have anything of interest for dinner, so he fixed a bowl of oatmeal. It, like mac and cheese, was his comfort food standby.

An hour on the Peloton and he hit the sack.

CHAPTER FOUR

RICH'S CELL phone rang at ten-thirty. Eyes still closed, he thought "Oh, crap. Here I go again.

He looked at the caller ID. Isabella Munro.

"Hi."

"Hi, Rich. I thought I'd better check on you. It's been several days. You okay?"

"Just busy and beat. How are you?" he asked.

"Feeling unloved."

"No need for such feelings. You are a gorgeous blonde who is smart, funny and an absolute doll. The whole world loves you."

"Very sweet! Not what I was looking for, but still sweet. How are the cases going?"

"The Lang case is looking good. We have someone in custody. The circumstantial evidence is strong. I think we can break him in a few hours of interview tomorrow. He has lawyered up, but we'll see."

"Think he is involved with Bill's murder, Rich?"

"He's related to the lifestyle group, but I seriously doubt he killed Bill."

"I know you cannot tell me, but it's killing me to know how the meeting with Monica went. I've met her, you know," Isabella said.

"Yes, it went fine, Isabella. Myra was unable to go due to food poisoning, so I had to wing it, which was fine."

"Have you ever conducted a police interview with a beautiful woman at an expensive steak house before?"

"Never. Not the ideal venue. Do you know the place?" he asked.

"I do. It's got some of the best food around," she said.

"Think it would be a good place for us to meet for dinner soon? I know it's a bit of a drive for you."

"I think the Mustang would make it if you were waiting there for me."

"How about letting me find out what the suspect and his lawyer are going to say tomorrow, then I will call you and we can agree on a date?"

"Okay."

"You do know the meeting room there is where the lifestyle group gets together every few weeks?"

"I do. When Bill stopped going to those meetings early on, I would go and have dinner alone in the main restaurant while Myra was attending the meeting. I apologize for earlier explanations. I was intentionally vague because I did not believe in or participate in Myra's lifestyle. Quite frankly, it embarrassed the hell out of me! Bill didn't either. He played along once and got so upset he just got up and left, Rich."

"No curiosity what went on behind closed doors?" he asked.

"None. I like my relationships straight forward and classic. I have enough self-confidence to not need a group to meet and enjoy wild times with someone with whom I have no other relationship."

"Me, too, Isabella. Though in learning more about this stuff, it strikes me it's more about being adventurous and daring and varied than it is lack of confidence," he said.

"Sounds like you have an interest."

"Not in the least. I am just trying to understand why folks do what they do. I was always impressed with a line Oklahoma lawman Bill Tilghman used as a caption in his early silent movie, The Passing of the Oklahoma Outlaws," he said.

"What did it say?"

"It was something like 'They did what they did because they were what they were' in explaining some of the worst outlaws in the West. Cold murderers like Red Buck. Others included Bill Doolin, Bill Dalton, Bitter Creek Newcomb, and Cattle Annie. The list goes on and on."

"Hmm. Elegant in its simplicity.

So, who did you arrest?" she finally asked. He had been waiting for it.

"Roland Kennedy."

"Isn't he…" Isabella began.

"Yes, he is," Rich interrupted.

"I didn't see that one coming. Are you sure he didn't kill my brother-in-law?"

"There are several tie-ins, but I am pretty sure he didn't," Rich said.

"Any luck finding the major Bill blew the whistle on?"

"No, unfortunately. The sheriff reached out to the feds for help, but nothing so far."

"I guess if my favorite investigator has solved one of two murders in less than a week he might be a superstar," Isabella said.

"To which he would tell his favorite blonde it was a

team effort with a lot of work and more luck than we deserved."

"You are going to call me tomorrow about our dinner date?" she asked.

"I am. Good night Favorite Blonde." She giggled and hung up without responding verbally.

"What on God's green earth am I going to do with Isabella Munro?" he asked himself aloud once his phone had gone dark. He still stung from having been caught unawares by Nurse Eleanor Moffitt unexpectedly taking a job in Texas and not telling him until the day before she moved.

What to do with Isabella would solve itself. Eleanor no longer resided on his radar screen. He went to sleep within minutes after putting the phone back on his bedside table.

Ray met Rich at the office at eight thirty the next morning.

"Is Jack in? I have big news. Rose should hear it also," Ray said.

"He has a meeting over in Quanah this morning. I'll get Rose," Rich said.

The three gathered. Ray advised them tests had already been run on Kennedy's .357 Sig and .38 Super. Neither had been used to murder William Strauss.

The public defender showed up earlier also. He had an expensive haircut and an Italian designer suit on.

Rich assessed him as one who would run for public office when his yearning to make seven figures a year turned to an ego-driven quest for power. He had the mannerisms and smile of a politician. It was pretty clear his required public defender duties were slumming. Rich was also sure he would represent his free client extremely well. His reputation depended on it.

Rose escorted the attorney to the interview room. Rich retrieved Roland Kennedy from the cell where he was finishing breakfast, they had gotten for him from the café down the street. Kennedy was handcuffed to the table.

They showed the attorney the location of the panic button and locked the two in for their initial consultation. They took forty minutes, then the attorney knocked on the inside of the door.

"We have a plea deal. I would like you to get your assistant DA or whoever you have nearby to join us," the attorney said.

There was a ADA at the courthouse. She came over and was briefed on the evidence.

Rose, Ray, Rich, and Assistant District Attorney Amy Wilson met with the public defender and the handcuffed suspect in the conference room.

"I am now quite familiar with the case. Mr. Kennedy and I have spoken. He is very contrite over his actions which were impacted by his post-traumatic stress disorder.

"We are prepared to enter a plea of guilty to shooting Henry Lang by reason of his PTSD and accept a fifteen-year sentence with no parole in lieu of trial. This plea is also conditioned by having no other charges brought against my client."

"I will submit your offer to the district attorney with one exception. We have enough on Mr. Kennedy to successfully prosecute him on the murder of Henry Lang. Neither of his relevant caliber handguns were used to murder William Strauss. However, we reserve the right to prosecute Mr. Kennedy for the Strauss murder should future irrefutable evidence come to light," ADA Wilson said.

"Please allow us a few minutes to discuss this change in private."

The four left the room and were motioned back in within a few minutes.

"Mr. Kennedy advises he was not involved in the Strauss murder. We accept the deal with your condition added."

"I will secure the DA's immediate approval or disapproval and be back here to report in a few minutes. The DA is standing by and awaiting my call.

"The Sheriff's Office will deliver our signed copy to the DA to sign and have it back here in one hour." The public defender looked at his Patek Philippe watch and nodded his head. For security, Kennedy was put back in his cell to wait.

Rich and Ray took the plea agreement signed by Kennedy and witnessed by his attorney to the DA's office. He was waiting, looked it over and signed it. He reminded them they should drop any other charges and charge him with the first degree murder of Henry Lang.

"Okay, Mr. Kennedy. Here is your signed plea agreement. You may look at it, but we will give an authenticated copy to your attorney. The original will be sent to the District Court.

"I will now formally charge you with the murder of Henry Lang. The resisting arrest charge will be dropped immediately.

"Roland Kennedy, you are under arrest for the First Degree Murder of one Henry Lang. A sentencing hearing will be held in the District Court covering Warrior County. In the hearing, the judge will formally sentence you for fifteen years in the state penitentiary without parole. This sentence is exclusively for the crime to which you have admitted guilt. You will remain in the regional jail until the sentencing," Rich said.

Because of the tight staffing at the sheriff's office, Rich transported Kennedy over to the regional jail later in the afternoon. Kennedy never said a word on the way over.

Back at the office, Tac caught him.

"I am the man with the word!" he said.

"Which word, Tac?"

"Responder!"

"Hey, one of my favorite words. You have delivery news?" Rich asked.

"I do. The price to receive the news is to be the first person to ride in it."

"Deal! Want me to cuff you?"

"Okay now, you have got to stop associating with the club in Norman. I'm starting to worry about you," Tac said, grinning.

"No cuffs then. You are on for the ride. When is it coming in?"

"Both yours and Jack's got in early. They were pretty well equipped with emergency equipment already. They are over at our contracted shop having the radios set to the correct frequencies, the locking chests bolted to the bed floor and the foldup tonneau covers attached onto the beds."

"Very good! Were all the lights and the siren package already installed?"

"They were. You have LED's primarily. They flash in the head lights, grill, rear view mirrors, windshield, rear window, rear lights, and upper brake light on above the rear window. There are also lights across the cladding under the doors. Lit up, you will look like a red and blue

Christmas tree. Unlit, you will look like a dark green F150."

It has the fastest acceleration of anything ever tested in the LA Sheriff's police comparison tests. I'm thinking it will equal or outrun your Mustang."

"Mine's not a regular Mustang. I saved almost every penny in the rangers. Especially the combat pay. My reward to myself for coming back whole was a Saleen Mustang. It's not only got engine mods but also a lot of handling tweaks.

"But, when can we take this ride?" Rich asked.

"Probably get your keys tomorrow afternoon."

"You have worked wonders. Which is Jack going to take, Tac?"

"He decided to take the off-white one and will have the star on the door and Warrior Sheriff insignias. He is going with a light bar. And, a crash bar. Yours will have a crash bar also."

"What made him change his mind, I wonder?"

"Politics, Rich. Come election time he will be driving a virtual ad. Pretty good decision, I'd say!"

"I agree. I kind of like the idea of the dark green. Looks like any other pickup. At least from a distance. Thanks again."

"You bet. Jack should be back anytime. I told him the FBI lady was coming by about now. Hopefully, if she's coming by it means she has something."

"Tac, I just saw a mid-size dark Buick pull into our front lot with one well-dressed female inside. I am betting it's her," Rich said.

He walked out to greet the visitor.

"Special Agent Louder?" She smiled and held out her hand.

"I am. I know you aren't Jack. So, I bet you are Sergeant Rich Ammon."

"I am. Come on in. How about some coffee?" he asked.

"Absolutely. Black please."

Louder was easily as tall as Isabella, though heavier. She was fit and muscular. Rich knew her suit had to be cut larger to hide her weapon. He knew agents carried extra mags and handcuffs in the field but not what else or exactly where. Her hair was brown and sensibly cut. She wore light makeup. Overall, she could have been a bank vice president or IT company CEO.

Rich led her back to the break room and poured her a coffee in one of their Warrior County Sheriff mugs.

"Keep the mug. Add it to your collection at the office," he said.

"Thanks. Good coffee, too."

"Let's go sit in Jack's office. He is returning from a meeting in Quanah and will be here any time."

"I guess you are who I read about in a bar incident a few days ago," she said.

"Could be. It was not the best of days. Except for the fact all the good guys got to go home."

"I'd call such a day a really good one, Sergeant."

"Rich is fine. I was a sergeant in an earlier life. I made it back to where I was seven years ago."

"I was an Army CID investigator. What were you?" she asked.

"75th Ranger Regiment. You are not Mary Lee Chang's immediate replacement are you?"

"No. She has already moved on to another division. It's our way of life," she said.

She nodded as Jack walked in.

"Hey, Cheryl. I see you met our investigator, Rich Ammon."

"I have. We just started chatting."

"Keep chatting while I get a cup," Jack said.

He returned shortly with a steaming cup.

"How have you been?" he asked.

"Well, you know how is with us federal employees, working only thirty hours a week and all," she joked.

"More like thirty extra hours a week," he said, knowing how hard his deceased agent friend worked. "Any luck with Willis?"

"Jack, I have a little something for you, but not much. I got stonewalled too. So, all of what I am going to say came from other sources.

"First off, I could not find a location on him. Second, this slip of paper is his federal probation officer's contact information. The information you were told was wrong. He was sentenced to eighteen years and released after fifteen. The PO is not Army, so he talked to me. Unfortunately, Willis has not reported for his first appointment. He's days from having a warrant issued.

"Third, I found out from Customs and Border Protection he crossed over into Mexico through Del Rio seventeen days ago. Willis is his father's name. Gonzales is his mother's name. He is fluent in Spanish and could pass for an illegal coming back in anywhere along Texas' twelve hundred fifty-four-mile border with Mexico.

"Or, he could have bought pretty good fake papers in Mexico and come back through as a legal. We would have nothing we could use to associate the name with Allen Willis."

"Thanks for trying, Cheryl. I am going to have my Texas Ranger buddy put out a Be On Look Out for him in Texas. Rich, why don't you do a BOLO for Oklahoma, too.

If Willis has gone to Mexico and skipped his first PO appointment, it looks like he's on the run. Which makes him a stronger suspect in my eyes."

"I can't think of anything else we could all do," Louder said.

"My question is, if he's our killer, why did he go to Mexico first? Why not pick up a gun here in the States, kill Strauss, then go to Mexico to hide," Rich said.

"Good point. If he had been incarcerated anywhere else, we could have found out who his cell mates were, who visited and sent him mail. Then we could talk to them.

Under these circumstances, we are walking in the dark, guys," Louder said.

"Thanks for trying, Cheryl," Jack said. She arose and shook hands with both and left cup in hand.

"Sounds like you and Ray have put the Lang murder to bed. Odd the way it ended up with the initial clues pointing us towards Strauss. But you showed good instincts Rich. I learned from Uncle Bud to always follow my instincts. They will seldom lead you wrong. Speaking of instincts, what are yours on the Strauss murder, given the fed information we just received?" Jack asked.

"My logic says it looks like Willis is our man. The motive seems there, the timing is right, and he's on the run," Rich said.

"Do I ever hear a big 'but' there!" Jack exclaimed.

"It's all too clean and pat, Jack. I would like to see what Zack finds out about whether Judge Munro's accident is something more. If so, it could be involved with Strauss. Since there is nothing I can really do on Willis until he pops up, I wish there was some way I could look around down in Texas."

"You know there isn't. No jurisdiction and you would risk insulting a good friend to all of us in this sheriff's office," Jack said seriously.

"I know. Just thinking ahead."

"Thinking is fine. Acting is not in this case, Rich."

"Myra could be the answer. I think she and Zack may have parted less than amicably. She seems to have a pretty open relationship with me. You cannot believe the detail she went into about Monica, Bill not performing. To say it was adult would be a gross understatement."

"I understand completely, Rich. But, unless she moves to Oklahoma, she is off-limits unless you need to phone her for clarification of something you discover or found while you and Ray were down in Wichita Falls."

They changed topics and chatted about their new county trucks, Rich having to practice with his new .45, and whether he was going to bring Isabella over for dinner at the Doolin's Cave Ranch.

"Lily said to invite you to a barbecue on Saturday. See if Isabella can make it. Rose is coming and Uncle Bud will be there. My neighbors Cindy and Julie too. I just left a message for Ray and his wife but haven't heard yet. The more the merrier," Jack said.

"You have an informal range set up don't you?"

"Real informal. You want to bring the .45 and try it out? Don't worry about paper targets. I have some steel targets strung at seven, twenty-five and one at eighty yards."

"Maybe I could come early and you could give me some pointers?" Rich asked.

"I'd be happy to. We'll have someone who killed his

first man with a .45 years before either of us were born there. He's the one who taught me."

Jack wrote something down on a scrap of paper.

"Here's Uncle Bud's phone number. He'd really like it if you called and asked him yourself. He's sharp as a tack, but his physical decline is starting to make him feel a lesser person. I think you asking his help would go a long ways."

"We've met several times, including at your wedding. I always figured he thought I was a piss ant deputy and paid no attention."

"You are very wrong. He pays attention to everything and everybody within gunshot distance. He and I have talked about you and your progress many times. He will know who you are when you call and identify yourself," Jack said.

"Thanks, Jack. I will do it. Maybe if Isabella comes, she can help Lily with the meal."

"I'm sure they will find something to talk about. Probably you. Lily had high hopes for you and her nurse. The way Eleanor left so abruptly upset Lily as much as I suspect it did you. She keeps asking me about Isabella and how you two are progressing together." Rich just shrugged and rolled his eyes.

He went back to his cubicle and called Uncle Bud.

"Bud Carey."

"Ranger Carey, this is Rich Ammon over at the sheriff's office. Nothing's wrong. If you have a second, I'd like to ask you some advice."

"Sure thing, Rich. Fire away."

"I am going to switch over from the issue Sig to a Colt 1911 .45. I bought a smooth old Commander model. Nobody I know has near the experience with one you do. What do you recommend? If you had time before the upcoming barbecue to give some pointers, I'd appreciate it."

"Bring your .45 over and a box or two of ammo. Shoot her a few times and I'll try to give you some pointers like I did Jack."

"Thank you, sir. I look forward to it!"

"It doesn't get much better than having a famous old Texas Ranger share forty years or more experience," Rich thought to himself.

He called Isabella's cell phone.

"Hi, cowboy," she answered as she often did.

"Hi, yourself. The sheriff just told me he and his wife are putting together a barbecue for a few close friends. It's Saturday and they have invited you to come too."

"I'll see if I can take Saturday morning off. Can I let you know in fifteen minutes?" she asked.

"Sure. I will wait for your call."

She called back in less time and confirmed her appearance at Doolin's Cave Ranch.

"Didn't you tell me it is an old homestead with a lot of history?" she asked.

"I did. The Doolin-Dalton gang hid out in a cave on the property. It is rumored Bill Tilghman and a deputy captured the teen girl outlaws Cattle Annie and Little Britches on the property."

"Oh! I can't wait to see it."

"I need to get there early. Maybe around ten in the morning. Jack's great uncle, retired Texas Ranger Bud Carey is going to give me some pointers on a new pistol. I am switching to it and he carried one like it several decades in the rangers."

"I might do a little Internet work on him. Is it 'ey?' or just 'y?'"

"It has an 'e' as I remember. He is quite a character. Imagine Zack Bodeway in his eighties."

"I will have to leave well before dawn," she began.

"You can come up on Friday night. You can ride over with me in the new Super Cop truck."

"Where should I stay? Are there any motels around?"

"Nope. Trust me. We'll work it out."

"Gotta go. Myra is ringing me. Later. Kisses!" And, she was gone.

"Is she just flirting? Or, is she working me?" he asked himself. He did not have an answer to which he gave much credence.

On Friday, Rich went into the office and confirmed with Tac the new truck would be in sometime during the day. He pulled the Chevy into the back of the fenced parking and removed his gear from it, making two trips inside to his cubicle. He had brought in his .30-30 deer carbine and had it by his desk. He put the AR next to it, since Jack wanted him to keep it in his new truck as a backup.

He worked on his computer, searching for any signs of former Major Willis. Rose Custalow came in with a big smile.

"Guess what's here?" she said and turned and walked away. Rich jumped up and followed her out the side door. Jack's truck was not there. It was having the lettering and door badges installed.

However, a very mean looking dark green F-150 pickup with a short bed and wide tires was sitting in the fenced lot. Rose tossed him the keys and he got in. She climbed into the passenger seat.

She did a radio check with Tac and checked the OHP channel and the several tactical use channels. He read a quick instruction guide and set the siren to sequence all of the sounds except the air horn by throwing a toggle switch and touching the horn. He could still selectively use individual sounds by hitting the appropriate button on the siren console. He blipped the air horn and tested the PA system.

Though the exhaust did not have the big V8 sound, it had a very un-police like burble.

"Rose, you know how hard Tac worked on these trucks. I promised him a ride."

"I'll spell him on the radio and phones and send him out," she said.

Minutes later, Tac came out in his tactical black wheel chair. Rich assisted him into the truck. The only gear he had put in was the Winchester lever action carbine.

They pulled out onto the main drag in town and the truck jumped up to the speed limit with no particular help on Rich's part.

"Investigator-1, can you take a patrol call?" Rose called over the radio.

"Investigator-1, what do you have?" Rich responded.

"Somebody just on the city limits hot-rodding a pickup, squealing the tires and so forth. Dark blue in color. Occupied by three young white males."

"Got it. On the way!" Still in town, Rich accelerated up to forty-five and began to watch for the offenders.

"What do you want me to do?" Tac asked.

"Work the radio if this turns into a pursuit. The lights and siren too when we see them. If it's a bunch of dumb kids, they might take off. I hope not."

They spotted the truck a few blocks ahead and Rich accelerated hard. The kids did not make the green truck out to be a police vehicle. They thought the truck was challenging their five-year-old Dodge hemi. Which is why, they took off.

"Warrior control, Investigator-1. They are running. It's kids. We are not going to engage in a high-speed pursuit. We'll follow at highway speed. Request you notify any of our units and OHP of our direction and location. Maybe a roadblock or stop sticks would be in order.

"Tac, light 'em up and throw the main siren switch."

Rich pulled it up to eighty and slipped in behind them. Blue and red LED lights appeared all over the exterior of the truck. Rich touched the horn button and the siren, alert and klaxon sequenced.

The driver turned on his right signal and pulled over, Rich following suit. They were a mile west of MacKenzie by the time both stopped. Tac called in their position.

Rich got out, glad the young driver showed some sense.

"Good morning. Driver's license, registration and proof of insurance, please."

The driver was shaggy haired with untreated acne. He was polite and apologetic.

Rich walked back to his truck and Tac used the in-truck computer to run wants and warrants on the kid. Nothing turned up. He returned to the truck.

"I just put a new carb on this and just wanted to try it out."

"The edge of town probably is not a good place to do it. Plus, you just burned a couple thousand miles of wear off your rear tires. Next time, go down to the drag strip and try it out there, okay?"

"I will deputy or detective. Will you answer a question for me?" Rich nodded.

"I never saw a truck move as fast as yours. What's in it?"

"Just a V6," Rich said. No need sharing the part about two turbos and four hundred horsepower.

"Keep it safe, okay? Next time I might not be so lenient." He went back to the truck and Tac and turned around.

"Investigator-1. Tac said into the mic.

"Go ahead, Investigator-1," Rose said back.

"Warning given. Back in service."

Tac grinned all the way back to the office. Rich finished moving his equipment into the truck. He wanted to leave a little early and pick up some items at the supermarket and clean his apartment. Isabella, who had not seen it, would arrive in several hours.

He accomplished his goals, including clean sheets and blanket.

The supermarket had a floral section and he picked up two arrangements in vases. Rich hoped having fresh flowers might impress his visitor.

He heard the rumble of her Mustang GT convertible at seven-thirty. He did a lastminute roll up of towels for the linen closet, ran his fingers unnecessarily though short brown hair and walked to the door.

Rich had a surprise as both Isabella and Myra greeted him.

"I know this is not what you bargained for," Isabella began. "But, Myra walked in the door as I was walking out. She has found something very important. So important I just brought her with me."

"Come in and tell me what's going on."

They sat in his living room kitchen combination.

"I have been going through Bill's stuff," Myra began. One of our bedrooms serves—served—as his office. I found a safe in there. Kinda like a small gun safe. He had a notebook of passwords and account numbers he kept in a lock box in his desk. It was not secret from me and I had the key. It had the combination to the little safe.

"I went into the safe and found a bunch of notebooks and photos and single page documents. I figured they would be related to the Arc business he was trying to get.

"They weren't! He was doing his own investigation of our parent's auto crash over six months ago! Bella and I thought it was an accident. Bill thought they were murdered and it was covered up. He was trying to track down proof of who did it. He had some suspects he was looking into.

He came up here to meet one of them," Myra was breathless with stress and took a gulp of air.

"Do you know who he was meeting?" he asked.

"No. I do have a couple names. I suspect it was one of them."

"And, you have all of these documents with you?"

"Yes! Every one of them," Myra said.

"Why didn't you tell Ranger Bodeway about them? The accident happened in Texas. He has the jurisdiction. I don't."

"But, Bill was murdered here where you do have the jurisdiction," Isabella said.

"Zack and I were an item a long time ago. I wanted more permanency than he was willing to give. We parted on bad terms. He's a fine man, but I don't want to spend any more time with him than is absolutely necessary," Myra said.

Rich was not about to tell them Bodeway was part of a reopened investigation of the fatal crash.

"Bring your things in. You both crash in the bedroom.

I will take the sofa. While you are bringing you bags in, I have to call the sheriff."

He immediately dialed Jack's cell phone.

"Hey. Sorry to bother you, but I have something which might be big."

"Shoot!" Jack said.

"Instead of just Isabella, she and Myra both just showed up at my door pretty excited.

"Myra found a small safe in Strauss's bedroom office and opened it. She found a whole bunch of information with his notes where he was investigating the wreck where his in-laws died. He believed it was murder and the authorities covered it up. Or, at least, some of them did. I have not mentioned Bodeway's investigation of it to them, nor do I plan to do so."

Jack paused for a minute, then let out the breath he had been holding.

"Here's what I propose. You call Ray and I'll call Zack. You go over the material tonight at your place. In detail. Do a summary. Ask Ray to come early. The same time you were coming to shoot with Uncle Bud. You can do the shooting after our conference call with Zack, Ray, Rose and us. Sound like a plan?"

"It does. They are going to take my bedroom. I will work on the files on the kitchen table and will see you around ten as planned. Please tell Ranger Carey about the change in time?"

"I will. Let's make our calls now. I know Zack will ask. Why did she bring them to you? Why not Zack?"

Rich looked out the front window. Both women were still at the Mustang, so he did not have to guard his response.

"I asked her. She said they had dated and she wanted more than he did. She said it did not end well and she harbors some ill feelings towards him. There was also some confusion whether since the murder happened here, evidence should be turned over to Warrior County for our investigation."

"I'll go with the latter excuse. Zack will likely know the other one without being told anyway. He spoke to her even before you all met with him and her in Wichita Falls. If there was coldness or hesitation, I am sure he felt it."

"I'll call Ray now and see you in the morning. Night!" Rich said and hung up.

The women had traveled with a minimum of luggage. Rich thought on Myra's part it was probably caused by the suddenness of her coming up to Warrior County.

"I know both of you are Peloton fans. There is a virtually new one you have probably already spotted in the corner. Have at it! I pretty much use the bedroom just for sleeping, so the only television is in here. Jack and Lily introduced me to British and Scottish mysteries. You can find those on Acorn and BritBox channels.

"After offering you the bedroom, I am going to use the bed for a while to spread the documents on and study them so I can prepare an executive summary for our impromptu conference call with the team tomorrow morning.

Myra, you've gone through this material thoroughly. Where do you recommend I start?" Rich said.

"Why don't I look over your shoulder to start while Bella does the Peloton?" she responded.

"And, since I don't have workout clothes, I will put my shorty PJ's on and work out. Before I do, you were a bit mysterious when I asked you about your non-official vehicle. Where is it?" Isabella asked.

"It's black. You parked three down from it. Here are

the keys in case you to take it for a spin. I never offered them to anyone before."

"I must be special."

"Must be," he said.

She walked out the door. They could hear the raucous rumble of the exhaust as she started the Saleen Mustang and the acceleration sounds as she reached the main road and took off. He smiled. Always the driver, he had never heard what it sounded to the rest of the world. "Damn good!" he thought instantly.

By the time she returned, Myra had assisted Rich in sorting the files, photos and individual documents into some semblance of order.

The photos particularly interested Rich. Some were of the wrecked Mercedes S Class the judge and his wife had been driving. Several focused on the right rear fender. It showed damage where someone had picked there instead of the very corner of the vehicle to hit for a PIT or Pursuit (or Precision) Intervention Technique.

Rich explained to Myra PIT pioneering had been done by the precision driving school at Summit Point, West Virginia and taught by the Fairfax, Virginia police department. It may have evolved from a "bump and run" cheating technique used by local stock car drivers to move a competitor out of contention.

Subsequent photos showed where the car had been pushed off the road at a curve on a rise. It had rolled, according to Strauss' noted, several times and crashed into a lake. It appeared neither Munro was wearing seat-belts and had only air bags for protection.

The rest of the material centered around the case of a man Judge Munro had sentenced to ten years for DUI and vehicular homicide and Strauss' efforts to track him after his release from prison seven months ago.

Rich realized this might or might not nullify Willis as a main suspect.

"The man who your late husband reported and the one he thought may be behind a retribution killing of your parents served in prisons hundreds of miles apart. As was the distance where he and the major served was relative to Wichita Falls.

"Based on those circumstances, I have a hard time believing there is any connection between the two. So, your information gives us a second logical suspect.

"The big questions to me are whether your late husband's theory was correct about it being a hit instead of an accident, and whether his choice of suspect is correct."

"Bill had his faults, Rich. But his life and his career as an engineer were both based on precision. His logic always impressed me. I was a philosophy major and studied some of the best and he still wowed me."

"I appreciate the insight, Myra, and will share it with our ad hoc task force tomorrow morning from Jack's ranch. You should go with us. I doubt you will find a more interesting assembly of folks anywhere. And, the ranch is an original homestead. It's like a museum. Jack even hid things like his television, the microwave and dishwasher behind cabinet doors. There is a small herd of bison who don't have to worry about becoming buffalo burgers, too."

Isabella walked in, her brief pajamas soaked with perspiration.

"Okay. The two machines I just enjoyed raise your desirability quotient even higher, Rich. I may just stay forever."

"Go to the second drawer in the chest over there. It has some tee shirts in it. Take one to replace the pajamas in which you exercised. If you want, you can hold them for my small washer and dryer. They are stacked behind a door in the kitchen. Myra can do the Peloton. By the time Myra has finished, y'all can wash your dirty clothes. I will be through here by then and make you dinner," Rich said.

"How about this? I will shower and put on the tee shirt and make dinner while you wrap up and Myra exercises?"

"Sounds like efficient time management to me," he said.

"And, she is a great cook," her sister added.

Isabella chose a white tee and draped it over the back of a chair in the bedroom before walking out. Myra took her pajamas out of her bag for exercise use and helped herself to a matching tee shirt. She laid hers over the corner of the bed as Rich developed his summary of Bill Strauss' investigative materials. He sat at his laptop in the bedroom and began his executive summary of the findings.

Isabella walked in wrapped in a towel and dropped it. She slowly put on the tee shirt, curtseyed and left walking silently in her bare feet.

He heard Isabella clinking pans in the kitchen and Myra turn on the shower as he was finishing his summary. Minutes later, Myra walked in wearing her towel.

She retrieved her tee shirt and walked over to him. Very close to him. And dropped her towel.

"Did my sister do this too?" she asked. He nodded.

"I bet this is the kind of thing teenage Rich fanaticized about, but thought would never happen to him, huh?"

He nodded again as she donned the tee shirt. She

215

padded out to help her sister. He could smell the body wash lingering in the air.

Rich blew out the air he had forgotten to expel and sat there. A few minutes later, Isabella called him to dinner.

Dinner conversation was relatively normal in view of the appetizer show which proceeded it. The sisters asked questions about the people who would be attending the barbecue.

Rich described the two neighbors, Julie and Cindy. He talked about how much he liked his Cherokee chief deputy. A lot of time was spent on retired ranger Bud Carey.

He spoke about Lily Landers, Jack's gynecologist wife and Ray who both had met.

"I have never seen nor met Ray's wife. I cannot tell you a thing about her," he said.

Our retired chief, Clive may be there with his wife. He was my early mentor as a deputy. He was actually Jack's too."

"Will you all want me to sit in on the call, in case there are questions?" Myra asked logically.

"Maybe, but it would be Jack's call.

The dinner is great Isabella. Far better than I could have done with the same groceries! I will clean up. Why don't y'all watch TV or go to bed?"

"The workout was longer than my usual and it took a lot out of me," Myra said.

She hugged her seated sister. Rich stood and she gave him a full body hug and a kiss. He thought for a minute it was for her sister's benefit, then decided she did what she felt like whether her sister was there or not. She walked into the bedroom and closed the door.

"You sure I can't help with the dishes, Rich?" Isabella asked.

"It's a small kitchen. We'd be bumping into one another. Which would hopefully lead to things we don't have the privacy to explore. Real soon, though?"

"Real soon. She gave him a kiss which eclipsed her sister's by several minutes.

"Night, cowboy!"

"Night, Isabella!"

CHAPTER FIVE

BREAKFAST WAS light in view of the probable spread they would face at the ranch. All slept well, though it took a long time for Rich to get the guests in his bed in the next room off his mind. The sofa was a bit short for his height, but he accommodated.

He put on a checked shirt and some uncreased jeans. He wore his backup gun, a small Sig 239 in .357 Sig. He liked the little gun despite its snappy recoil and ear-spitting crack and thought he would maintain it even once he transitioned to the .45.

The beautiful sisters came out of his bedroom dressed in cowboy boots, sundresses and hats not unlike his own. Texas dreams personified. He told them so and was rewarded with memorable looks and smiles.

"Should we drive separately or together?" Isabella asked.

"Either is fine. I got a new county vehicle yesterday. Since we are both Mustang fans, I suspect you will like riding in it. It's not at its best yet since I have not had time to break it in."

They walked out and he led them to his "police parking" sign

"It's a green F-150. No offense, Rich, but what's so special about it?"

"It's one of the only pursuit-rated trucks ever. And, it has four hundred horsepower."

He watched Isabella's eyebrows rise. Myra was clearly not impressed.

"Rich, will we be anywhere near where Bill died?"

"I can take you by to see it if you want."

"May I steal some of your fresh flowers and make a little bouquet to leave on the spot?" Myra asked.

"Of course, use all of them if you need. I just bought them to impress your sister."

"You mean the sister who is standing here listening?" Isabella asked.

"Yes. You. Did they work?" he asked.

"I cannot tell you right now."

"Why?"

"Since we are in a public parking lot, you'd have to arrest us both."

"I am going to take your response as a positive."

"I know my sister better than anyone does. You should take it as an absolute superlative," Myra said as she climbed into the rear seat after going back in and getting the flowers. She took an elastic hair band from her purse and secured the flowers into a very presentable bouquet.

Rich took them to the crime scene and stopped on the shoulder. He flipped on his LED array and they got out. He pointed out where the shooter had stopped and where Strauss's truck had come to rest. Myra put the flowers there. She mentioned she had a specialty firm clean it and had the passenger window replaced. A dealer friend had the scratches on the doors buffed out and sold it to a wholesaler who sent it out of state for her. She got less money wholesaling it, she said, but did not care. She really did not want to see it on the streets of Wichita Falls. Ever.

Rich looked at his watch. They had spent more time there than he thought. He would have to rush to reach Jack's in time.

"We are a bit behind, so I am going to have to push it," he said once all were in and seat-belted.

He noticed a wide grin spreading on Isabella's tearstained face.

Rich turned around, got up to enough speed to maintain traction and punched it.

The Responder's V6 roared as the twin turbos cut in and delivered all five-hundred-pound feet of torque to all-wheel drive.

"Wow," Isabella mouthed silently. Rich heard Myra say something in the back seat. He could not quite make it out, but it sounded irreverent.

"Rich?" Isabella asked sweetly.

"May I have your truck?" He just grinned at her and concentrated on driving.

They pulled into the gate for Doolin's Cave Ranch on time and drove up to the house.

Jack and Lily walked out.

"She is the most beautiful woman I have ever seen," Isabella said with quiet sincerity. "She is absolutely perfect."

"I thought so too. But both of you give her a run for her money."

"If I can't have your truck, I'll take you," she said.

After introductions, Myra saw the small herd of

bisons grazing and she, Jack and Rich walked over to the fence.

Uncle Bud came out, looking like the ranger he was, even with the walker.

"You must be the legendary Bud Carey!" Isabella said.

"I don't know so much about legendary, Missy, but I am all that's left of Bud Carey all right."

"My Rich has talked so much about you. You know you are his hero?"

Bud grinned and Lily focused on the "my" part of the sentence. She was quickly and studiously appraising her guest. She had seen the young deputy risk his life crawling into precarious wreckage after a tornado to save two elderly people. She had seen him repeatedly clear the ground at every hill in his patrol car, responding to help her with comatose Jack. She had seen him at their wedding where Jack was shot. And she knew this week he had killed a man to save her husband's life. He would always be very special to her.

Lily Laughton Landers considered him a priceless hero, close to her husband in stature. She had equity in him and his future as far as she was concerned. He was family to her, a five-year younger brother. Probably the next sheriff of Warrior County when Jack's inevitable call to return home with her to his ancestral Cinco Peso Ranch came.

Lily flashed back to the present as Isabella turned to her.

"I don't mean to embarrass you, Lily. I said to Rich as we pulled in you are the most perfectly beautiful woman, I ever set eyes on."

Uncle Bud spoke before Lily could respond.

"My niece, Georgia has always been the most beautiful woman alive. Even as a little girl I called her the

Yellow Rose of Texas. Then Lily appeared. One day she will be co-owner of the Cinco Peso Ranch and the Red Rose of Texas. Now, here you are. There are three beautiful women I know. How lucky can one man be?"

"Thank you. You make me very proud, Ranger. If I am one of the three, you now have four. Wait until you see my sister who's with Rich and Jack looking at the buffalo."

"I'm not sure my heart can take a fourth," Bud said with his still strong, commanding bass voice.

Ray and his wife pulled in before Bud had to test his heart. He perked up as he heard Ray introduce Isabella to his wife, saying "and she was a Tulsa police officer."

The other guests were not due for an hour. Rich and Ray came early for the conference call about Myra's findings.

Jack gathered everyone for the call, including Myra. He had spoken with Bodeway earlier. Isabella would have loved to participate but knew the only reason Myra was on the call was in case they misinterpreted something in the documents. Even had she still been a sworn officer, she knew her personal connection would have prohibited her appearance.

"Uncle Bud has kindly offered the use of the bunkhouse for our call. We have something installed in there not present in the ranch house. It is a landline and I have attached a speaker. Let me call Zack and I will tell him who is listening in with me," Jack said.

He dialed the ranger.

"Zack Bodeway."

"Zack, it's Jack. I have our usual call or Zoom participants plus two others. Let me list everyone with me at Doolin's Cave Ranch.

I have Rose Custalow, Ray Colton, Rich Ammon, Myra Strauss, and Bud Carey," he said.

"Hi, everybody. First off, let me congratulate you for making an arrest and getting a confession on the Lang murder. Turning around a murder in a week based on good detective work without paying a family member to squeal on the perpetrator is fantastic.

"Now, let me admit something to you, Myra. Several days ago, I uncovered some disparities in your parent's accident reports. I had to go all the way to Austin and we have an Inspector General looking into it and I have been assigned a DPS accident investigator from out of the area to help me investigate the accident. I am eager to hear what Bill Strauss found."

"Okay. I am going to ask Rich to give us an executive summary of the material Myra brought to us. Myra, please feel free to elaborate or correct as necessary," Jack said

"Good morning. This, if Bill Strauss' suspicions and suspect is correct, gives us a second suspect along with former Major Allen Willis. Willis, by the way, entered Mexico several days after leaving prison at Leavenworth and has not been seen since.

"I am a little leery of going into name detail on an open conversation. If Bill Strauss chose the right suspect, there is a lot of money, influence and power involved. Enough to eavesdrop our conversation.

Let me begin. Written copies will supplement my somewhat abbreviated conversation here.

"Strauss obtained the accident report and suspected a coverup. He located the trooper, who would not speak with him and appeared nervous and or scared. He also located the Mercedes. The insurance company sold it to a junk yard specializing in selling parts of wrecked expensive cars. It is still at a lot in Wichita Falls. The written materials identify the location of the car.

"Zack, I will overnight you the full package. You might want to secure the car for your investigation.

Bill photographed it. The right rear panel shows evidence of a badly done PIT maneuver. It is a color photo and it appears the striking vehicle was dark red or maroon.

"We all know how tough a good PIT can be with variables like escaping driver's abilities, road surface, strike point and the like. The person attempting to PIT in this case struck the rear panel several feet ahead of the bumper, not the normal target, which is the corner of the vehicle.

"The application of the technique was at the perfect place to make it a murder. It was a curve on a hill. There was either a stream or lake below deep enough to submerge the car at the bottom of the hill. I cannot tell which it is from the picture I have.

"Let me stop for a moment and ask Myra a couple of questions.

Do you know where the 'accident' occurred and where your parents were coming from? Finally, was the route consistent with them returning home from the location?" Rich asked.

"They were at a bar association awards dinner. I know where the accident occurred. You can get to their house from the bar dinner by taking the route they did. However, I thought at the time it was one of the least direct options. My father was a stickler for taking the shortest, easiest way. He did not enjoy driving and just wanted to get from point A to point B in the least amount of time. I doubt he would have taken the road he died on," Myra said.

"Myra," Zack said, "was your father's cell phone returned to you?"

"We received his wallet, watch, cell phone, a short-barreled revolver, and Mother's jewelry and purse from the trooper," she said.

"Did you try to turn on the phone?" Zack asked.

"Yes. I did. It came on fine. Though it had been underwater for a short period, it was one of the new models which was factory waterproof without a separate case."

"And, you still have the phone?"

"I do. The battery may have run down, but the charger should be on his desk at the house. Isabella has been living there since she returned from Tulsa. She could get it."

"Thanks. It's either an Apple or Android so we can get it charged without the charger. I'd like to pick it up as soon as possible to have it studied to see where his last calls were to and from. Before this angle presented itself, there had been no need to look at it. Now there is," Zack said.

"Zack, any more questions?" Rich asked.

"Not this minute. Pray continue."

"Having concluded there was a coverup with the accident, Bill Strauss then looked for the best candidate for retribution on Judge Munro and came up with one with connections to organized crime in Texas and Oklahoma.

"The trial was several years ago.

The charges were a variety of crimes including several murders. The case was heard in Judge Munro's court and the individual charged was found guilty. The judge sentenced him to twenty-five years on a plea bargain and he is still in prison. His criminal empire in the two states is crumbling with his son running it. The news articles Strauss included on the son suggest he is a borderline psychotic. He is who Bill Strauss identifies as his primary person of interest."

"Rich, with the criminal enterprise being in two states, why did a Texas district attorney handle it instead of a US Attorney?" Jack asked.

"According to Strauss' noted, the US Attorney for the relevant district of Texas turned it down. He did not know why but suspected the worst.

I am now handing each of you a more detailed version of the summary I have just given.

It includes the names of the convicted gangster, the primary company involved in the two state crimes and, most importantly, the son's name.

"Zack, I am emailing it to you right now on a secure email I am aware you have. Please take a look at the name. If it rings a bell, email me back, okay? We will be reviewing it in person here," Rich said.

Unless anyone has further questions let's curtail this call and put our thinking caps on."

Nobody wanted to discuss anything without reading the summary and thinking about it.

Zack sent Rich an immediate reply on the encrypted email. Rich shared it with the group in Oklahoma, sans Myra.

"I know the son by reputation. He travels with a lawyer and a qualified bodyguard. He is extremely dangerous and equally crazy. It would not surprise me if he did the hit on the Munros and Bill himself. If Bill spoke to anyone on his payroll, official or otherwise, it would make Bill an immediate threat to eliminate. Such is the danger of untrained civilians playing cop."

Rose summed up the feelings of the group.

"Well, crap!"

"Let's go have brisket and everything else. There are tubs of iced down beer and lots of sweet tea. Anybody goes home hungry, it's their fault!" Jack said.

On the way out the door, he said to Rich, "Good job. I sure would like to lure him back to Warrior County and put the cuffs on him here."

"Me, too, Jack. I'll try to make it happen."

JACK'S NEIGHBORS Julie and Cindy arrived, then retired chief deputy Clive Bottoms and his wife.

After a heaping plate and some beer, tea, or Jack's Diet Dr. Pepper by all, Bud approached Rich.

"Now, boy, I know it's not yet time to see you fire some rounds out of the 1911. But, I'd sure like to handle it and check it out for you."

"You wait right here, Ranger and talk with these two blonde ladies. I'll go get it from the truck," Rich said.

If there was anything Bud liked better than a good .45, it was a beautiful blonde. Or, two.

Rich came back and took out the sixty-five-year-old .45. He dropped the empty mag and locked the slide back, checked it was empty and handed it butt first to the old ranger.

"First off, boy, I'm Uncle Bud to you. Lily says you're family, so it's a done deal. I might have to adopt Isabella and Myra here too!" Both smiled. The man had class and charisma.

Bud looked into the empty chamber and squinted down the barrel. He dropped the slide and pulled the trigger.

From twenty feet away, Jack touched Lily on the arm.

"Come watch a maestro in action. He handles a .45 like a Stradivarius." They edged over and Rose walked with them. Then, Ray and his wife. Clive was stretched out in a lawn chair and not about to get up. Julie and Cindy were next to join the audience.

Bud looked Isabella in the eye and began to speak about the weather. Without looking down, he field stripped the automatic into its primary parts.

He picked up the slide and examined the inside.

"Everything looks good. No worn areas."

He looked at the frame, then picked up the barrel. Holding it up to the bright sky, he took a long look.

"I would replace it with a professionally fitted Bar-Sto or other top barrel. I'd have the same gunsmith put a brass bead front sight on her and a rear sight you could hook in your belt or jeans or boot to rack in case you don't have use of your off hand. Might cost a little, but it would be worth it. This is a Colt. It has tradition. It's worn in to have an action slicker than the boots of a fat man on an icy sidewalk.

"Then, when you win the lotto, get a nice pair of stag grips. Ivory is too slick unless you have a thick eagle scrimshawed on it. Pearl looks like a soiled dove's gun.

"When you get it back, you'll have yourself a gun which kept American military and lawmen safe since WWI and still does. Look at the one in my boy's holster. It has more credits than I ever wanted to put on it. And, my boy had to put more on than I ever did. Same is true for Bodeway and other rangers."

As niece Georgia Landers was his "daughter," her son was his boy. Neither would ever want it to be any other way. They worshiped this man like the worst Texas outlaws had feared him.

"Do you know a fine 1911 gunsmith for me to seek out, Uncle Bud" Rich asked.

"As it happens, I do. He's in Texas, but we can arrange for him to get the gun and fix her up nice for you. Carry your Sig. You've proven yourself with it to the world and used it the other day to look out for one of the two people I care the most about.

"Everybody here knows he came at Jack with a big knife. Jack had his hands full of bad hombres. And, you cancelled all the rest of the knife wielder's Christmases. The Sig will do until you get this one just right. The gunsmith, whose name is Smith of all things, is about fifteen miles southeast of Wichita Falls. I hear you make some trips down there now, so dropping it and picking it up won't be an inconvenience. I'll call him later and have him waiting for you. Just call him the day you are going," Uncle Bud said.

Bud nodded at the parts. Rich reached down and did what he had practiced. He looked the old man straight in the eye and assembled it without breaking gaze.

Bud didn't say a thing. But, Rich and Jack both saw the flash of approval. Rich nodded. It was enough. The two lawmen understood each other.

The barbecue wound down and people gave their best regards and drifted off. Uncle Bud headed to the bunkhouse and to bed, Rich and the sisters joined Jack and Lily in the main house.

Jasmine crawled up in Myra's lap and purred herself to sleep as Isabella reached over and rubbed the little cat's forehead with two elegant fingers. The sisters accepted an invitation to retire to the second bedroom. Rich took off his boots and belt and stretched out on the old rawhide sofa. He finally found one to comfortably accommodate his length.

Coyotes howled in the distance. The bison were silent as were the three horses in the stable.

Best of all, neither lawman's phone interrupted the night.

JACK AWOKE at five and so did Rich. They silently made coffee, the aroma of which awoke the women. The small black and white cat continued her beauty sleep a bit longer on Lily's pillow. The three women claimed mugs of coffee and took them back to bed.

Jack took a Yeti mug of hot coffee over to the bunkhouse and left it capped and hot for Uncle Bud, who no longer had need to beat the roosters up in the morning.

The sheriff and his sergeant sat on the front stoop in rockers older than either of them. They drank coffee and strategized about how to get the gangster son trapped for a warrant to be served in Warrior County. The man's name was Elbert Ingles, Jr. A computer inquiry made on the computer in Rich's new truck gave his arrest record, physical description and truck information.

He was as tall as Jack or Rich, but forty pounds heavier. His arrest record went back to the time he was young enough to have his first eighteen years sealed. From eighteen on, it included fighting, evasion, a broad variety of misdemeanors. Resisting and assault against law enforcement officers was a charge generously sprinkled throughout his rap sheet.

"How can this piece of crap have a rap sheet looking like an enforcer for the mob, yet no charges stuck?" Rich asked almost, but not entirely, rhetorically.

"It appears to me the Ingles family has a great deal of

influence in high places in Texas. Until, perhaps, they bumped into Judge Munro," Jack opined.

"I wonder why it took so long, Jack?"

"It appears their primary base of operations was outside of Wichita County. It worries me they broke all sorts of laws here in Oklahoma too, without being successfully prosecuted for it. If they have hands in so many pockets over a two-state area, we are going to have a dangerous investigation and have to be really alert and careful."

"I was just thinking the same thing. Tougher for you with Lily. Maybe even Uncle Bud. Plus your folks are in Texas," Rich said.

"Well, everybody but Dad signed on with me. But if someone was to come after Mom or him or the Cinco Peso, Dad would rain hell down on them. As we get into this, I will mention it to them.

"I worry about the Munro sisters. One already lost a husband. We don't know if it was in retribution or to stop his investigation. For a non-cop, he did pretty well. What he sucked at was not understanding the risk and not preparing for it," Jack said.

"Either of us could get sniped from a distance. But we're a helluva lot tougher targets than Bill Strauss," Rich said. "Perhaps he could be scared a bit…."

"What do you mean, scared? Sounds like he's too mean and stupid to be scared."

"Oh, nothing. Just thinking aloud," Rich said, thinking of ranger sniper tactics, but then dismissing them. His job was to enforce the law, not break it. He was no longer in the no-man's land of Afghanistan.

Isabella walked out with what must have been her second cup of Jack's strong cowboy coffee. She had on jeans and a tee shirt and was barefooted.

"Morning, cowboys," she greeted the two former cowboys.

"Good morning, Isabella," Jack said. "Did you two sleep well?"

"We did. Last night and the night before at Rich's were the first two times we had slept together since being teenagers. I had forgotten what a bed hog my sister is!"

"And I had forgotten you snored!" came a voice from the doorway.

Ever the cop, Rich withdrew a small leather-bound pad from his jeans and wrote "snores" on a page, closed it and put it away.

"Oops!" Myra said and grinned broadly showing no remorse at her disclosure.

Isabella shot her a look of unfeigned displeasure.

"Everybody snores sometimes, I am sure it had to do with all this amazingly fresh ranch air," Rich said. "What schedules do you ladies have for today and the rest of the weekend?" he asked deliberately changing the subject from sleeping noises to something without controversy.

"I have nothing on my schedule until Monday morning," Isabella said.

"I have nothing on my schedule until a hair appointment in two weeks," her sister replied.

"I wish we had more horses for a trail ride," Jack said. "We have three and my horse, Remington. He can be a bit tricky at times."

"I wouldn't mind a long walk. Your ranch is beautiful, Jack. Rich told me about a cave where the Doolin-Dalton gang used to hide from the law," Isabella said.

"You can walk there in twenty or thirty minutes or take a four-wheel drive down. One person took a Dodge

Charger almost there at high speed, but he was worried about a friend."

"I bet there is a real story there," Myra said.

"Only about how to destroy a perfectly fine police car, I am afraid," Rich offered.

"Lily thought it was well worth it. I did too, when I found out a few days later."

"Me, too, Jack. I'd do it again in a heartbeat. Just don't give me the chance!"

"You have a deal, compadre!"

They talked for twenty more minutes until the aroma of more coffee and of bacon frying drew everyone in and Bud Carey transiting between the bunkhouse and the main house.

Jack, Lily, and Bud had started taking many meals outside except in weather with precipitation. There were a couple heavy wooden tables out there from a roadside flea market. They looked like a bunch of cowboys used them, an image probably not too far from the truth.

The breakfast was perfect and Rich offered to clean up the dishes while the ladies talked and Jack checked the horses.

Before the walk down to the cave, Julie and Cindy pulled in. The former was driving her dually Diesel GMC and pulling a double horse trailer.

"We are going to pick up a new Morgan mare in Oklahoma City. Anybody want anything from there?"

They chatted for a minute and pulled off without a shopping list.

"If y'all want showers, there is one in the bath. It is a room I had to add on. The original pioneers had a Johnny house and not much need to wash, I guess. There is also one around the corner of the house outside. The

G. WAYNE TILMAN

water is propane heated and the temperature has a finer adjustment than the one inside," Jack said.

"I'm for outside in the fresh air! Can you see the buffalo from the shower?" Myra said.

"Maybe later. I think they are grazing too far to the left currently."

"Nonetheless. Are there soap and shampoo outside also?" she asked.

"Yes. There is a box I put on the side of the house near the controller for the shower. Everything you need should be there except for towels."

Myra got up and went in for a towel.

"Me, too, if she doesn't hog all the hot water," Isabella said, following her.

Lily smiled and said nothing. She would have a special shower tomorrow when they were alone, she thought and smiled again. Jack caught the smile and nodded imperceptibly. She read it loud and clear. As he would have said over the radio in his Coast Guard days, "I have you lima charley."

"We should take advantage of some down time to call Zack once it's a decent hour to call," Jack said to Rich.

"There is a lot more we need to find out about the Elbert Ingles senior and junior criminal enterprise. Especially the part here in Oklahoma. Where is it? What do they do? And, how can we catch them here and get a confession out of him?" Rich said as he headed in to wash dishes.

An hour later the two sat in Rich's new Responder and called Zack on a cell phone through the truck's speaker system. For security, they used the talk feature on an encrypted message service app on their cell phones. Something which would have been insufficient for the crowd on the recent conference call.

234

"Just the two Texans I wanted to talk with, notwithstanding you took jobs over the state line," Bodeway began.

"I've have been busy and driven to Austin and back twice. The trooper I have working with me on the accident is one I have known for years. I trust him implicitly. The Inspector General's investigator is a ranger who retired due to a disability. It slows him down too much for ranger work, but not for what he does now. I have also known him for years and would trust him 'til the cows come home.

"Based on Rich's information, we have located the Mercedes and taken it into custody. Bill Strauss was right about the damage. The car was knocked off the road and has the mismatching maroon paint in the damage to prove it. Our lab is studying samples now.

"My trooper buddy sent it in as an accident investigation without naming what accident.

"There are insiders here and we don't know their identities yet, so we have to be careful.

"We are getting close to one. We have identified the probable person who modified the original accident report and recorded the new version. The person is a records supervisor in the HQ of the region in which the Ingles family lives. She was the only person with access to change a final computer accident report.

"The three of us will be interviewing her today.

"Elbert junior goes by Bertie or Bertie Boy. His pre-eighteen cases were sealed. I just happened to read the arresting city detective's personal notes on his most egregious arrest before he hit eighteen.

"The court mandated a psychological evaluation. A panel of three psychologists deemed him a paranoid schizophrenic. I read it to mean batshit crazy in my untutored cop mind. Almost every subsequent unsealed arrest involved violence.

"We have to be real damn careful with this guy. The good news is he probably thinks he has eliminated his primary threats related to the car crash. So, he isn't going anywhere immediately. Give me a week or so and I think I can provide you with sufficient evidence for an Oklahoma murder warrant. And too many embarrassing arrests in Texas of people on the state and municipal payrolls. I have full support from Austin on this."

"One question, Zack," Jack said. Does he have any illicit business in Warrior County which would cause him to come here?"

"I don't have everything on their criminal enterprises yet. The answer looks like 'yes.' It appears he has an interest in the tribal casino just outside Quanah."

"It's reservation property with its own police. We have no jurisdiction there. So, we will have to take him on the way in or out," Rich said.

"Yes. Again, things are moving fast and I think I can give you what you need in a week. Maybe you can dismiss former Major Willis as a suspect by then. I am pretty sure Bertie Boy is your man for Bill Strauss and my man for the Judge and Marie Munro," Zack Bodeway said and hung up.

"Lots of luck on Willis in a week," Jack said to his sergeant.

Rich nodded his head. They climbed out of the truck and Jack went into the house.

Jack returned in a minute with two sets of shooting earmuffs, a box of .45 ACP target ammunition and his own stag handled automatic.

"Why wait until you have Smith work on your gun? It's gonna be exactly like this. He did this one just before

Uncle Bud retired. We'll walk down to where the steel targets are, and you can shoot some. I know your shooting from a few days ago and requalifying you months ago. I just want to see your comfort level with a 1911," Jack said.

Jack took three empty magazines and put them on a wooden bench. He and Rich loaded them.

"Okay Rich, put the belt and holster on. I think it will fit fine. On 'now' I want you to draw shoot at all of the steels until you knock them down and do a combat reload."

Rich put Jack's gun belt on, racked the slide on the new mag, and nodded.

"Now!"

Rich drew, dropping into a crouch. He flipped the safety off as he drew and brought his left hand up to support his shooting hand.

The second his pistol ceased to rise, he fired and was rewarded with a "clang" and it was followed by eight more clangs as he hit the steel targets in fast succession.

Rich hit the mag release. As the empty was falling to the ground, he slid the fresh mag into the butt of the gun and dropped the slide. Within a split second, he double-tapped the remaining steel and came to low ready with his gun still in two hands, but pulled in towards his chest and pointed several feet in front of where he stood. He turned his head right to left to check for hostiles.

"I guess we can save the rest of the ammo unless you want to shoot for fun. I knew you could shoot like a house on fire. Now, I know you can shoot a 1911 just fine. Consider yourself qualified," Jack said.

Rich went to find the sisters for the walk they wanted to take. Both had been covertly watching the show from around the corner where the shower was located.

He walked up on them standing by the shower, which was now turned off. Myra treated him with a soaked wave and the identical looking Isabella ducked behind her. Rich darted back around the corner from whence he had come.

Their walk became more of a hike. Like the foot pursuit in Tulsa, it was not good news to a man whose only footwear available was cowboy boots. It was not they were uncomfortable. They are very comfortable. However, the soles and heels were not made for climbing hills of rocks and red clay. Or sprinting down sidewalks.

After slipping and sliding up one last rise, he determined he would keep a pair of old running shoes or stall mucking boots in the covered bed of his patrol truck. And wished he had figured it out before getting stranded again without them.

"What did Zack say?" Myra asked.

"We are narrowing down on a suspect in both your parent's murder in Texas and your husband's murder in Oklahoma. We think it is the same person. It is directly from the information you found yesterday and delivered to us.

"Zack is doing background investigations because the man lives in Texas. He lives a ways from Wichita Falls, which was not detailed in Bill's materials. Until we get enough information out of Texas, we cannot swear out a murder warrant in Oklahoma. Which of course is not what he said, but is the gist of our situation we discussed," Rich said.

His response was intentionally vague.

The sisters were intimately involved. However, they were not sworn law enforcement officers on the case. Like he knew from his Army days in the rangers, the access to sensitive or classified information depended on two things: the clearance to know; and the need to know.

Myra Strauss and Isabella Munro had neither.

"Can't you be more detailed?" Isabella asked.

"Not at this time. There are too many things up in the air to try to make sense out of them," Rich said with finality.

"Can you say whether Allen Willis is still a suspect?" Myra asked.

"He is, technically, but I like the new one more."

"Is it the man in prison, Ingles?" Isabella asked.

"He could have ordered it. Or, not. We don't know. He is not the suspect though. This is all I can say right now. Sorry. It's just the way it is."

Myra frowned and Isabella just jutted her lower lip out. Neither said more for the duration of the walk.

Rich was learning important things about the sisters. Things better learned now than later.

THE TEXAS RANGER made faster and better inroads into his part of the investigation than he thought he would. The people assigned to him were good. The Texans worked as a cohesive team.

They interviewed the woman who altered the DPS accident report to sanitize it. What she did was not as beneficial to them as the last thing she said in the interview. She said it in front of a public defender, not an Ingles-supplied attorney. Bodeway had made a point of scooping her up quietly before the Ingles knew about it.

"I would never have done such a thing," Maddie Stokes said.

"My work has been spotless and honorable for thirty years. Love screws you over every time. It did here. If it had not been for the bodyguard, I would not be here now with my retirement in jeopardy."

"Please tell me what you mean by the bodyguard," Bodeway said in a non-threatening tone.

"I fell in love with him. The first man since my divorce ten years ago. He was great. He is great. He said he had been told to contact someone to modify the accident report then file it permanently.

"He was disgusted with Bertie. Said he was a wacko. A psycho. He was going to get his next pay and disappear. He couldn't take me with him because I have to finish out my time to collect my retirement. But, I could visit him in Mexico until then. The Ingles did not know about us or who he was going to have modify the report. We'd be safe!" she said.

"What's the bodyguard's name?" the ranger asked.

"Bob Udell."

"Is Bob still with the Ingles?"

"Yes, for another week. He needs to get his end of the month pay before he bails."

"Where does he live?"

"Are you going to arrest him?" she asked.

"I don't know. Being a bodyguard certainly is not against the law. Has he done other illegal things for the Ingles?"

"I don't think so. The old man hired him to rein in and protect Bertie. Bertie is crazy."

"Was Bob present when the accident occurred?" the ranger asked.

"Yes. He told Bertie to stop. He said what he was doing would put him in prison just like his old man. He said Bertie was in some sort of irrational rage or something. He was out of control. Bob said he thought he was going to die in the chase and accident."

"Did they stop when the car rolled into the water?"

"No. Bob begged him to stop and help the two old people. He said Bertie cackled like a rooster. He did not try to imitate a rooster. His laugh was crazy and he naturally sounded like one," she said.

Zack Bodeway made a quick decision.

"Counselor, I believe your client is in danger from Bertie Ingles. Serious danger. We cannot have her contact him or anyone else for a brief period today. We need to speak with Bob Udell and hope he is as forthcoming as your client has been.

"I would like her to stay here with us in protective custody. She is not under arrest. I will press the prosecutor to look at her actions as breaking rules versus breaking the law. You are welcome to stay here with her for the few hours I am requesting. You may discuss it if you wish.

"At ten-fifty-three AM, the interview is finished and we are now turning the audio and video off," Zack said.

The woman and her attorney huddled in the corner whispering. The attorney looked up and shook his head.

"Will you have a deputy stay with them in the lounge until we get back?" the ranger asked Investigator Joe Soames from the Inspector General's Office.

Once the soon to be former DPS supervisor and her attorney were sequestered, the ranger, investigator and trooper met in the interview room. Soames called his boss and brought him up to date. The IG said he would speak with someone in the attorney general's office about deals to offer Stokes and Udell in return for full cooperation.

The accident specialist trooper on the team obtained

Udell's photo and address from his driver's and concealed weapon licenses. The photos were taken two years apart, but same person. The addresses matched exactly.

"We have a real break here guys. We also have an immediate dilemma. I believe we can offer this guy a deal to testify against crazy Bertie. The dilemma is timing. Getting him at home alone would be ideal. But, as a bodyguard paid by the old man to rein in Bertie, his hours are probably pretty erratic.

"So, we need to get him on a traffic stop with or without Bertie. Today. ASAP," Zack said.

Both team members agreed.

Investigator Soames went with Bodeway and the trooper, who had an unmarked Tahoe, followed. He called in and had several DPS troopers move in and follow just out of sight as they headed to the building which was the headquarters of Ingles Enterprises.

"Unless these guys have brown paper bag lunches, or have food delivered, I think one of our vehicles ought to set up surveillance and have the other three Tahoes stay just out of sight," Zack said on the agreed upon tac radio channel. "It's lunch time and I'm betting they head out. We will need to separate Udell from any attorneys on the lunch run," he added. "It's going to be hard, since he usually travels with one."

Zack parked his tan pickup where he had a clear view of comings and goings at the Ingles building but was not noticeable.

"Do you think this idiot's maroon Buick is the one he knocked the judge off the road with almost seven months ago," Investigator Joe Soames from the IG's office asked.

"We'll know soon enough. With any luck it will be in the lab this afternoon," Zack said.

A maroon Buick LaCrosse left the rear of the building and pulled onto the main road.

"Target maroon Buick is pulling out now. Occupied three times," Zack said into the radio. He looked at his watch. They had waited twenty-seven minutes. He hoped it was worth it.

The tan truck, unnoticeable in Texas, pulled in behind him but held back. They pulled onto a limited access four lane with a median.

"Troopers, take him down!" the ranger ordered.

Two marked Tahoes roared by. As they closed on the Buick, they energized full lights and sirens.

"What the hell?" Bertie screamed raucously as he stomped the accelerator.

"Bertie, don't do it. You will make it worse or get us killed!" the attorney in the rear seat said.

Bertie Ingles was already approaching sixty. The Tahoes were faster and one was moving in.

"Bertie! Don't do it man!" Bob Udell yelled.

"Shoot out the window at those bastards, Bob! You heard me!"

"No way. I am not starting a gunfight with troopers and die for you! Slow down," he yelled as Bertie continued to accelerate.

"We have a clear spot ahead. He is an endangerment. I'm gonna move on him!" the closest trooper said as he employed a Pursuit Intervention Technique.

Zack and the IG investigator watched the perfectly executed PIT from four cars back. Both were former troopers and appreciated the precision as the push bar on the Tahoe tapped the right rear corner of the Buick, slammed on brakes to keep out of the way and send the maroon car spinning off out of control.

The spot selected for the PIT was perfectly flat and the car spun in revolutions without overturning. It came to rest in a cloud of dust and burnt tire rubber.

Three troopers jumped out, Sig 320 pistols drawn and at high ready as they approached the car.

Udell was out, hands raised. The attorney rolled out and fell over. He stood up shakily and puked on his shoes.

Bertie Ingles came out running towards a trooper who was aiming his 9mm directly at his chest. Before he got to the trooper, a second one hit him from the side on the fly and knocked him to the ground. The third trooper helped the second one pull Bertie to his feet and slam him against the Buick to cuff him.

The lawyer approached and yelled "I am his attorney!" He thumped the trooper who had put away his gun on the chest.

The trooper grabbed the thumping hand, turned it into a painful come along and frog walked the lawyer to the Buick and bent him over the trunk face first as he handcuffed him.

"You, counsel, are under arrest for assaulting a police officer. And, it's all on the dash cam you performed for. You have the right to remain silent. You have the right to have an attorney present during this or any future interview. If you wish to have an attorney but cannot afford one, one will be appointed for you by the court. Do you understand these rights?"

"Of course I do! I am an attorney!" he interrupted.

"Then I suggest you start acting like one. Walk over to my vehicle with me and I will seatbelt you in the back."

"This is unnecessary!" he said struggling in front of the camera recording video and audio.

"Sir, it became necessary the second you struck me."

At the same time, Zack had approached Udell, his .45 at low ready.

"Ranger, I am a bodyguard and legally armed."

"I know, Mr. Udell. Where do you keep all weapons so we can remove them for the safety of all concerned?"

"Glock 19 behind right hip and Glock 42 on left ankle. Folding knife clipped in right front pocket."

Zack nodded to Joe Soames who moved in and disarmed the man.

"We have been talking with Maddie. Come with us quietly and we may have a deal you won't turn down. We know you want to get away from Ingles," Joe Soames said quietly.

Udell agreed and was placed cuffed in the rear seat of the ranger's pickup. The troopers took their prisoners to their district office for booking. Udell went to the regional office to talk.

And talk he did. Udell was disgusted with his crazy boss and wanted to get a deal for himself and Maddie, for whom he genuinely cared.

He testified without lawyering up. He told about Bertie killing the two old people by running them off the road into a lake and not stopping.

He said Bertie had bragged to them about eliminating Bill Strauss as a threat with his Sig 226 in .357 Sig caliber.

"It was worth the trip up to Yahoo, Oklahoma to kill the bastard," he told me.

"Was anyone else there who heard him?" Zack asked.

"Only the slimy lawyer who was with us and was stupid enough to thump a trooper on the chest."

245

"Bob, where does he keep the Sig?" Zack asked.

"I watched him put it in the glove box of the Buick as we left for lunch. It's gotta still be there," Udell said.

Bob Soames got up immediately and went and called one of the troopers who had helped.

"Are you still on scene?"

"Yep. Standard procedure search of the Buick. Guess what I just found?"

"Oh, a Sig 226 like we carried possibly?"

"How did you know?"

"It is an Oklahoma murder weapon. Bag it my friend and Ranger Bodeway and I will pick up it from you. How long will you be there?"

"Probably a half an hour longer. I am waiting for a flatbed wrecker to tow the Buick."

"Good! Have the wrecker driver stand by until we get there to tell him where to tow it. The car is a murder weapon in a dual murder too."

"That ole boy was crazy as a loon, wasn't he?"

"Crazy enough to go down for murder of an elderly judge and his wife in Texas and their son in law in Oklahoma. See you in thirty minutes or less." Soames hung up.

"We have a Sig in hand. Right caliber. We need to get back to the scene and get the gun and have the Buick towed to the regional lab as evidence in a murder trial.

"Good! Let's tell Udell quickly and keep him here until we get back to finish the interview," Zack said.

They arrived back where the apprehensions were made, took possession of the pistol after having the trooper sign as first in chain of evidence on the evidence bag he had placed the pistol in. They instructed the wrecker driver to haul the Buick to the regional lab.

They had an eye level view of the left front of the

bumper from where the car was sitting on the flatbed wrecker. The Buick still had paint matching the Mercedes' on it from where Ingle hit the judge's car.

It and Udell's testimony would contribute to a long incarceration for junior. Daddy could not buy or bribe this one away. Additionally, the killing bullet in Oklahoma tying back to the Sig owned by Ingles junior should get him capital murder in Oklahoma. The state having the highest per capita of executions nationally.

They spoke with Udell for several hours and ended not charging him with any crime. He was not an accessory to running the judge and his wife off the road. He was more like an unwilling witness, who signed a statement saying so and stating Bert Ingles Jr. was the driver and intentionally did it and refused to stop to render aid.

With respect to the murder of William Strauss in Warrior County, Oklahoma, he said in a signed statement Ingles bragged about shooting Strauss and described the crime scene and said Ingles told him he used the weapon now in possession of the Texas Rangers.

Zack had the statements signed and sent copies to Sheriff Jack Landers along with copies to Rich and Ray. Zack stated if one of them would get an Oklahoma murder warrant and come down, he could arrest Ingles in jail and return with the gun as evidence.

At dinner time, Rich called Jack and Ray on a conference call from the truck.

"Did you receive Zack's email to Jack and cc'd to Ray and me?" he asked excitedly.

"No, I have not had a chance to look at emails yet today, both responded."

"Zack arrested Bertie Ingles for eluding and assaulting an officer. He has a statement in our email

247

from Ingle's bodyguard saying Bertie killed the Munro's in his presence and later boasted about killing Bill Strauss with his .357 Sig. Said pistol is awaiting our pickup when one comes down to formally charge Ingles for murder one."

"Our ranger has been busy. All this in one day?" Jack asked.

"I don't know for sure. Sounds like it," Rich said.

"I will go to our ADA and see if she and I can go to the judge with it and get a warrant. You can charge him without one, but a warrant makes everyone happier .... except Ingles, of course," Jack said. "Y'all decide who wants to go. I am running down the street to try to get a warrant in the meantime."

The sheriff rang off, leaving his sergeant and the OSBI agent to talk.

"It's your case, buddy. If you can slip down to make the arrest and pick up the pistol, go for it." Ray said.

"If you want, we will go together and figure out a way to both charge him."

"No thanks. I have a full plate. I am still finishing up on the jewelry store robbery and dead owner. And, I have a PTA meeting tonight I faithfully promised my wife I'd attend with her. Besides, you can go see Isabella."

"There is Isabella. I have mixed feelings there. I am not ready to commit to her. Or, her sister. They play some competitive games which worry me. I sure would like to keep Isabella as a fun date, but no more for a while," Rich said. "I just got burned badly and could see it happening again too soon with Isabella," he said.

"Nothing wrong with going slowly. If she won't go slowly with you and takes off, you know it was not meant to be. My Martha and I dated four years before committing. You have known these two a week or so."

"I appreciate the guidance, Ray. I really do. I'll keep you up on this soap opera. In the meantime, I will pack a bag and put some premium in the truck for a fast run to Tejas!"

Jack called back a half hour later. He had the warrant in hand and suggested Rich pick it up at his ranch which was closer to his route south than going to the office.

Rich started immediately and swung by. He put the warrant in his briefcase and turned eastwards then south on Interstate 44 to Texas. He left a voicemail for Jack saying he was on the way and would apprise Zack as he got closer.

"Myra. It's Rich. I don't know whether Zack Bodeway has called you, but he has Bertie Ingles in custody. We have sufficient evidence for me to be en route to Texas to formally charge him with your husband's murder in Oklahoma. I will leave it to Zack to share other Texas charges pending on the suspect. Call if you want. You have my cell number. I am in the police truck and driving fast right now."

Rich called Isabella next.

"Hi, it's me, your last minute friend. I am southbound on I-44 heading towards Wichita Falls. In the morning, I will go east and formally arrest Bertie Ingles for the murder of your brother-in-law. I will be getting there too late to take you to dinner, but how about dessert?" He hoped Isabella would get the voicemail soon though he had almost three hours yet to drive with Warrior factored in.

One last call to make. To the man who solved the case, or at least caught the suspect.

"Zack. It's Rich Ammon. I am on the way to Texas with an Oklahoma murder warrant in the name of Bertie Ingles. I am not exactly sure where he will be tomorrow morning, but I need to formally arrest him and to pick up the Sig pistol for the OSBI lab to compare with the bullet which killed Bill Strauss. Please text me the location to charge him and the whereabouts of the gun. Thanks for all you have done."

Those tasks accomplished, he concentrated on driving. He flew past a stationary OHP trooper and flipped his red and blues on for a second without slowing down. He got a flash of headlights and drove on into the encroaching darkness.

"How did this happen so quickly? I just brought you the material yesterday!" Myra exclaimed into the truck's speakers since Rich answered the phone on them.

"We got together after the call and formulated a strategy. Most of it was in Texas. Zack already had a team working on the murder of your parents being retribution. The suspect ran and was apprehended. We had inside information and were able to use it.

Your parent's murder has trial priority over the one in Oklahoma. I am not sure the Oklahoma one will ever come to trial. He is looking at a long time in the Texas penal system, Myra."

"Have you let my sister know?" she asked.

"I left her virtually the same message. But I called you first. You lost parents and a husband and your diligence going through Bill's records led us to today's actions."

"If you were here, I'd .... oh, well no need saying it. I bet you can imagine."

"I am sure I will imagine all the way to Texas."

"Are you staying with Isabella?" she asked. "Because you are welcome to stay here."

"Thanks. I don't have plans and I have not spoken with her live yet. You are very kind," he said.

"Well, consider my offer. You would not regret it!"

"Indeed," he said and told her goodbye.

He received a text from Zack saying the prisoner and the gun had been moved to the Wichita County Sheriff's Office since the Texas murder had been there. Zack would be there at ten in the morning to meet him for the charges and passing the evidential gun to him.

Still no Isabella. Rich thought it was odd yet was not in any hurry to speak with her.

She finally called at nine o'clock.

"Sorry to be late. I've been wondering how to best meet. I came up with meeting for drinks at the bar I just texted you. I don't know exactly when you get in, so you can either grab a room first or after. Not much happening in town this week, so finding one won't be a problem. Let me know by text what you want to do. I am heading out for a run now. Bye."

"Well, Ms. Munro. I guess you told me a couple things between the lines in your brevity. One was where I was *not* being invited to stay. Another is you want to see me to tell me something. And thirdly, you don't want to discuss it over the phone.

"I get the message. It's probably for the best. I am getting used to being let down, so it's okay," he thought aloud.

He was a bit relieved. There was something off-putting about the sisters. How could one have a girl-friend when her almost matching sister was overtly hitting on him at every opportunity? A lot of guys would think it was a dream scenario. Rich knew he just was not wired for it. He kicked himself for allowing the relationship with Isabella to grow so fast so quickly. Perhaps she was thinking the same thing and taking the adult steps?

Or perhaps he was simply overthinking things and needed to tell his mind to shut the hell up and see how things developed? He was pretty confident they would significantly evolve at the bar tonight.

Harkening back to his rodeo days, maybe he should just ride the horse he drew.

Rich let out a long breath, unaware until then he had been holding it in.

An hour later, he was crossing the Red River into Texas. It always gave him a sense of being home to cross the line.

He began to look for the bar and found it.

Rich had driven down in his duty pistol and vest. He was on the way for official business with a Texas Ranger and did not have to worry about identification as an Oklahoma lawman. The bar was a whole different animal. It was too hot out to wear a covering jacket unless it was a sport coat, which he did not have.

In the dark parking lot, he took off the vest and the gun belt, leaving the smaller Sig backup in his boot holster. Slow to pull, but totally invisible. He unclipped the star on his belt and put it in his pocket.

Rich put the gear he removed in the locker under the bed tonneau and walked across the parking lot. It looked like a mugger's paradise to him. Why had Isabella picked such a rendezvous point?

When he walked in, he was a tall Westerner in a white Resistol, white shirt, creased jeans and rodeo buckle. Right off a movie set.

He spotted Isabella at a corner table. She was back to the wall like he would have chosen to sit.

She obviously planned this change in relationship to be memorable because of her outfit. If he never saw her again, he would always remember the vision of her sitting there in a mini skirt, cowboy boots, and a low-cut Western blouse. The cowboy's fantasy. He wondered how many drinkers she had to fend off before he arrived.

Isabella saw him as he walked in and smiled. He did not detect anything hesitant in the smile. It was about as come hither as a smile could be. Was she playing with him?

He gave her his best hero grin and sauntered over.

She stood and embraced him. He got a kiss which made every patron in the bar, male or female jealous.

"Hi, Isabella. You look stunning."

She smiled beautifully.

"You, too, cowboy."

Rich sat down and a waitress rushed over. He ordered a Dos Equis which matched the one sitting unsipped in front of her.

"Nice drive? Must have been pretty fast," she ventured.

"I started in a hurry to see you. After your call, I slowed down."

She looked puzzled.

"Why?" she asked.

"It was short and curt and the major message was 'get yourself a motel room, cowboy'."

"I didn't mean it to be short or curt. I wanted to speak with you seriously and figured afterwards you might prefer to not spend the night with me," she said and took her first sip of beer.

He took one also.

"Guess we better get into it then."

"No warm up, then?"

He just looked at her pleasantly and did not answer.

"Okay. I have been following a dream. Let me go back to Tulsa for a minute to explain.

"My goal has always been to become what you are. A

253

sheriff's investigator or major city detective. I was well on the way, being fast-tracked at Tulsa. Then I fell in love with my sergeant. His wife would have been my boss as a new detective.

"As I was in the midst of my quandary, my folks died. Now I know they were murdered. I moved home. I started taking a course of study to transfer my Oklahoma peace officer training credentials over to Texas.

Then along comes this dream cop. I fell in love with him. 'Him,' of course is you!

"Rich, I don't want to move to Warrior County and have another work relationship. They never work. Never."

Rich could see a tear forming.

"I have been wrestling with this as long as I've known you. A whole week and a half. Myra knows. She thinks I should step aside and let her become your girlfriend. At thirty-four, she's certainly age appropriate. Not even old enough to be a cougar!"

"A couple of days ago, I finished my compulsory training and got an offer to be an investigator with the Wichita County Sheriff's Office.

"I accepted it to start Friday which is a payday. I did it with the trepidations I would lose you!

All of this is why my invite tonight was short and mysterious.

"I am happy over the job and terrified you will stand up and walk away right now."

Rich sat there absorbing what he had heard and thinking hard. Both logically and with his heart.

"Congratulations on the job offer. I know you will be a fantastic investigator. I watched you chomping at the bit not being included in our investigation. One which directly impacted you and your family.

"We have been moving real fast, Isabella. Who could not?

"You are smart, funny, beautiful. In short, a dream girl in cowboy boots.

I don't want to give you up. I really don't.

"What if we stayed in an exclusive relationship with the deal, we would immediately tell the other before the exclusivity changed? You investigate crimes here, I investigate crimes in Oklahoma?

"We talk, we spend wild weekends, we take vacations together and see how it goes? It seems like a win-win until it isn't."

"Rich, let me accept your plan and add an addendum?"

"Okay."

"Forget the damn hotel room tonight. Let's start what you described right now! Just don't expect to get much sleep!"

"You're on, Isabella!" he said, his superhero grin clinching the deal.

He dropped a ten on the table and they walked out, hand-in-hand.

THEY LEFT the Munro estate together the next morning. Both were tired and happy. They may have slept a couple of hours during the night, but neither cared. They agreed it could not have been more perfect.

Rich was back in a dress shirt, creased jeans, white hat, boots, and the .45 in a carved saddle color belt holster. His new normal.

They both parked in Police Parking at the sheriff's office. Isabella had to drop off one last set of papers and talk with several HR people. Rich had to arrest someone for murder in the first class.

Rich saw Zack's tan Responder backed in. He backed his green one in beside it. He went in with Isabella.

Zack was talking in the hall with a man Isabella introduced as the sheriff. He, in turn, introduced her to the ranger as his newest detective, starting on Friday.

"Congratulations! Rich, did you know this?"

"I just found out and am really pleased about it," Rich said.

"Chief, this is Sergeant Rich Ammon. He's a friend who works with another friend, Jack Landers, Sheriff of Warrior County, Oklahoma."

"Aha! The other gunfighter!" the sheriff said.

"Rich is one, too. Someone came at his boss a few weeks ago with a knife. Jack had his hands full with three other bikers. Rich drew and did a failure or Mozambique on the man and he was dead before he hit the floor. I notice he is wearing a 1911 now, too," Zack said.

"My heroes have not always been cowboys. They are three lawmen I know who are famous for their .45's," Rich said, "one is standing here and two are in Oklahoma. But all four of us were born in Texas."

"Willie ought to make a new song with those modified words," Isabelle said before walking off with the sheriff.

"You got the warrant?" Zack asked. Rich nodded. "Leave it with me and we will have it when it's time to extradite. I have arranged for a photo op. I'm going to have a little crowd. The sheriff should be in it and Isabella with a borrowed badge. The headline will be 'Oklahoma lawman arrests Ingles for murder.' Some good publicity never hurts."

They walked down to the sheriff's office and Zack asked about adding Isabella to the news plans they had discussed. He agreed and got her a badge. Rich stuck his backup Sig in her waistband right behind the badge.

The news people were already standing by and the prisoner brought up in orange overalls.

Zack announced off the record he was going to re-arrest Ingles for the photos. The media photographers got to the right side of the two lawmen. It gave them clear shots of guns, badges of the ranger and the investigator as well as frontal shots of the sheriff and the strikingly beautiful female investigator.

Bodeway spoke first.

"Mr. Ingles, I am Texas Ranger Zack Bodeway. You are under arrest for the murder of Judge James Munro and his wife Marie in Wichita Falls on January 18th of this year." He stepped aside.

"I am Sergeant Richard Ammon, Investigator for the Warrior County, Oklahoma Sheriff's Office. I hereby arrest you for the first-degree murder of William Strauss, the son-in-law of the Munros. The murder was done less than two weeks ago in rural Warrior County, Oklahoma."

"You can't arrest me, asshole! I been arrested already!" Ingles screamed out crazily.

"I just did, Mr. Ingles," Rich said amid chuckles from bystanders and the press.

Bertie Ingles went berserk and was led away by deputies with the video cameras flying.

The sheriff, with Isabella silently standing between him and Rich, and the ranger each answered questions. The sheriff and the ranger were used to media questions and having their words twisted to meet a journalist's agenda or simply to make for more exciting news. Rich knew this happened and it infuriated him. He kept his answers brief and noncontroversial. The two older lawmen were legendary. One of the media members had followed up on the bar fight in Warrior and knew Rich was the one who saved the sheriff and asked him about it. He answered simply and Zack jumped in and gave an exciting rendition, saying the best heroes are always modest.

Isabella was an investigator nobody in the press or television news knew. She was the source of a lot of questions the sheriff did not answer, raising speculation through the roof.

Out of sight, Isabella returned the loaner badge and Rich slipped the compact Sig back in his boot holster.

"Y'all probably could use some coffee? I know I could. Sheriff, got a few minutes for coffee? The Rangers could even stand you for a donut or two if you wanted," an ebullient Bodeway said.

"I have a meeting and have to get too it. Raincheck? Take care of my new investigator, ya hear?"

"We will though I think she could do a fine job of taking care of us!"

They took Rich's truck and Isabella led them to a coffee shop which was not vegan like her sister's haunt.

"As a cop once again, and one who ran three miles last night and had the best work out of my life afterwards, I am having a chocolate donut," Isabella announced.

"Well, after burning all those calories, you deserve at least two donuts!" Rich added keeping their joke going. The ranger in the front seat was not so easily fooled.

Seated and enjoying really good coffee and fairly good donuts, Zack asked Isabella about her new position.

"Initially, I will be handling crimes against children and spouses and be backup on robberies and other assaults. Rich's first investigative assignment was homicide. I'd like to practice first."

"Just remember domestic cases are right up there with routine traffic stops as the most dangerous things a peace officer does," Zack said.

"I know from my patrol years in Tulsa. I hated both on scene. I am thinking it will be a bit safer after the event."

"And you, Rich? What are you going to do? Head back to Oklahoma?"

"No, I am going to take my new old 1911 over to a gunsmith nearby named Smith. He redid Uncle Bud's just before he retired. Bud wants me to get the same barrel and sight replacement and action job."

"Well, he's exactly who did mine too. There's a guy with the same last name in Florida and these two are the best 1911 guys I know. The one here is getting pretty old, so you are doing this at the best time. Maybe the only time.

"Then back to Oklahoma?" Zack asked.

"At high speed. I guess we can dismiss Willis from interest and just let the federal probation officers look for him."

"I'd guess so. You have your murderer. Are you and your sister satisfied, Isabella?"

"We are Zack. I told Rich it drove me crazy not being involved in the case, but I understand why," she said.

They finished and the ranger paid.

Rich rode them back to the sheriff's office and Bodeway took off at a high rate of speed. The only one he seemed to know.

Rich walked Isabella back in, her left thumb hooked

into his right hip pocket. Something a news photographer snapped for a sidebar article he had in mind. One about the two which appeared across Texas and Oklahoma the next morning along with more about Zack and Rich.

RICH FOUND his way to the gunsmith's. The man said he was contemplating retirement but would take on this job for his old friends Bud and Zack. He could see he was talking with their next generation.

"I'll put the brass bead on the front sight, if you want. But, there is a better night sight option now. Trust me with it and I promise you won't regret it," he said.

"You are the master. Both mentors said go with whatever you suggested."

"I'll fit a new high quality barrel with a longer polished feed ramp. Jonathan Browning did not envision our evolved hollow points in the early 1900's when he was designing this gun. I will replace all the springs and put a square rear sight to allow racking the slide with one hand. Do you want it refinished?"

"No, sir. I kinda like the patina."

"I do, too. Since I probably won't be doing any more, how about some nice stag grips? I have one pair left and will give you a deal on them."

"I plan on carrying this gun for a long time and keeping it handy once the badge is retired. Yes. Add the stag grips. Bud Carey's gun has them and I see it in his great nephew's holster every day. Bodeway's too."

"Yep. I installed the stag grips on both guns. Yours will be part of three of a kind. The three best Colt Commander .45's I ever made."

"Thank you sir. I can't wait. When do you think it will be ready for me to come back down and pick up?"

"A lot of what I do is by feel. But my eyes are declining fast. I will hustle without shortchanging you. Usually I'd say three months. I will do it a lot quicker and will call you, okay?"

"Yes sir. Would you like a deposit?"

"Sure. Whatever you can do."

"Here is three hundred cash. Is it okay?"

"It's fine. See you soon, Sergeant Ammon."

Rich left and got a smaller saddle color floral carved belt holster out of the back of the truck for the small Sig 239 and threaded it on. He climbed into the cab of the truck and headed back to Wichita Falls to cross the river on Interstate 44 northbound.

His phone rang. It was Zack.

"Where are you?"

"About three miles out of Wichita Falls, then planning to cross the Red River."

"Good! Step on it! Ingles just shot two deputies. Killed one. He has two guns and is running. He has taken a white county works Chevy pickup. His current location is unknown and people are running amok looking for him. I will be back to Wichita Falls in about three minutes."

"I'm right behind you! Has anyone called the OHP?"

"Unknown. Better do it. I am heading towards I-44. Just a hunch."

"See you there, Zack!"

Rich switched the radio to the OHP frequency and got their regional dispatcher.

"OHP! This is Warrior County Investigator-1 in Wichita Falls, Texas. Emergency call!"

"Warrior Investigator-1, what is nature of your emergency?"

"OHP, an Oklahoma murder suspect has shot two Texas deputies and may be heading north across the Red River. Can you saturate I-44 in the area?"

"We have two cars I can put in the area right away and a couple more I can start your way."

"Thanks, OHP. Suspect vehicle is a white Chevy pickup. I am heading to the area in a dark green F-150 with lights energized. A Texas Ranger is assisting in a tan F-150 with lights also. Hot pursuit rule."

"Roger. Will advise responding units."

"OHP, one last: subject has been charged for three murders before today and has at least two handguns from the deputies he shot. He is armed and dangerous."

"OHP copies and will relay." Rich knew units in the area could already hear his traffic.

He saw the tan Responder speeding across the Red River Bridge a quarter of a mile ahead of him. He took the onramp at ninety with full lights and siren and punched it.

At one-fifteen on the speedometer, he was closing on Zack slowly. He pushed it up to one-twenty.

Zack must have known something to make this much of a commitment to Interstate-44.

Both were in the left lane passing traffic. He saw Zack's brake lights flicker and looked ahead of the ranger.

He saw it! A white pickup going fast with Zack approaching it at speed. He saw Zack drop back in speed then accelerate and hit the Chevy from behind. The Chevy spun off the highway and did a three-sixty on the shoulder and grass beyond.

The driver, Ingles, wrestled the wheel and started off across pasture land.

The Chevy was a six-cylinder county work truck with rear wheel drive and skinny tires. It was not equipped for fast use off road.

Rich watched Zack gun the police truck and hit the Chevy hard again. The truck skidded sideways and stopped. Zack could see Ingles reaching for the door handle. Since the truck had slid around, its passenger side was facing the ranger. He only had one choice and took it. Zack crashed the heavy duty push bar of his truck into the passenger door of the stolen one. On a hill, it toppled the white truck over with Ingles still in it. Though Zack's truck was protected by the push bar, the blow of the collision inflated the front air bags in his face. Since he had unbuckled to have his pistol more accessible, he was knocked backwards and took the full brunt of the air bags' velocity.

Rich could not see inside the dark windows of Zack's truck yet.

As Rich neared to within several hundred yards, he saw Zack's truck had rolled to a stop and appeared to be immobile. As he approached, jumping hills better than his Charger had done at Jack's ranch, he saw why. Zack had hit something hard enough to energize his front air bag. He was sitting stunned in the truck.

Rich came to a stop and watched in horror as Bertie Ingles staggered out of his stolen truck and walked erratically towards the semi-conscious ranger a stolen Glock in each hand.

Rich rolled out, his 1894 Winchester .30-30 in hand. He leaned the carbine against his open door.

"Bertie! Drop both guns. Drop them now!" he yelled across the broad space.

Bertie Ingles trudged on mechanically. Rich knew his one goal was to kill the ranger.

Rich levered the gun and put the front sight in the middle of the groove on the buckhorn rear sight.

The ranger sniper pressed the trigger back from well over a hundred yards away as Bertie raised both guns towards Zack.

Rich felt the butt hit his shoulder and watched a pink spray cloud from behind Bertie Ingles head. He knew, like many times before in Afghanistan, he had a kill shot. This one saved a ranger friend too. Just a different kind of ranger.

He heard the sirens and saw OHP vehicles closing in. They saw the man in a white Resistol and carrying a rifle at its balance point walk towards the tan truck.

A man who looked just like him from a distance fell out of the truck, then rose to his feet. The other man, who they knew to be an investigator for a sheriff's department upstate, leaned his rifle against the tan pickup and steadied the Texas Ranger.

Two troopers, guns drawn approached the man on the ground. Two Glock pistols were laying on the ground on either side of him. The hole above his left eye was gruesome. The back of his head was far worse.

Rich held Zack up bodily. The ranger focused for a second and said something in a low voice before temporarily going limp. Rich sat him down, leaning his back against the truck. Rich knew he was okay. Just stunned from the airbag hitting him in the face at around four thousand feet per second. He had a small trickle of blood from one nostril. It was to be expected.

"What did he say?" the approaching trooper asked as he holstered his gun.

"Vengeance is mine, sayeth the Lord."

A LOOK AT HONOR AND BLOOD: THE MACLACHLAN THRILLERS

BULLETS FLY AND KEEP YOU ON THE EDGE OF YOUR SEAT IN THREE ACTION-PACKED THRILLERS.

One of the deadliest men alive, Mack MacLachlan is a security contractor for the intelligence community. Mack MacLachlan has spent the past 25 years as the conceivably deniable fixer for the US Intelligence Community. When the US needs something fixed quietly and permanently, somebody calls MacLachlan.

From kidnappings to tearing down business empires, MacLachlan longs to fade away from the danger and into retirement…but that's not happening anytime soon.

Honor and Blood includes: Honor Above All, Unsanctioned and Highlands Blood.

AVAILABLE NOW

ABOUT THE AUTHOR

G. Wayne Tilman is a full-time author. He is retired from the Federal Bureau of Investigation. Prior to the FBI, he was a Marine, bank security director, deputy sheriff, investigator, and security contractor.

He holds baccalaureate and master's degrees from the University of Richmond and has been an adjunct faculty member there and several other universities as he has moved around America.

Mr. Tilman holds the internationally-recognized Certified Protection Professional board certification, generally accepted as the highest in the security profession. He also earned a US Coast Guard 50 Ton Inspected Vessel Master Captain's license.

He writes espionage thrillers, mysteries, and Westerns. Mr. Tilman's impetus to write in those genres comes from both personal experience and heritage.

A direct ancestor was a sheriff in Virginia Colony in 1680. Another ancestor was the lawman who brought in outlaw Bill Doolin (Desperado of song fame) singlehandedly and helped to neutralize the infamous Doolin-Dalton outlaw gang.

Closer to home, his mother was a counterintelligence agent for what is now the Defense Intelligence Agency or DIA.